the
SAVAGE
humanists

the SAVAGE humanists

edited and with an introduction by

Fiona Kelleghan

Robert J. SAWYER BOOKS

Robert J. Sawyer Books Published by
Red Deer Press
A Fitzhenry & Whiteside Company
1512, 1800–4 Street S.W.
Calgary, Alberta, Canada t2s 2s5
www.reddeerpress.com

Edited for the Press by Robert J. Sawyer
Copyedited by Chris Szego
Cover and text design by Karen Thomas, Intuitive Design International Ltd.
Earth photo: NASA
Printed and bound in Canada for Red Deer Press

Financial support provided by the Canada Council, and the Government of Canada through the
Book Publishing Industry Development Program (BPIDP).

Canada Council   Conseil des Arts
for the Arts   du Canada

Library and Archives Canada Cataloguing in Publication
The savage humanists / edited by Fiona Kelleghan.
ISBN 978-0-88995-425-0
1. Science fiction, American. 2. Science fiction, Canadian (English).
3. Short stories, American. 4. Short stories, Canadian (English).
5. American fiction—21st century. 6. Canadian fiction (English)—21st century.
I. Kelleghan, Fiona, 1965-
PN6120.95.S33.S38 2008   813'.087620806   C2008-903799-5

Publisher Cataloging-in-Publication Data (U.S)
The savage humanists / edited by Fiona Kelleghan.
[304] p. : cm.
Summary: Writing on the human condition.
Includes authors: Kim Stanley Robinson, Connie Willis, James Morrow, Jonathan Lethem, and
Robert J. Sawyer.
ISBN: 978-0-88995-425-0 (pbk.)
1. Short stories, American. 2. Short stories, Canadian (English).
3. American fiction – 21st century. 4. Canadian fiction (English) –21st century.
I. Kelleghan, Fiona, 1965- . II. Title.
813.56 dc22   PS648.S5.S283 2008

This book is dedicated to Mickey Gomez;
and Mickey knows what,
and Mickey knows why.

ACKNOWLEDGMENTS

I wish to thank Sabrina Heath, Gary Heath, Bryn Neuenschwander, Adam Salazar, Kristin Salazar, Fred Salazar, Thomas Voccio, Aidan-Paul Canavan, Andy Weir, and Alex Irvine for invaluable contributions.

CONTENTS

INTRODUCTION

A DEFINITION OF SAVAGE HUMANISM, WITH AUTOBIOGRAPHICAL ANECDOTES

Savage Humanism is a term I coined to describe the works of several authors who share key themes, chief among them a cry for reason to prevail over irrationality and hypocrisy, a preference for the scientific method over credulity and faith, and a certitude that, with Reason and Science (as much tools as modes of thought), it may yet be possible that the plight of most humans on this planet and the ongoing despoliation and ruination of the resources of Planet Earth — our only home, yet also the only home of billions upon billions of other creatures and the countless beautiful wonders of nature — might be ameliorated and even remedied.

I have tagged them with the prefatory "savage" because the satirical style of their best work — indeed, the best science fiction written today, as evidenced by the awards, nominations, and critical acclaim these writers have earned over the decades — is colored by a facetiousness of tone and a violence of plot development expressed as both subtextual and projected anger at the perfidies of modern society and contemporary science fiction.

Some other characteristics of Savage Humanism include:

- An awareness of the history and evolution of science fiction that often reveals itself in allusions to earlier works in the field.
- A familiarity with the history and evolution of human civilization that often reveals itself in alternate histories or fictionalized biographies, rather than as, say, neo-pulpster Gosh-Wow adventure tales, lost-civilization romances, and other fanciful, Lovecraft-influenced tales not grounded in scientific and anthropological research.
- An ambition for literary quality that reveals itself as polished, thoughtful prose with allusions to earlier acclaimed writers such as Mark Twain, Herman Melville, Charles Dickens, George Orwell, Franz Kafka, and particularly William Shakespeare.
- A suspicion of the heroic qualities of the traditional Campbellian hero — that is, not the mythic quest-figure of Joseph Campbell, but the two-fisted man of macho science that appeared so frequently in *Astounding Science Fiction*, under the editorship of John Wood Campbell, Jr.
- A frequent use of irony and satire in a dystopian setting.
- A fondness for depicting spectacular disasters at the climax of "If This Goes On" extrapolative stories.
- A conviction that skepticism is healthy.
- A vision of progress that includes expansion of global human rights and better husbandry of our natural resources (as opposed to, say, turning Earth into the third mall from the Sun).

As a scholar and a librarian, I know that literary categories are not beloved by everybody. Nor do I claim that the motifs listed here pertain to each of the nine authors collected in this volume, or that they use identical methods and styles to dramatize which motifs they do share.

However, those characteristics which *are* shared help to make these authors the wittiest, most caustic, most significant writers we have today. (A clever copywriter wrote for the dust jacket of Jonathan Lethem's 1996 collection *The Wall of the Sky, the Wall of the Eye* that its "pages are not acid-free.") My category does not rely on story furniture or on setting, in the way that cyberpunk, steampunk, military science fiction, post-apocalyptic adventure, space opera, and other varieties do. Instead, I am identifying a set of attitudes that can appear in science fiction or fantasy and a group of authors who have, to greater or lesser degree, these sensibilities in common to explore, articulate, and dramatize their ideas.

Most of these authors reside on the Eastern Seaboard of the United States. They follow national politics and world news closely and vote for Democratic candidates. They care deeply about the suffering of humans who are affected profoundly by social conditions and change; and, for the most part, they reject super- or supranaturalistic explanations for the fact that the universe exists and that its denizens can be good or evil, can experience suffering or joy, because they consider reason, human dignity, and progressive human achievements to be of greater value than any explanations that occult reckonings can provide.

— • —

In his novel *Good News From Outer Space*, John Kessel has a scene in which a televangelist speaks with the heroine whom he has kidnapped. The Reverend says, "It's hard sometimes to know, when things happen to us, whose will is being done." She replies, "Some dickhead's." [1] It's a funny moment, it's savage, and it's philosophically rationalist.

In November 1991, I met John Kessel and Gregory Frost at Kessel's home. A few months later, I had read everything they had written that I

1   John Kessel, *Good News From Outer Space*. New York: Tor Books, 1989, p. 279.

could get my hands on. I realized there was more to their importance than their close friendship; there was also something similarly and significantly angry in their work.

But the anger goes hand in hand with humor and humanism. Indeed, if you go to Kessel's website (www4.ncsu.edu/~tenshi), you can read his joking essay "The Education of Gregory Frost," in which he reminisces,

> At first I hesitated: did I want to be seen in public with this man? After all, I was a newly hired English professor — were I to be associated with him it might have the direst consequences for my career. However, I have never failed the call of simple humanity, and I did not then. Greg and I became friends.

John and Greg are still friends, and both hear the call of simple humanity. More, they answer it.

As I continued to read in the field, I found myself grouping them and some of their friends into a circle that I thought of as "Savage Humanists." In the Philadelphia area there were Frost, Timothy R. Sullivan, Michael Swanwick, James Morrow, and Gardner Dozois (under whose editorial tenure these writers were frequently published in *Asimov's Science Fiction*). These writers are connected in different ways, chiefly through friendship. Many of them regularly attend(ed) the Sycamore Hill Writers' Workshop. Frost and Kim Stanley Robinson studied at the same year's Clarion Science Fiction and Fantasy Writers' Workshop, at which nearly all of them have since taught at least once. Sullivan and Frost roomed together in Philadelphia; others, such as Kessel, James Patrick Kelly, Jonathan Lethem, Swanwick and Sullivan have collaborated severally and often. Sullivan volunteered an extra connection when he remarked to me in 2002, "All of them really believed in the ideals of the 1960s and were disappointed when those ideals never crystallized."

These authors had already self-identified as humanists. To give an example, Kessel commented on a presumptive squaring-off between cyberpunk and other authors, "By the way, one of the complaints us humanists made about cyberpunk circa 1985, that we got roundly slammed for at the time, was that the cp future ignored people who had jobs and were part of the structure of society. See the scene where the characters are watching TV in the middle of K. S. Robinson's 'Down and Out in the Year 2000.'" [2] Elsewhere, he adds,

> In the midst of the cyberpunk-humanist dustup of the mid-eighties, when the conventional terms of the debate held that no writer could be interested in both traditional fiction of character with the gloss of high art and in cutting edge technology with an anticultural bent, Kelly was the only writer in the humanist camp to be included in *Mirrorshades*, the definitive cyberpunk anthology. He can do hardheaded extrapolation to rival Bruce Sterling, twist a plot as well as Connie Willis, develop characters as convincingly as Kim Stanley Robinson, and fashion a sentence as beautifully as Karen Joy Fowler. [3]

And, in an interview with Nick Gevers ("New-Fashioned Romantic James Patrick Kelly Smokes, but Never Inhales," Scifi.Com online), Jim Kelly confirms,

> When *Cheap Truth*, the cyberpunk propaganda organ, started lumping me in with my friends John Kessel, Connie Willis and Stan Robinson as literary reactionaries, while claiming the bleeding edge for the cyberpunks, I was at once flattered and annoyed. I did have more in common with the folks some were calling the humanists, but I wasn't at all ready to cede

2   "Postcyberpunk Manifesto reactions," in *Nova Express* 4:4 (Winter/Spring 1998), p. 13.
3   "Foreword" to *Think Like a Dinosaur* by James Patrick Kelly. Urbana, IL: Golden Gryphon Press, 2003, p. viii.

the future of the genre to Messrs. Gibson and Sterling. I thought then that cyberpunk was more an attitude than a revolution. My story "Solstice" (1985) was intended to demonstrate that the literary techniques I had been developing with John Kessel, in our collaborations worked just fine when applied to the cyberpunk tropes. "Rat" (1986), on the other hand, was clearly intended as a satire of the cyberpunk antihero.

Many of the Savage Humanists share a dislike for two seminal and very popular works, Tom Godwin's story "The Cold Equations" (1954) and, to a lesser extent, Orson Scott Card's *Ender's Game* (1985).

About the former, Michael Swanwick wrote to me in an e-mail (May 10, 2002), "It's the sort of work that's embarrassing to reread as an adult. You feel a horror that you might have once been taken in by it. Sort of the way second-graders feel about Barney."

Jim Kelly earned the Hugo Award and a Nebula nomination for his 1995 novelette "Think Like a Dinosaur." Its critique of Godwin's fictional murder of a stowaway girl, who must be thrown off a spaceship because there is not enough fuel to carry her weight, is outraged. As readers might consider, Kelly's story also recalls Algis Budrys's ingenious 1960 novel *Rogue Moon* in its focal dilemma: Kelly's protagonist, Michael Barr (whose name suggests Budrys's reduplicated character, Al Barker), operates a device (known familiarly to *Star Trek* fans as a transporter) which murders the "original" person being transmitted, although Kelly's aliens, informally called dinosaurs, who share this device with humankind, pretend that an identical person arrives at the destination. Kelly's sympathies parallel Budrys's; both recognize the enormity of the execution and the sacrifice when their characters die that others may live. In *Rogue Moon*, the sacrifice is noble; in "Think Like a Dinosaur," our sadness bears an ashen taste, because Michael must put the "redundant" (i.e., original) woman to death. His is a literary and sophisticated anger, where that of John W. Campbell, the prime mover behind

Godwin's story, could be called scriptural; "Think Like a Dinosaur" is ironic and multisyllabic where "The Cold Equations" is bathetic and simplistic. Kelly takes issue with the notion that a pretty young girl should die for the sake of a lecture about the coldness of the laws of physics.

You can find a veritable orgy of postmortemizing by some Savage Humanists in *The New York Review of Science Fiction* (*NYRSF*) if you read a multi-issue conversation that begins on page 22 of issue #54 (February 1993) with John Kessel's letter in response to Brian Stableford's essay "The Redemption of the Infimal" (#52, December 1992). In the Screed (letters column), Kessel writes,

> I want all the fans of Tom Godwin's "The Cold Equations" to recognize that they like it because it's a social darwinist parable about how the homeless don't belong anywhere else than the gutter they find themselves in, and that this is not social injustice but a simple working out of absolute laws of nature. Most of all I want them to admit the satisfaction they get when the dumb bitch gets heaved out the airlock, admit that they think the little tart gets exactly what she deserves for not understanding the cold laws of the universe that we tough-minded men have to struggle against every day of our frontier lives while they sit home on their cute asses eating bon-bons. This story is about as coolly rational and impartial as the Wannsee Conference.

Frequent *NYRSF* contributor Taras Wolansky takes exception to this in issue #58 by considering the 1950s context of the story and Campbell's influence (June 1993). Author Catherine Mintz defends Kessel with a screed in #60 (August 1993). Kessel again confronts Stableford[4], reasserting that fans of "The Cold Equations" "like the politics of this story" and that it

---

4   Kessel, John, *New York Review of Science Fiction*, 1993.

"supports their view of society. It's not a case of 'good' sf vs. 'bad' sf, it's a case of my values vs. yours." Kessel charges Stableford with confusing "the law of gravity with the Republican party platform" and sarcasms, "Sorry to have messed up your nice clean genre. But it was never as clean as you thought it was." *NYRSF* dedicated five pages of the #66 issue to further discussion, and the arguments continued through April 1995. Many of these screeds contain *ad hominems*, many argue the literary and scientific merits or lack thereof of the Godwin story; all of them reveal passion and anger.

When I queried some of the contributors to this volume about their current feelings about "The Cold Equations," I received these responses, quite varied:

"Deep-seated antipathy." (James Patrick Kelly);

"Well, at 12, I thought, 'Wow, I can't believe he did this.' Now it's more a sense of ambivalence because I think the moral dilemma it predicates is entirely false. The either/or that really wasn't an either/or at all." (Gregory Frost);

"My short answer is sympathetic weariness." (Robert J. Sawyer, with a longer explanatory commentary in his weblog at sfwriter.com/2008/03/thought-experiments-in-ethics.html);

"I hold with Damon Knight's great critique of the story, which shows that the story itself reveals in its incidental details that there is enough non-crucial stuff inside the spaceship to equal the weight of the little girl (closet door, etc. etc) and so the whole story is a bogus concoction, stupidly trying to justify cruelty against other humans for supposedly higher ends. Very much right-wing "hard" (attitude) science fiction. God bless Damon Knight I say. It's the best critique I've heard of concerning that mendacious and mean story." (Kim Stanley Robinson);

"Actually, my feeling has always been that anything as iconic and impossible to forget as that deserves a certain respect. Campbell's overt agenda was sort of horrendous, but the resultant embodiment of paradoxical feelings is a perfect example of what fiction does best..." (Jonathan Lethem);

"I would predict that we Savhums feel a collective weary disdain toward that particular story." (James Morrow):

"I've always wondered whether John Campbell got the idea from Robert Heinlein's novel or the subsequent 1950 film adaptation of *Destination Moon*. The characters face the same challenge, but they solve it rationally by jettisoning what can be jettisoned to save the life of a man who actually volunteers to remain behind, if I remember it correctly. Maybe Campbell decided that such logical "warm" thinking about the equations was mawkish." (Tim Sullivan).

I cannot help but think of Tom Stoppard's 1972 play, "Jumpers," which parodies this willingness to sacrifice others. In his play, the tragic history of the race to the South Pole (which Roald Amundsen won and in which Robert Scott's British team lost their lives), is reduplicated in a televised program of the first British landing on the Moon. Historically, Scott was unprepared and overly optimistic about an easy triumph; and Lawrence Oates, part of his team, realized on March 16, 1912, that his extensive debilitation due to frostbite, scurvy, and hunger was hampering the chances of the rest of the team to reach their Cape Evans base camp. In a brave act, Oates told the others, "I am just going outside and may be some time." They understood it was a determined self-sacrifice. In Stoppard's play, the captain of the lunar mission is named Scott and his subordinate is named

Oates. When they realize that their lander has been damaged and contains enough oxygen for only one man, the two scuffle at the foot of their rocket, and Scott pushes Oates off the ladder, then calls, "I am going up now. I may be gone for some time." As the historical Scott and Oates are both considered heroes to this day by the British, Stoppard's brutally satirical reinterpretation mirrors the disgust that so many of the Savage Humanists feel toward "The Cold Equations," for the way Campbell demanded that it be written by Godwin (four times, by some accounts).

Turning now to *Ender's Game*, by Orson Scott Card, who for years has preached that the only correct way to write is "the plain tale, plainly told" (see "Uncle Orson's Writing Class: On Rhetoric and Style," May 12, 1998, at Card's website, hatrack.com) — by which dictum he indirectly assaults the Savage Humanists, who write with subtlety and literary finesse. The boy Ender Wiggin is trained throughout the novel to attain the skills and anthropocentrism that allow him to exterminate a planet of sentient beings, yet Card embeds Ender in such circumstances that the sympathetic reader will cry, "It's not his fault!" The Savage Humanists who have written or spoken about it — primarily John Kessel — find this popular novel inherently two-faced and unscrupulous, and some of the reasons for the antagonism between them and Card are listed in Kessel's 1990 essay "Demonizing Literature" and his 2004 "Creating the Innocent Killer: *Ender's Game*, Intention, and Morality" (both are available at Kessel's website).

In the latter, Kessel writes, "Presumably, someone can kill hundreds, thousands, even billions (Ender eventually "kills" an entire race) and not be a killer. A killer is motivated by rage or by selfish motives. To be a killer you must intend to kill someone. And even if you do intend to kill, you are still innocent if you do it for a larger reason, "selflessly," without personal motives. And if you feel bad about being forced into doing it."

Frost adds, "OS Card and company call us the humanists, which is like being tarred 'liberal.' It takes something that by definition cares about humanity and makes it sound like you're some sort of mutant fungus ...

That's a very powerful book. Lots and lots of sf readers point to it as a great novel, an important novel. Intelligent people do. They seem somehow blind to the inherent corruption of the book" (Frost, e-mail to Kelleghan, March 29, 2002).

A recommended read is Michael Swanwick's parody "Under's Game," in which young Under behaves like any normal prepubescent boy suffering from attention-getting-deficit disorder, whining for snacks, dismissive of the weepy pleas of the general, and shrugging off his easy demolition of the Invaders. When it turns out that Under has also unwittingly arranged for the destruction of Earth, he responds to the general's horror with a careless, "Hell, it's only a game." The story is available in Swanwick's *The Periodic Table of Science Fiction* (Hornsea: PS Publishing, 2005) and in *Year's Best SF 7* (edited by David G. Hartwell, New York, NY: HarperCollins/Eos, 2002).

Author Bryn Neuenschwander suggested that a very useful word for my Rationalist authors is "sacrilicious." In other words, their caustic views on right-wing politics and organized fundamentalist religion, and how those two forces have conspired to damage Earth's natural resources, are delicious to read. The Savage Humanists are guerrilla ideologists, sniping at the censors of liberty, but not with the anomic savage humor of a Marquis de Sade or a Jonathan Swift. They are fully invested with care for their fellow inhabitants of the planet.

The writings of Gregory Frost, John Kessel, Tim Sullivan, James Morrow, Robert J. Sawyer, and James Patrick Kelly form the core of my notion of Savage Humanism.

Perhaps Frost's body of work is central to that core. His tour de force 1993 novel *The Pure Cold Light* is an exciting turmoil of amnesia victims and alien invasion set in a shockingly decayed alternate Philadelphia. It was described, in an interview with Frost on the HotWired website (April 2, 1996), by Jonathan Lethem as a "gritty urban cyber-thriller." I have disagreed[5], because the novel finds the kiddie thrills and cat-burglar posturings of

---

5   Kelleghan, "Postcyberpunk Lost: *The Pure Cold Light*", Nova Express 4:4 (Winter/Spring 1998): 16-17.

cyberpunk abhorrent. Its heroine is an undercover journalist who begins her investigation by working out in a gym on an orbiting station:

> The only constant point of reference was toward the screens, where the TV, at whatever angle, displayed the loud opening credits of "The President Odie Show."
>
> [The people exercising] stared slackly at the screens to forget themselves, to escape the excruciation of weightless workout by shutting off their brains and acquiescing in scripted idiocy. Odie and Vice President Schnepfe felicitously dished up a story as lurid as a plate of intestines.
>
> "Normally, you know," chimed the President, "we just have on board your and my favorite celebrities. And we do have with us the juggling prime minister of Lithuania later, so don't switch satnets on me yet, folks. But our first guest — I gotta tell you, this woman's story really moved me. I think Schnepfe had a movement too."[6]

George Bush Sr. was President while Frost was writing *The Pure Cold Light*. When he shows the White House turned into a TV program for bathroom jokes, you see what Gregory Frost calls "the angry dark side of the Savage Humanist — the cynic who's a cynic because he sees what's going on" (Frost, e-mail to Kelleghan, March 29, 2002). He feels betrayed by leaders who do not display leadership qualities, and he would agree with the politician in Kim Stanley Robinson's *Fifty Degrees Below*, who says of his political climate as portrayed by its media, "we are a real foxhole fraternity, shelled daily as we are by Fox."[7]

Frost is always identifiable as the narrator, too. When he says a few paragraphs later, "The time had long since passed where fraud looked any different from truth,"[8] he shows his unending astonishment at the fact that

---

6   Frost, *The Pure Cold Light*. New York: Avon Books, 1993, p. 7-8.
7   Robinson, *Fifty Degrees Below*. New York: Bantam, 2005, p. [370].
8   Frost, *The Pure Cold Light*, p. 9.

in the information society, few are capable of profound thinking and fewer are capable of distinguishing what is presented by our many media from solid, verifiable truth.

Frost has a gift for the bitter aphorism. "There would always be a percentage of humanity that did not mind letting everybody else clean up after them." Or: "You don't kill corporations, they kill themselves." He never pauses for a second to show why believers are to be pitied and why televangelistic omniscience is a risky position to stake out.

He says,

"I despise stupid, incompetent, nationalistic pseudo-patriots who wrap themselves in God and a flag and then accuse me of hating my country because I question *their* motives and *their* intelligence and *their* competence. You want my allegiance? Earn it. As someone wiser than me said, I love my country as an adult, not as a worshipping child. Can my country do wrong? You bet your Aunt Fannie. And it should be called to task for it. Punished for it. It should have to stand in a corner and shut up. The neocon Nazi attitude is summed up in the [2004 film] *Team America: World Police* theme: "America — fuck yeah!" The trouble is, there's a toad-IQ part of America that doesn't realize that film's a satire. If you want to boil it all down to one statement, it's willful ignorance I despise. Has no party stripe, no denomination, no social stratum in particular. A rich asshole weaving an SUV through traffic while talking on a cell phone is as worthy of contempt as a cretin who thinks the world is 4000 years old and that God buried those dinosaur bones to test our faith. You can almost randomly pick anything Mark Twain said regarding American culture and I would stand by it. Really, nothing has changed since then" (Frost, e-mail to Kelleghan, April 8, 2008).

Of Frost, Karen Joy Fowler has written:

In addition to rich, sensory writing, Greg's work evokes: my sense of justice, my sense of wonder, my sense of horror, my sense of humor ... Greg is both a funny writer and an angry one. His sympathies are usually clear; his heart is usually fully engaged. Some people can't get justice in this world and Greg's characters tend to locate themselves among them. Sometimes Greg provides different worlds, places where different justices are possible. But the work is never simple, never thin, never escapist. You can't miss the writer's unhappiness with the real state of things; the real, unjust world exists as visibly as a shadow to every sentence. Things are not as they should be and, if we allow ourselves the temporary solace of pretending otherwise, still Greg's anger reminds us that we are only pretending. [9]

Kessel concurs:

Frost's fiction is charged by an awareness of the idiocies, cruelty, prejudice, and ignorance of what Mark Twain called "the damned human race." I sometimes think that his sensitivity to these sad realities gives him physical pain, and if I were allowed no more than one word to describe the large body of Frost's fiction, the word would be "angry."

Stories like "The Madonna of the Maquiladora" are powered by rage at the injustices we visit upon each other, or that are visited upon us by God (if She exists). Frost identifies villains in high (and low) places. He excoriates organized religion. He reveals to us "The secret inner life of the masses," and what we see there is seldom pretty.

---

9   *Attack of the Jazz Giants and Other Stories*, by Gregory Frost. Urbana, IL: Golden Gryphon Press, 2005, p. x.

Yet what I like about Frost's stories is the bruised heart they reveal beneath the rage ... What captures me is how these stories tread the edge of a decent and humane despair: despair at the way we destroy ourselves, at the yawning gap between what we might be and what we all too often become, at the ways we might reach out to one another, and at our common failure to do so. Frost tells certain hard truths about America. I see him falling in a line of storytellers from the American gothics Poe, Hawthorne, and Melville, through Twain in his supernatural mode ... [10]

Kessel adds that Frost is a cool observer

of the American scene, horrified by its callousness, who turn to fantasy to depict a reality that cannot be caught in social realism. Before this all gets too grim, however, let me say that if you allowed me a second word to describe Frost's work, that word would be "funny." Sometimes Frost's humor can be very dark indeed, as in "The Girlfriends of Dorian Gray," but in another mood Greg can deliver "The Road to Recovery," a farce that no one else could write, the best Road Movie never made. [11]

Frost's books are full of adventure and destruction (note that the plural term for wildcats is "a destruction of wildcats," and Frost is certainly a wildcat of the fantastic fiction world). Yet his fiction is not just a big bacchanal of mau-mauing those he despises. He suggests that we begin to improve our world by questioning the wisdom we receive from politicians, corporations (from the CEOs down to the lackeys), advertisers, religious leaders, and especially television. In such fiction as his 2002 novel *Fitcher's Brides* and "Madonna of the Maquiladora," Frost warns us that when our

10   Ibid.
11   "Afterword: The Damned Human Race," by John Kessel, *Attack of the Jazz Giants and Other Stories*, p. 343.

leaders display a sense of entitlement, we should distrust them. Frost sees that the intricacies of the modern American hierarchical system provide a natural order for the exercise of sadism. The God of those in charge is the protector of rich white men. Their justice is the punishment of the ill-born and disadvantaged and it is meted out on the say-so of the powerful.

"Madonna of the Maquiladora" (2002) is a sad and trenchant fable about American corporate hegemony in Mexico. A photojournalist investigates fraudulent appearances of the Virgin Mary among poverty-ridden Mexican workers in an American factory. The heroine says to the photojournalist that the Madonna's message is "To be patient. To wait. To endure their hardships. To remember that they will all find Grace in Heaven more beautiful than anything they can imagine." The photojournalist replies, "That wouldn't take much of a heaven." The insight is both funny and painful. The narrator adds that the Virgin "sells accommodation. It's always been her message and it's the message of the elite, the rich, a recommendation that no one who actually endures the misery would make."[12] The heroine also says that these visions are spreading. "There are always stories once it starts. People who don't want to be left out, who need to hear from her. That can be a lot of people."

Fitcher's Brides is a retelling of the story of Bluebeard, the man who enjoyed murdering each of his wives and then pricking the curiosity of the next by ordering her never to open the locked door of his secret room. Behind that door are the bodies of the previous dead wives. Most authors, deciding to retell a fairy tale, would find enough meat in the legend of Bluebeard to satisfy, and I imagine that most would set him and his unhappy wives in the medieval period so popular in fantasy. Frost, however, chooses the New York frontier of 1843, and instead of treating this as a story about disobedient wives, he stalks evangelism.

His Bluebeard is an evangelist named Fitcher, who says things like, "To stay in good with God, you must stay in good with me."[13] He tells his last

12   All quotes from "Madonna of the Maquiladora," *Asimov's Science Fiction* (May 2002): 62-63.
13   Frost, *Fitcher's Brides*. New York, Tor, 2002, p. 305.

wife, Kate, "Some things in life should be accepted without question, because they are too great to be questioned. That is the definition of faith." Kate, who stands in for Frost, replies, "On the contrary, Mr. Fitcher. I believe the greater the promise, the more closely it must be scrutinized. The largest promises govern our lives. I'm unwilling to embrace blindly that which I've not considered to the fullest." [14] The two previous wives, Kate's older sisters, succumb to Fitcher's charms and evil; Kate survives and beats Bluebeard because she is a skeptic.

As in so much of Frost's work, the themes of unworldly upheavals, transformations, and near lunatic disarray overturn the bourgeois world of sanctimonious normalcy and daily mediocrity. His humor is revolutionary, seeking change in American society and presenting an arena in which value is pitted against value and disposition is pitted against disposition, and if the good guys don't always win, at least they seriously frighten the bad guys. His work gestures toward hope of better things in a sort of helical ascension. Alfred Lord Tennyson's Ulysses said that "something ere the end, some work of noble note, may yet be done, not unbecoming men that strove with gods." Frost has certainly striven with a number of arrogant and rapacious authorities in his fiction, if not with gods.

Equal anger toward politicians and religious leaders can be found in the works of Nebula nominee Tim Sullivan, which often turn to classical history and mythology to dramatize his concerns about contemporary American culture — although the historical settings suggest a Santayana-esque view of our so-called post-historical era. *Destiny's End* (1988), his first novel, is based upon the Greek myths of grandfather Acrisius, mother Danaë, and hero Perseus, and unflatteringly depicts the children of privilege in a very distant future who, like the billionaires of corporate America, are never satisfied with what they've already got. No one in the group is better than Sullivan at portraying a *mal du siècle* (or, in this case, *du éternité*) such as John Ruskin once described — "On the whole, these are much

14   Frost, *Fitcher's Brides*, p. 363-364.

sadder ages than the early ones; not sadder in a noble and deep way, but in a dim wearied way, — the way of ennui, and jaded intellect, and uncomfortableness of soul and body. The Middle Ages had their wars and agonies, but also intense delights. Their gold was dashed with blood; but ours is sprinkled with dust"[15] — though, happily, his fiction is always as plot-driven as theme-driven, and sublime delights fill our senses. Sullivan's Perseus character, Deles, fulfills one destiny after another, and he learns the final one will be to reveal a surprising secret to humanity, but he does not know how to uncover that secret. His revelation comes with a bourgeois realization: *"No one is happy here."*[16]

The Martian Viking (1991), which tackles both the science fictional genres of inner space and space imperialism, describes a New World Order of forced labor, a penal colony on Mars, and a hallucinogenic drug that allows the hero to see a bizarre and excitingly unpredictable truth behind his horrifying reality. Sullivan's is not the romantic red planet of Ray Bradbury — in fact, it presages Kim Stanley Robinson's *Mars* trilogy — being a tale of the political struggles between some brave but ordinary humans who just want to get along in life (hoping for an occasional shot at the pleasures of creativity and parenthood) and a dictatorship of bureaucrats. He opens the book, sans irony, with a Scandinavian precept: "To the guest, who enters your dwelling with frozen knees, give the warmth of your fire; he who hath traveled over the mountains hath need of food, and well-dried garments." And yet Sullivan, and the world he depicts, do not allow the guest/reader any such welcome. How unfriendly our world has become is made explicit in the first few pages of the novel:

> Johnsmith ... reflected on his previous feelings about the draft. He'd always thought it sort of unfair, but had continually reminded himself not to worry too much about it. The government frowned

15   John Ruskin, *Modern Painters, Volume 5*. London: Smith, Elder and Co., 1856-1860, p. 321.
16   Sullivan, *Destiny's End*. New York: Avon, 1988, p. 233.

on activism, and you might end up in front of the Selective Space Service yourself, if you raised too much of a fuss about the injustice of it all. Besides, what good would it do? The poor were always with us, weren't they? (Not anymore, actually; now they were on the moon, or, in a few cases, on Mars or the Belt; but the principle still held.) He had happily maintained this ambivalent outlook until it became clear that he was soon to be eligible for the draft himself. That had radically changed his perspective. [17]

Like Deles, the protagonist Johnsmith discovers what he needs — courage — when he discovers love, as he tells his ex-wife:

"You think I'm a fool," Johnsmith said. "But the truth is, I've loved someone besides myself, and you never have."

Ronindella turned on him in a rage. "I love God," she snarled.

"That's a convenient excuse for acting with almost complete selfishness," he said calmly. "As long as you can convince yourself that you're closer to God than the rest of us, then you can treat us like shit. Well, I'm not buying that anymore." [18]

Sullivan cares deeply about his characters. His books are viciously funny in a deadpan way, as is his story "The Mouth of Hell" (2003), an alien invasion-cum-peplum-epic novella in which the protagonist describes Christianity, straight-faced, as a "death cult" [19] — which it is. Almost any of these authors, in challenging contemporary politics and the hypocrisies of religious leaders, could have written these lines:

"David, do you think this is a sideshow? Do we really want the media distorting the truth about what's happened here?"

"It is traditional in our country to take that chance," David said.

17 Sullivan, *The Martian Viking*. New York: Avon, 1991, p. 2.
18 Sullivan, *The Martian Viking*, p. 214.
19 Sullivan, "The Mouth of Hell." *Asimov's Science Fiction* 27:8 #331 (August 2003): 60.

"Mr. Albee, you are very naïve."

David glared at him. "And you, Secretary Flanagan, are very cynical."

Flanagan colored. "You can believe what you like about me, but I know I'm doing the Lord's work, and I'm doing it for the good of the greatest country on Earth."

"Well, at least you're willing to grant that I can think what I like about you. That's a step in the right direction."

"Your sarcasm is not helpful." [20]

Yet, as *Buffy the Vampire Slayer*'s Rupert Giles would say, sarcasm can be an end in itself [21], and Sullivan has a talent for it. Sullivan was writing this aliens-and-dinosaurs novel, *Lords of Creation* (1992), during the Ronald Reagan presidency, which was succeeded by the George Bush Sr. presidency. His character "the famous, telegenic Christian Millennialist Jaffrey Flanagan" serves, or, more precisely, rules in the "new cabinet post [given] as a sop to the religious right — the Department of Morality." [22] The novel is set in 1999, just two years before George W. Bush established The White House Office of Faith-Based and Community Initiatives, a real live Department of Morality. Sullivan's protagonist, David Albee, muses:

> Paleontology had been only a small part of the Millennialist assault, of course. Art deemed offensive to "community standards" was under attack throughout the nineties, followed by the sciences that conflicted with the views of the religious right. In other words, anything that logically argued against creationism — the notion that God had created the Earth and everything on it four thousand years or so ago — was fair game for fundamentalist

20   Sullivan, *Lords of Creation*. New York: Avon, 1992, p. 98.
21   *Buffy the Vampire Slayer*, Season 4, Episode 8, "Pangs," November 23, 1999.
22   Sullivan, *Lords of Creation*, p. 34.

fanatics after they had managed to foist a weak administration into creating the Department of Morality — good old D.O.M., the bane of secular humanists everywhere. [23]

When I asked Sullivan how he had predicted the rise of John J. Di Iulio Jr. (the first director of the "Initiatives") and John Ashcroft, Bush's Attorney General (a Pentecostalist) who, famously, in 2002, ordered that the partially nude female statue of the Spirit of Justice be covered with curtains at a cost of $8,000, Sullivan shrugged and said, "I just knew that it was where the country was headed. We even did have a Secretary of Morality [Di Iulio], although he quit the post when he learned what it was that Bush wanted him to do."

In a later scene, Liz, the love interest for paleontologist David, badgers the Secretary of Morality to see how much he will tell her about his motives:

> "So now the hatchlings are from hell, right?" Liz rolled her eyes.
>
> "There are more things in heaven and earth —"
>
> "Is that what you tell the President and the congressional leadership when you make them toe the line, Reverend?"
>
> "The men you speak of so contemptuously are doing God's work," Flanagan said.
>
> "Sure they are, by letting you and your flunkies take away the rights that people died for in the past. That's what God wants, is it?"
>
> He looked at her with a superior expression on his handsome face, an expression that suggested she was too much of an infidel to understand the complex intricacies that link church and state. Liz wanted to throw her cranberry juice at him. "The President and the congressional leadership are protecting the rights of the

---

23 Sullivan, *Lords of Creation*, p. 7.

majority, seeing that community standards are upheld all over our country. They stand for what Lincoln called our better angels."

"Have you noticed that our country is sliding further and further into decline while you and your political bedfellows watch our better angels dance on the head of a pin?"

"Our economic difficulties are a result of the licentious waste that went before."

"Still blaming it on the liberals? They haven't been in power for nearly twenty years. Good thing for you we don't have free elections anymore."

"We most certainly do have free elections, and the people have made their wishes known."

"Sure, they vote for the candidate they see most often on TV, and his ads are paid for by megacorps, who don't give a damn about anything but profit. I never heard the people say we should have only two classes, and that only one of those classes should have any rights." [24]

The American Constitution and Bill of Rights have long been misinterpreted for self-serving reasons or completely ignored by those in power. After all, the Founding Fathers omitted to plan ahead for Creationism or Intelligent Design, because the theory of evolution hadn't been invented yet; and even two centuries later, as Kim Stanley Robinson comments, "Christian *Realpolitik* isn't really a supercoherent philosophy." [25] Sullivan's fiction, time and again, recalls the outcry from U.S. Army attorney Joseph Welch to Senator Joseph McCarthy during the 1954 Army-McCarthy hearings: "You've done enough. Have you no sense of decency, sir, at long last? Have you left no sense of decency?"

Among the great opening lines in a field rife with them is the first

---

24   Sullivan, *Lords of Creation*, p. 122-123.
25   Robinson, *Forty Signs of Rain*. New York: Bantam, 2004, p. 317.

sentence of James Morrow's first novel, *The Wine of Violence* (1981): "*There was a time, believe it or not, when human beings did each other harm.*" Thus began a career in satirical examination of the idiocies of theodicy and other pseudo-intellectual flights of fancy that testify to the human mind's capacity for self-deception, social irresponsibility, and theorems that rely on circular reasoning to prove all sorts of things with no pertinence to reality. When you prefer the fallacy of personal credulity to the scientific method, everything proves everything else: Reverend X is tight with God, and Senator Y is tight with Reverend X, therefore Senator Y and all his friends are tight with God, due to the transitive property of tightness. Their ambitions, therefore, are unquestionably approved by the Divine Rubber Stamp and so cannot be questioned with impunity.

Like the fiction of Sawyer, Sullivan, Robinson, and Willis, Morrow's often features scientists and other truth-seekers as protagonists. Morrow self-identifies as an "atheist, scientific humanist," [26] and he has said, "Manichaeanism, I feel, is perhaps the single worst idea our species ever invented. The human race does not divide neatly into the Forces of Light and the Forces of Darkness, and endless misery has accrued to the supposition that it does" (interview with Nick Gevers, "A Conversation with James Morrow," Scifi.Com, November 2000).

Friedrich Nietzsche first proclaimed the death of God in his *Die fröhliche Wissenschaft* (1882) — "*Gott ist tot! Gott bleibt tot! Und wir haben ihn getötet!*" ("God is dead! God remains dead! And we have killed him!") — though he meant it figuratively. Morrow literalizes the death of God in his acclaimed *Godhead* trilogy, composed of the novels *Towing Jehovah* (1994), *Blameless in Abaddon* (1996), and *The Eternal Footman* (1999). In the first novel, God's two-mile long body falls from the skies into the Atlantic Ocean. This, naturally, raises a multitude of questions, from "Is He really dead?" to "What will humans do now?" In *Blameless in Abaddon*, the protagonist, Martin Candle (note the various connotations of his name), who

---

26   "James Morrow: Having It Both Ways," in *Locus* 41:2 (August 1998): 67.

is having several personal crises, including the recent death of his beloved wife and the discovery that he has metastatic prostate cancer, decides to put God on trial for crimes against humanity.

Morrow, like Robert J. Sawyer, is notable for his dramatizations of both disasters and of trial proceedings. In *Blameless*, the trial of — not the century, nor of the millennium, but of the whole history of humanity — Candle v. God is fascinating for its catalogue of atrocities, both scriptural and historical; this catalogue is perhaps matched only by Kim Stanley Robinson's "A History of the Twentieth Century, With Illustrations." Martin, a contemporary Job, loses his case because the Jury, to the contempt of Martin and his friends, concludes:

> "...To wit, only by building random annihilation into the scheme of things could the Defendant [God] have secured a world containing charity, compassion, courage, patience, self-sacrifice, and ingenuity."
>
> "Not to mention the March of Dimes," snorted Randall.
>
> "Easter Seals," grunted Esther.
>
> "Jerry Lewis telethons."
>
> "The Ronald McDonald House." [27]

And, in the final book, *The Eternal Footman*, the Corpus Dei explodes until only the head remains. God's skull goes into geostationary orbit above the Western Hemisphere, and in its shadow a new plague is visited upon humanity. [28]

In his same interview with Nick Gevers, Morrow said, "At base, the satirist is a moralist — often an angry moralist. He doesn't know how to fix the world, but he knows that it's in a lot of trouble, and he's anxious to share his diagnosis. Just as the first step in treating a disease is coming up with a

27   Morrow, *Blameless in Abaddon*. San Diego: Harcourt, Brace & Co., 1996, p. 368-369.

28   For further discussion, see Michael-Anne Rubenstien's "The Godhead Trilogy," in *Classics of Science Fiction and Fantasy Literature, Volume 1*, edited by Fiona Kelleghan. Pasadena, CA: Salem Press, 2002.

correct diagnosis, the satirist believes that the first step in ameliorating a social ill is naming it accurately."

In all of his works, from his first novel *The Wine of Violence* to *The Philosopher's Apprentice* (2008), Morrow happily clashes with received wisdoms about politics and religion, and finds most of them to be ill-conceived. In an interview with me, Morrow said, "That's my ultimate critique of so much belief, whether we're talking about New Age mysticism or orthodox church-going — or Marxism. At a certain point, the practitioner is not asking the tough questions that have to be asked. I always liked a truism about George Orwell, which was that the Right Wing hated him because he was a Socialist, and the Left Wing hated him because he told the truth. I don't see myself as a truth-teller, but do I see myself as an ambiguity-monger. Somebody who says that a question is always better than an answer" ("War of the World-Views," *Science Fiction Studies* online, March 2003). Further:

FK: How and when did your opposition to irrationality arise? Give examples.

JM: Boy, these doctoral defenses are harder than they used to be. My opposition to irrationality arose through irrational means. It sounds like there's a paradox in there, and maybe even some hypocrisy on my part. But there's a sense in which — and I hope I'm not sounding remotely mystical — there's a sense in which those literary voices spoke to me: the voices of the skeptics, the world-view that's going on in Voltaire's *Candide* or in the plays of Ibsen, in the satire of Jonathan Swift, and in the honest atheism of Camus.

The word "honesty" is pivotal for me. These writers seemed like honest voices when compared with the voices of Belief and Irrationality, and with the Theistic Claims, and with Anti-Darwinism. It became so clear that something disingenuous was driving the believers' agenda. The proselytizer was not coming clean, was not asking questions of himself or herself, tough questions — questions like, "Why have I been appointed to go out and tell people about Jesus? Why does God permit such a deranged state of affairs, where some people become privy to ultimate truth, while others remain in the outer darkness? Why do I keep gunning for Darwin? Is God so weak that he can't even make his presence felt in a crummy biology classroom? Is that a deity worth worshipping, this being who needs this pathetic press corps running around, these spin doctors for the divine?"

He goes further in *The Last Witchfinder* (2006), set in the heady period when the Renaissance is evolving into the Enlightenment, the age of Benjamin Franklin and Sir Isaac Newton. Jennet Stearne, daughter of England's last Witchfinder General, sets out with her lover, the young Franklin, to disprove the existence of demons and thereby bring an end to the hunting and killing of so-called witches. Their task is not easy, though it is eased by their falling in love — and their love-making is highly humorous in their pillow-talk after Ben Franklin has tried to convince her that lightning and electricity are one and the same:

Naked, they scurried to the bed-chamber and collaborated in the construction of a fire. With the fevered intensity of a poet choosing a new quill, his original having cracked in mid-composition, Ben selected an adder-bag from his cache, which he kept beside the mattress in an earthenware jar. Her cunny was a wet as a peach. Sheathing his manhood, they set about exhibiting their deathless devotion to the cult of electricity.

"Ne'er have I felt such sparks," he said as his ardor gained admittance to its object.

"Mr. Franklin, you make me crackle," she said, rotating on the axis of his manhood. "I declare our experiment a triumph."

"Absolutely."

"*Quod **eros** demonstrandum*," she said. [29]

But because Jennet is smart and courageous, soon there are enemies who want to see that she will herself undergo imprisonment and trial. Remembering the unerasable minutes of her dear aunt's own death at the stake, Jennet is brave. And having herself been sentenced to execution for witchcraft, simply because she's intelligent enough to write a book excoriating the wizened old witch-fearers who run the world, she has a few moments in prison to share these words with her beloved Ben Franklin:

"The sufficiency of the world, that's the demons disproof lies hidden in the bowels of the *Principia Mathematica*, whether Mr. Newton knows it be there or not," Jennet said. "When Aunt Isobel cried out from the pyre, screaming of Aristotle's elements, she meant only that I must look closely, so very closely, as everything my senses embraced. She was instructing me to scrutinize the universe, Nature with her winds and tides and lodestones and sunbeams — her air and water and earth and fire."

Ben brushed his lips across their son's brow. "You have wrought an ingenious conjecture, dearest. Though I fear your enemies will say that in making Creation sufficient, you have rendered the Creator superfluous."

"If I must murder God to save a Marblehead hag, then that is what I shall do." [30]

29   Morrow, *The Last Witchfinder*. New York: William Morrow, 2006, p. 262-263.
30   Morrow, *The Last Witchfinder*, p. 356.

There are multiple puns in play here; Morrow's joke about the transliteration of "Q.E.D." is sexily playful; and if, in the second passage, the reader is happy enough to discover an implication that Jennet's fellow-accused women have heads filled with rocks, that will do.

Yet Morrow's ending gestures towards hope. As he says,

> The Enlightenment gave us two great gifts: the gift of reason and the gift of doubt. The problem is, reason without doubt inevitably leads to disaster. Today, it's really fashionable to piss on the Enlightenment. I think what people are really pissing on is the way our more immediate ancestors have fetishized reason and completely missed the other half of the program ... Now, for all this, I am willing to defend reason per se up to a point, because I'm not sure that reason was tried, really. It's not that reason was tried and found wanting. I'm not sure that you can say it was seriously tried. I think we're all kind of waiting for the Age of Reason! I don't know if it's just around the corner. And I hope it is, as long as it's tempered by doubt, as I said earlier. But at the moment we live in the Age of Nonsense, where any kind of charlatan with a pseudo-science will get a hearing on the Internet or in the bookstores. ("War of the World-Views," *Science Fiction Studies* online, March 2003)

In Morrow's next novel, *The Philosopher's Apprentice*, philosophy graduate student Mason Ambrose self-sabotages his thesis defense before the doctoral committee after realizing that his thesis is unlikely to be granted:

> "Why," I persisted, "would this same divine serial killer have begun his career spending thirteen billion years fashioning quadrillions of needless galaxies before finally starting on his pet project: singling out a minor planet in an obscure precinct of the Milky Way

and seeding it with vain bipedal vertebrates condemned to wait indefinitely for the deity in question to disclose himself?"[31]

Mason's daring showmanship in calling God a "serial killer" is what persuades a mysterious employer to hire him for a job at a privately owned island off the coast of Florida, where he is asked to school a brilliant heiress in the history of ethics, as her mother has been unable to inculcate her with any sense of morals. Morrow has rather perversely if proleptically named this pupil Londa Sabacthani, the last name referring to the alleged Jesus Christ on the cross, and his alleged penultimate words: "Eli, Eli, lama sabachthani?" that is, "My God, my God, why have You forsaken me?" (*Matthew* 27:46). Mason's first meeting with Londa suggests that she is a feral child, but he soon has her reading the historical ethics-philosophers. Mason is challenged when Londa declares that she dislikes Immanuel Kant's theorem for God's existence.

> "Do you prefer some *other* proof of God's existence?" I asked.
>
> "I guess you haven't heard the news," she replied. "I'm going to stop believing in God."
>
> "You're going to *stop*?"
>
> "If it's all the same to you."
>
> "It's all the same to *me*, but it's hardly the same to *most* people. The leap into disbelief is not a step one takes lightly. It will put you at odds with the rest of the world."
>
> "I'm *already* at odds with the rest of the world ... I know that the God hypothesis has its partisans, but, oh, what a *boring* idea. Where did the universe come from? *He* did it. How do we account for rivers and rocks and ring-tailed lemurs? *He* made them. Ho-hum."[32]

31   Morrow, *The Philosopher's Apprentice*. New York: William Morrow, 2008, p. 13.
32   Morrow, *The Philosopher's Apprentice*, p. 108.

Mason has to admit that "spiritual" is his own least favorite word, and when billionaire Londa decides to use her wealth to finance a scientific city based on Rationalism, Mason is against the idea, but acknowledges the "splendid projects" that Londa undertakes: "providing contraceptives and small-business loans to women in underdeveloped countries," "running to earth the architects of various international prostitution rings," and "tirelessly lobbying against the user-friendly fascism, feel-good theocracy, and creeping [Philistinism] that now dominated the American political landscape." [33]

However, Londa later decides upon a daring abduction of three hundred of America's top Philistines — corporation presidents, Congressmen, lawyers, judges, arms merchants, misguided professors, government advisers, political operatives, theocrats and lobbyists — and imprisons them on a cruise ship, where she invites them to see how much their employees enjoy toiling at "monotonous but spiritually rewarding jobs." [34]

> "In your former careers as corporate heads, you collectively outsourced two hundred and thirty-four thousand manufacturing jobs to atrociously run factories in Asia and Latin America. But hear me now, masters of the universe ... in our compassion we've decided to retire all our stokers and offer you their jobs at four lucres a day. True, the boiler rooms are an austere environment — quite similar, in fact, to the sweatshops that figure so crucially in your corporations' prosperity: long hours, foul air, hazardous working conditions, infrequent bathroom breaks. The temperature is one hundred and ten degrees Fahrenheit in the shade. But at least you'll be gainfully employed ... But here's a late-breaking story to cheer you. Despite frenzied efforts by well-funded lobbyists, we shall continue to bless all G-deck residents with free health insurance." [35]

33 Morrow, *The Philosopher's Apprentice*, p. 167.
34 Morrow, *The Philosopher's Apprentice*, p. 322.
35 Morrow, *The Philosopher's Apprentice*, p. 334.

The plutocrats are set to work in the boiler rooms and kitchens; she underpays them, starves and dehydrates them, and poisons their working and living atmospheres with the introduction of lead, mercury, sulfur dioxide, carbon dioxide, and carbon monoxide — after all, these men had, all along, campaigned against environmental extremism with "right-wing" scientific evidence that dismisses "left-wing" studies arguing that heavy metals and hydrocarbons are deleterious to human health.

After weeks of this treatment, the elite see the light: they discover in themselves shame at their former lives of greed and cruelty; they declare that they will improve working conditions, donate fortunes to schools, and protect rain forests. Pleased with their rehabilitation, Londa frees the three hundred; yet it takes only a few more weeks for the plutocrats to return to their corrupt ways, and, naturally, they go after Londa and her City of Reason with murderous intent.

Morrow sums up his attitudes very well in a *Locus* interview:

There was certainly a hope that I entertained for a while, that science could replace the magical, mystical, transcendent element of religion, because after all, this cosmos is astonishing in its scope and beauty, and we've only begun to probe it. That seems not to be working out, though. I'm a scientific humanist, and I still believe that world-view is the most valid of all possible world-views, but I don't think it can work for very many people, because science is something you cannot practice unless you're part of that very small sub-population of investigators ... Maybe people will come to see that the given world, the given universe, is itself so astonishing and mysterious that we don't have to live under this sort of dictatorship of tradition, this allegiance to myths ... And I particularly value science fiction because it's not afraid of these big questions. Certainly politicians don't want to talk about the Big Questions. [36]

36   "James Morrow: Having It Both Ways," in *Locus* 41:2 (August 1998): 67.

Robert J. Sawyer tackles these and other Big Questions throughout his work, fiction and essay alike. In an interview with Steven H. Silver, he said that, although "some problems are inherently insoluble," nevertheless, "What's left for us to do is fight the good fight about the value of rationalism over superstition, of openmindedness but not credulousness over dogma. Certainly, that's what I'm trying to do in my books" ("A Conversation with Robert J. Sawyer," *SF Site* online, July 2002).

He says elsewhere:

> One of the things that's bothered me over the years is that "science" is a turn-off word for a lot of people, and the science fiction audience is declining. I think a better name for most ambitious science fiction is "philosophical fiction." It's fiction about big ideas. Where did we come from? Why are we here? Where are we going? If you ask somebody if they are interested in quantum computing or cloning, they'll say "No." But if you ask, "Are you interested in what it means to be human, whether there's life after death, whether there was ever any intelligent intervention in the creation of human beings?," almost everybody is interested in that. I never downplay the science in my books and I call myself a science fiction writer, but the philosophy and the metaphysics (which I don't think is a dirty word) are the most interesting to me these days. [37]

These themes appear in all of his books, notably in the *Quintaglio Ascension* trilogy, consisting of the Homer Award-winning *Far-Seer* (1992), another Homer Award winner, *Fossil Hunter* (1993) and *Foreigner* (1994), and in the *Neanderthal Parallax* trilogy, consisting of the Hugo Award-winning *Hominids* (2002), the Hugo-nominated *Humans* (2003), and *Hybrids* (2003).

---

37   "Robert J. Sawyer: Quantum Metaphysics," in *Locus* 50:2 (February 2003): p. 93.

The *Quintaglio* novels are set on another planet where intelligent dinosaurs live, though, as he told Silver, they "were only peripherally about dinosaurs, anyway; they were really about science versus superstition ... [They] metaphorically told the story of the dawn of modern science." *Far-Seer* tells the life of the saurian version of Galileo Galilei, whose scientific accomplishments supported Nicolaus Copernicus's heliocentric, rather than geocentric, cosmology. *Fossil Hunter* in turn imagines a Charles Darwin, a Quintaglio geologist who must prove that his theory of evolution is true in order to save his world. And *Foreigner* describes the rise of psycho-analysis with a saurian Sigmund Freud. As a Quintaglio historian sums:

> Historically, there have been three great blows to the Quintaglio ego.
>
> First, Afsan delivered the cosmological blow by taking God out of our skies and moving us from the center of the universe to one of its countless backwaters.
>
> Then, Toroca dealt us the biological blow, showing that we were not divinely created from the hands of God but rather had evolved through natural processes from other animals.
>
> And, finally, Mokleb administered the psychological blow, proving that we were not rational beings acting on lofty principles but are in fact driven by the dark forces that control our subconscious minds.[38]

Sawyer's dinosaurs were transported from Earth to their planet by an alien race. Though they share many of humanity's foibles — religious credulity, violent territorialism, discomfort with new modes of thinking — Sawyer has them reach Enlightenment within a single generation. The clear implication is that humans should be doing a bit better. In fact, as Sawyer expressed it:

38   Sawyer, *Foreigner*. New York: Tor, 1994, p. [13].

The philosophy of my books has always been rationality as the most prized of human virtues. *Far-Seer*, *Fossil Hunter*, and *Foreigner* took three of the turning points in human intellectual development ... All three of those are interesting for us, but they aren't crucial. As much as I decry the Creationist movement getting evolution out of the schools, what you believe doesn't actually affect anything in the world. I wanted to write novels where that was desperately important, and the species would die if they did not learn to understand the subconscious forces that were driving them as a species to violence. [39]

The *Neanderthal Parallax* trilogy deals with similar themes at greater length. The premise is that, in a parallel universe, the Neanderthals developed intelligence, while *Homo sapiens* became extinct. When two Neanderthal physicists tinker with a quantum computer, one of them, Ponter Boddit, is unintentionally removed from his world and lands in ours. He is befriended by Mary Vaughan, a geneticist who specializes in recovering DNA from ancient specimens, Reuben Montego, a physician, and Louise Benoît, a postdoctoral physics student. The four spend several days in quarantine at Reuben's house, and as Ponter develops the ability to speak English, he asks questions about this Earth where he must presumably spend the rest of his life.

He is astounded to learn that there are over six billion humans on the planet; the Neanderthal world, where society is based on hunting and gathering, has under two hundred million. Mary explains to him how the human reliance on agriculture led to unrestrained overpopulation.

"You manage to comfortably feed six billion people with plants?"

"Well, ah, no," said Mary. "About half a billion people don't

39   "Robert J. Sawyer: Quantum Metaphysics," in *Locus* 50:2 (February 2003): 92-93.

have enough to eat."

"That is very bad," said Ponter, simply.

Mary could not disagree. Still, she realized with a start that Ponter had, to this point, been exposed only to a sanitized view of Earth. He'd seen a little TV, but not enough to really open his eyes. Nonetheless, it did seem that Ponter was going to spend the rest of his life on this Earth. He needed to be told about war, and the crime rate, and pollution, and slavery — the whole bloody smear across time that was human history. [40]

Ponter also learns about human religions; his people are entirely atheistic rationalists. Mary must explain to him about her Catholic beliefs, including her God, the son of God, life after death in a Heaven or a Hell, the soul, the immaculate conception; and Ponter grows more and more bewildered.

"Well," replied Mary, "not everyone on Earth — on this Earth, that is — believes in an afterlife."

"Do the majority?"

"Well ... yes, I guess so."

"Do you?"

Mary frowned, thinking. "Yes, I suppose I do."

"Based on what evidence?" asked Ponter. The tone of his Neanderthal words was neutral; he wasn't trying to be derisive.

"Well, they say that ..." She trailed off. Why did she believe it? She was a scientist, a rationalist, a logical thinker. But, of course, her religious indoctrination had occurred long before she'd been trained in biology. Finally, she shrugged a little, knowing her answer would be inadequate. "It's in the Bible." [41]

40   Sawyer, *Hominids*. New York: Tor, 2002, p. 268-269.
41   Sawyer, *Hominids*, p. 290-291.

Later, Ponter is surprised to hear about human belief in the cosmological big bang, which he dismisses as yet another creation myth.

> "Well," said Mary. "I don't think you're going to convince many people that the big bang didn't happen."
>
> "That is fine. Feeling a need to convince others that you are right also is something that comes from religion, I think; I am simply content to know that I am right, even if others do not know it." [42]

Ponter again challenges Mary, and the United States government, when she takes him to Washington, D.C.

> She looked away from the black wall and waved her hand at objects in the distance. "This whole mall is filled with memorials. The pair of walls here point at two of the most important ones. That spire is the Washington Monument, a memorial to the first U.S. president. Over there, that's the Lincoln Memorial, commemorating the president who freed the slaves."
>
> Ponter's translator bleeped.
>
> Mary let out a sigh. Evidently there was still more complexity, more — what had she called it? — more dirty linen to be aired.

And when they visit the Vietnam Veterans Memorial:

> "And the reason to not forget the past," said Ponter, "is so that the same mistakes can be avoided."
>
> "Well, yes, of course," said Mary.
>
> "So has this memorial served its purpose? Has the same mistake — the mistake that led to all these young people dying — been avoided since?"

42   Sawyer, *Hominids*, p. 363.

Mary thought for a time, then shook her head. "I suppose not. Wars are still fought, and —"

"By America? By the people who built this monument?"

"Yes," said Mary.

"Why?"

"Economics. Ideology. And ..."

"Yes?"

Mary lifted her shoulders. "Revenge. Getting even."

"When this country decides to go to war, where is the war declared?"

"Um, in the Congress. I'll show you the building later."

"Can this memorial be seen from there?"

"This one? No, I don't think so."

"They should do it right here," said Ponter, flatly. "Their leader — the president, no? — he should declare war right here, standing in front of these fifty-eight thousand, two hundred and nine names. Surely that should be the purpose of such a memorial: if a leader can stand and look at the names of all those who died a previous time a president declared war and still call for young people to go off and be killed in another war, then perhaps the war is worth fighting." [43]

Sawyer wrote these novels during the years in which the George W. Bush administration had sent troops to invade Iraq without provocation. Ponter's declaration cannot be misunderstood: President Bush, or his advisors, should have realized from historical precedent that they should have reconsidered whether "the war is worth fighting."

Jonathan Lethem claimed to express little in the way of political commentary in his early science fiction stories, saying in an interview with me that stories such as "Walking the Moons," (1990), "'Forever,' Said the

43   Sawyer, *Humans*. New York: Tor, 2003, p. 189, 198-199.

Duck" (1993) and "How We Got in Town and Out Again" (1996)

come out of the *Galaxy*-Frederik Pohl-C.M. Kornbluth-*New Maps of Hell* tradition where the skeptical 1950s-style science-fiction writer takes a debunking position on his society's infatuation with technological development, usually in light of some instinctively Marxist sense of how capitalism corrupts the reception of radical technology ... I grew up reading dystopian and skeptical science fiction passionately, and I write that way by default. Most of my stories work from a ground assumption that dystopian realities are plausible ones, that we're probably living in a dystopia ourselves at the moment. That's my vocabulary. So any specific skepticisms that arise are against that ground. ("Private Hells and Radical Doubts," *Science Fiction Studies* online, July 1998)

He adds about the characters in his 1995 novel *Amnesia Moon*, "They've exchanged freedom and awareness for some kind of organizing principle or explanation. And it's usually a bad deal."

FK: A related question takes note of the fact that what organizing principles or explanations there are in your stories do tend to be handed down from above, so my next question was whether you consider yourself a political writer.

JL: Well, I'm very uncomfortable with the idea that I'm a political writer ...

FK: I mean political in the anthropological sense of power structures, not in the specific sense of the modern American political system.

JL: I inherited a skepticism. My parents were war-resisters, and I grew up, I came to consciousness in the early 70s, during Watergate, essentially, so as with my relativism, it's a ground I stand on, that powerful skepticism. But I'm equally [aware that] there's a tremendous susceptibility to conspiracy theories out there. Those always seem to me as naïve about the way the world works as utopian fantasies. They're equally attempts to understand the world according to one vast, organizing principle, which is a betrayal of the complex and ambiguous and, most importantly, the uncontrolled nature of our experiences. Conspiracy theorists believe that things feel chaotic and out-of-control only because someone bad is controlling them, which is one fiction among many fictions that people use to feel less out of control.

When you ask me if I'm political, what you're really saying is, "Do you identify your critique of everyday life as a political one?" It seems to me a politics of consciousness and a politics of awareness are so lacking in most of what are considered to be political viewpoints, that I'm not sure I want to call it politics. Before I can begin to discuss the kinds of questions that people normally call "politics," I would have to solve perceptual and mental and emotional confusions that seem to me to so surround every discourse that I certainly haven't gotten anywhere close to "politics" yet.

FK: I was thinking of politics in that more general sense, just because you are so keenly aware of rhetoric. I thought that you might be interested in the linguistic aspect of politics.

JL: I'm very interested in the linguistic aspect of our struggle to control or understand our experience of everyday life.

That's a kind of politics, a root kind. It's a politics of everyday life and a politics of perceptual coping that underlie what seem to me to be the falsely dichotomized arguments that are carried on instead of these deeper interrogations. That stratum of falsely dichotomized arguments seems to me to be "politics."

FK: "Light and the Sufferer," it seems to me, describes the urban life of the junkies as a series of choices about whether to behave as predator or as prey. *Gun, With Occasional Music* describes what is tantamount to a police state, where the civilians are victimized by the Inquisitor's Office ... now that I think about it there aren't that many *predators*, but I feel as though a lot of your characters feel that they're *victims'*.

JL: They do. A lot of my characters feel that they're victims, and ... I usually end up complicating it, and, demonstrating the "victim's" complicity with the "oppressing" apparatus or personalities, whether it's a family or a society. Their complicity with the structure that makes them feel victimized.

Undeniably, however, works such as *Motherless Brooklyn* (1999), *The Fortress of Solitude* (2003), and *You Don't Love Me Yet* (2007) are more overtly political in that they are placed in modern and real-life settings, in which the politics of race, the politics of sexual relations, and even the politics within a musical group rise above subtext. They are also far less dystopian and far more humorous than his earlier works which were earnest, but earnest in a different, more needing-to-prove-quality way than the later, more auto-biographical novels. His landscapes are haunted and policed by inscrutable, punitive spaces such as prisons, barrios, xenophobic colonies, even exclusive scientific or technologized communities. The opposite of a conspiracy paranoiac, he warns in works such as *Gun With Occasional Music* (1994), *Amnesia Moon*, and *As She Climbed Across the Table* (1997) that we have become not only menaced but deafened with information turned into noise.

Meanwhile, Connie Willis criticizes government by showing how politics can infect quotidian lives at the personal level; her protagonists are bedeviled by ineffectual busybodies who attempt to run society or who meddle with personal liberties as well as with scientific progress: pseudo-scientists with all the answers, inept nurses, middle-managers and conference organizers, control freaks, overbearing do-gooders, hypocrites and political-correctness zealots of all stripes. For example, in her Hugo and Nebula winner *Doomsday Book* (1992), a team of time-travelers in the History Department is preparing a "drop," or transplantation of a history student, Kivrin, from the 21st century to the 14th. Professor Dunworthy wants to delay the drop, as he believes the Middle Ages are far too dangerous. He asks a colleague where Basingame, the Head of the History Faculty is, and is told the man has already departed on Christmas vacation. Dunworthy says, bitterly,

> "He is, and Gilchrist maneuvered to be appointed Acting Head in his absence so he could get the Middle Ages opened to time travel. He rescinded the blanket rating of ten and arbitrarily assigned rankings to each century. Do you know what he assigned the 1300s? A six. A six! If Basingame had been here, he'd never have allowed it."

And:

> "... Gilchrist is sending Kivrin into a century which is clearly a ten, a century which had scrofula and the plague and burned Joan of Arc at the stake." [44]

44   Connie Willis, *Doomsday Book*. New York: Bantam, 1992, p. 5.

Because of Gilchrist's self-righteous meddling, the drop is mis-managed: Kivrin winds up, not in 1320, the drop destination, but in 1348, the year when the Black Death reached England. And because of another scientists's mistake, a pandemic influenza is let loose in contemporary England.

Kivrin is taken in by a family and forced to watch helplessly as they and the rest of the villagers die agonizingly from bubonic plague. The last survivor, Father Roche, who believes Kivrin to be a saint, breaks her heart with his dying words.

> "Bless me, Father, for I have sinned," he began in Latin.
>
> He hadn't sinned. He had tended the sick, shriven the dying, buried the dead. It was God who should have to beg forgiveness.
>
> "— in thought, word, deed, and omission. I was angry with Lady Imeyne. I shouted at Maisry." He swallowed. "I had carnal thoughts of a saint of the Lord."
>
> Carnal thoughts.
>
> "I humbly ask pardon of God, and absolution of you, Father, if you think me worthy."
>
> There is nothing to forgive, she wanted to say. Your sins are no sins. Carnal thoughts. We held down Rosemund and barricaded the village against a harmless boy and buried a six-month-old baby. It is the end of the world. Surely you are to be allowed a few carnal thoughts.
>
> She raised her hand helplessly, unable to speak the words of absolution, but he did not seem to notice. "Oh, my God," he said, "I am heartily sorry for having offended Thee."
>
> Offended Thee. You're the saint of the Lord, she wanted to tell him, and where the hell is He? Why doesn't He come and save you? [45]

45   Willis, *Doomsday Book*, p. 410.

In 1982's "Fire Watch," another Nebula and Hugo Award winner set in the same universe as *Doomsday Book*, a student friend of Kivrin's, Bartholomew, has prepared himself for four years to meet Saint Paul the Apostle, and is told two days before the drop that he will, instead, be sent to 1940 London to help save Saint Paul's Cathedral from the bombs of the second World War's Blitz. Bartholomew is unprepared for his new job of fire-fighting, but he falls in love with the cathedral, befriends a girl named Enola as well as a cat, the first living pet he has seen in his life, and is suspected by another fire watch man, Langby, of being a Nazi spy. For three months he lives through fear, sleepless exhaustion, the blackouts, lostness and loss. Returning from this grievous practicum, he receives with shock his final exam papers. In one of the most celebrated rants in science fiction, Bartholomew demonstrates Willis's humanism.

I looked down at the test. It read, "Number of incendiaries that fell on St. Paul's————Number of land mines———— Number of high explosive bombs————Method most commonly used for extinguishing incendiaries————land mines————high explosive bombs————Number of voluteers on first watch———— ——second watch————Casualties————Fatalities————" The questions made no sense. There was only a short space, long enough for the writing of a number, after any of the questions. Method most commonly used for extinguishing incendiaries. How would I ever fit what I knew into that narrow space? Where were the questions about Enola and Langby and the cat?

I went up to Dunworthy's desk. "St. Paul's almost burned down last night," I said. "What kind of questions are these?"

"You should be answering questions, Mr. Bartholomew, not asking them."

"There aren't any questions about the people," I said. The

outer casing of my anger began to melt.

"Of course there are," Dunworthy said, flipping to the second page of the test. "Number of casualties, 1940. Blast, shrapnel, other."

"Other?" I said. At any moment the roof would collapse on me in a shower of plaster dust and fury. "Other? Langby put out a fire with his own body. Enola has a cold that keeps getting worse. The cat ..." I snatched the paper back from him and scrawled "one cat" in the narrow space next to "blast." "Don't you care about them at all?"

"They're important from a statistical point of view," he said, "but as individuals they are hardly relevant to the course of history."

My reflexes were shot. It was amazing to me that Dunworthy's were almost as slow. I grazed the side of his jaw and knocked his glasses off. "Of course they're relevant!" I shouted. "They *are* the history, not all these bloody numbers!" [46]

He earns a "first," with honors, for proving himself a true historian.

Far more humorous, though depicting the same level of outrage, is Willis's Hugo- and Nebula-nominated *Passage* (2001), in which two scientists attempting to discover the neurological basis for the near death experience (the "light at the end of the tunnel" phenomenon) are plagued by a popinjay whose best-selling books dish up "proofs" of a paradisiacal afterlife and who corrupts the factual testimony of patients at Mercy General Hospital by convincing them, before they can be scientifically interviewed, of his specious irrationalities.

"He's a famous author," Mrs. Davenport said. "He wrote *The Light at the End of the Tunnel*. It was a best-seller, you know."

"Yes, I know," Joanna said.

"He's working on a new one," Mrs. Davenport said. "*Messages*

46   Willis, "Fire Watch," in *The Science Fiction Century*, edited by David G. Hartwell. New York: Tor, 1997, p. 457-458.

from the Other Side. You know, you'd never know he was famous. He's so nice. He has a wonderful way of asking questions."

He certainly does, Joanna thought. She'd heard him: "When you went through the tunnel, you heard a buzzing sound, didn't you? Would you describe the light you saw at the end of the tunnel as golden? Even though it was brighter than anything you'd ever seen, it didn't hurt your eyes, did it? When did you meet the Angel of Light?" Leading wasn't even the word.

And smiling, nodding encouragingly at the answers he wanted. Pursing his lips, asking concernedly, "And you don't remember hovering above the operating table? You're sure?"

They remembered it all for him, leaving their body and entering the tunnel and meeting Jesus, remembered the Light and the Life Review and the Meetings with Deceased Loved Ones. Conveniently forgetting the sights and sounds that didn't fit and conjuring up ones that did. And completely obliterating whatever had actually occurred.[47]

As Bryn Neuenschwander would say, "sacrilicious" is exactly the word. Willis's contempt with this sort of generation of false data recalls that, in Sawyer's *Golden Fleece* (1990), "mystic" is used as a curse-word.

Elsewhere, Joanna and her colleague, Dr. Richard Wright, joke about the fact that "messages from the beyond" are not worthy of interest, much less belief, as they always consist of banal platitudes: There is never a sublime quotation from the beyond, never a fascinating insight from, say, an Egyptian princess or a European king. No, the messages from the beyond are always the same humdrum promises that the dying body will release a soul which will live in a pudding of happiness ever after.

In stark contrast with to Connie Willis's satires about the banality of evil, Kim Stanley Robinson, the eco-thriller novelist *par excellence*,

47   Willis, *Passage*. New York: Bantam Books, 2001, p. 4-5.

uses fearless *romans à clef* to expose and harass the architects behind the controversial USA PATRIOT Act (in full: "Uniting and Strengthening America by Providing Appropriate Tools Required to Intercept and Obstruct Terrorism Act of 2001") and the even more controversial Global War on Terrorism, both of which allowed the George W. Bush administration to justify spending trillions of dollars in ongoing wars and their concomitant atrocities, particularly in Afghanistan and Iraq, while pursuing punitive domestic policies such as the misnamed Clear Skies Initiative and the rejection of the Kyoto Protocol. In Robinson's works, natural weather, behaving as it naturally will do, also stands in for political weather, representing those forces, which we cannot restrain, that inhibit proper conservation of our environment. Throughout his oeuvre, and most excitingly in *Antarctica* (1997), *Forty Signs of Rain* (2004), *Fifty Degrees Below* (2005), and *Sixty Days and Counting* (2007), the disastrous consequences of global warming signify the poisoned corollaries of turn-of-the-21st-century political developments.

Each of these novels features ecologically conscientious Senator Phil Chase, who will eventually run for presidential office and win. Chase is not only a door-always-open politician, he actually answers e-mails from individual citizens, and he takes his job and commitments and his personal history seriously, as is shown in this excerpted segment of an e-mail, "*Response to Response 1 to Response to Response 5,692*":

> So I see a fair bit of resentment. You old Vietnam vet, I see their eyes saying, you old hippie, you got lucky and were born in the right little window and got to grab all the surplus of happiness that history ever produced, and you blew it, you stood around and did nothing while the right reaganed back into power and shut down all possibility of change for an entire generation, you blew it in a ten-year party and staggered off stoned and complicit. You neither learned to do machine politics nor dismantled the machine.

Not one of you imagined what had to be done. And so the backlash came down, the reactionary power structure, stronger than ever. And now we're the ones who have to pay the price for that. [48]

I see the same sentiments expressed, less or more explicitly, in some of Tim Sullivan's works; I'm thinking particularly of his disaster-and-post-apocalypse novel *The Parasite War* (1992), a title which unambiguously declares sides of battle, a novel in which the alien invaders seem to a Vietnam veteran (Sullivan's older brother died in Vietnam) very much like an army of easily replaceable yet relentless Republican warriors:

It was so unfair, being able to die while your enemies could hardly be killed ... No matter how many pieces you blew them into, they kept coming. They would feed, recombine, and grow, and be just as threatening in a matter of days, or even hours. All you could do was slow them down, make them a bit more manageable, but if you didn't get away from them they'd mire you down and eat you alive. [49]

The doughty real-world Republican-turned-Democrat founder of the watchdog organization Media Matters for America David Brock would approve, as he would approve of Phil Chase. In *Forty Signs of Rain*, good guy Charlie Quibler, political advisor to Senator Chase, must strive against villains such as the President's science advisor, who

in Charlie's opinion was a pompous ex-academic of the worst kind, hauled out of the depths of a second-rate conservative think tank when the administration's first science advisor had been sent packing for saying that global warming might be real and not only

48   Robinson, *Sixty Days and Counting*. New York: Bantam, 2007, p. 250.
49   Sullivan, *The Parasite War*. New York: Avon, 1989, p. 5.

that, amenable to human mitigation. That went too far for this administration. Their line was that no one knew for sure and it would be too much expensive to do anything about even if they were certain it was coming — everything would have to change, the power generation systems, cars, a shift from hydrocarbons to helium or something, they didn't know, and they didn't own patents or already existing infrastructure for that kind of new thing, so they were going to punt and let the next generation solve their own problems in their own time. In other words, the hell with them. Easier to destroy the world than to change capitalism even one little bit.[50]

In *Antarctica*, Wade Norton, who, like Charlie, works for Senator Chase, has been sent to the continent at the South Pole to investigate what global warming is doing to the Antarctic ice shelves. In a conversation that dramatizes the integrity of these two men, the Senator expresses his worries that the 1991 environmental protocol for preservation of that continent is being undermined by the Republican administration:

> "I swear I cannot understand why the American people elect guys like him, it's absurd. Congress from one party and President from the other, they do it more often than not, what can they be thinking? All it does is make it impossible to do anything!"
> "That's the point. That's what they're hoping for."
> "But why hope for gridlock? No one likes to see it in traffic."
> "They're hoping that if the government can't do anything, then history will stop happening and things will always stay just like they are right now."
> "What's so great about right now!"
> "Not much, but they figure it can only get worse. It's a

50   Robinson, *Forty Signs of Rain*. New York: Bantam, 2004, p. 143.

damage-control strategy. They can see just as clearly as anyone that the globalized economy means they're all headed for the sweatshop."[51]

And it is this kind of fatalism and battle fatigue that launches *Antarctica*'s eco-saboteur on his way:

> He saw more clearly every day that the big slogan-ideas like democracy, free markets, technological advancement, scientific objectivity, and progress in history, were all myths on the same level as the feudal divine right of kings: self-serving alibis that a minority of rich powerful people were using to control the world. Modern society, like all the societies before it, ever since Sumer and Babylon, was a giant fake, a pyramid scheme in which the wealth of the world funneled up to the rich; and its natural environment was laid waste to bulk the obscenely huge bank balances of people who lived on private islands in the Caribbean. [52]

Robinson has used in various books the term "Götterdämmerung capitalism," by which he means that entirely free-market, entirely deregulated capitalism in the United States can lead only to disaster, for the world's people and for the world's environment, and this group of novels about sustainability and ecotage showcases Robinson's angered wit at its finest. After damage-control strategy fails in *Forty Signs of Rain*, resulting in the Californian coast-lines beginning to crumble into the Pacific Ocean and widespread flooding on the Eastern Seaboard, Charlie Quibler is astonished at how the news media try to toe the party line and remain upbeat in their reports on daily natural disasters:

51   Robinson, *Antarctica*. New York: Bantam, 1998, p. 35.
52   Robinson, *Antarctica*, p. 37-38.

The media meteorologists were already in a lather of anticipation and analysis, not only over the arctic blast but also in response to a tropical storm now leaving the Bahamas, even though it had wreaked less damage than had been predicted.

"'Unimpressive,' this guy calls it. My God! Everyone's a critic. Now people are *reviewing the weather*." [53]

Robinson opens the sequel, *Fifty Degrees Below*, with a funny yet not-at-all cynical summation of the new state of the union:

Nobody likes Washington, D.C. Even the people who love it don't like it. Climate atrocious, traffic worse: an ordinary mid-sized gridlocked American city, in which the plump white federal buildings make no real difference. Or rather they bring all the politicians and tourists, the lobbyists and diplomats and refugees and all the others who come from somewhere else, often for suspect reasons, and thereafter spend their time clogging the streets and hogging the show, talking endlessly about their nonexistent city on a hill while ignoring the actual city they are in. The bad taste of all that hypocrisy can't be washed away even by the food and drink of a million very fine restaurants ...

So naturally when the great flood washed over the city, wreaking havoc and leaving the capital spluttering in the livid heat of a wet and bedraggled May, the stated reactions were varied, but the underlying subtext often went something like this: HA HA HA. [54]

As *Fifty Degrees Below* sees yet further devastating extremes of climate, the American president, never named but always already and increasingly identifiable as George Bush, tackles the problems with idiosyncratic vernacular certitude:

53   Robinson, *Forty Signs of Rain*, p. 319.
54   Robinson, *Fifty Degrees Below*. New York: Bantam, 1998, p. [3].

The president announced on the campaign trail that he had inherited this problem from his Democratic predecessors, particularly Bill Clinton, and that only free markets and a strong national defense could battle this new threat, which he continued to call climatic terrorism. "Why, you can't be sure you won't wake up someday to find the world spitting in your face. It's not okay, and I'm going to do something about it ..." [55]

Elsewhere in this novel, another of Senator Chase's aides mocks a phrase in a campaign speech, saying, "We'll join humanity? ... What's this, Democrats as aliens?" [56] In the face of such determined blindness to the reality of disaster and death, Charlie Quibler's wife Anna exclaims, "There's so much information out there. And so many organizations! ... We know, but we can't act." [57]

Robinson tops himself in style, rhetoric, and allusion in these novels. Having turned "reagan" into a verb, he one-ups it by noting that "capitalism continues to vampire its way around the globe, determined to remain unaware of the problem it's creating," and, recognizing William Shakespeare as a fellow diversionist in disaster, cheerfully tosses out quips such as "now is the winter of our wet content" [58] and "[they] called for a particular protein to come out from the vasty deep of a particular gene, and it would have come when they called for it." [59]

If Robinson tops my list of very ecologically concerned yet also very funny authors, I must give credit to Rob Sawyer for rivaling him.

Granted, few settings in my decades of reading science fiction can match the horror of the presumably paved-over world in Kessel's "Not Responsible! Park and Lock It!" (1981), in which individuals, families, generations live only to drive as far and as fast as they can on an apparently

55   Robinson, *Fifty Degrees Below*, p. [367].
56   Robinson, *Fifty Degrees Below*, p. [175].
57   Robinson, *Fifty Degrees Below*, p. 253.
58   Robinson, *Sixty Days and Counting*, p. 265.
59   Robinson, *Sixty Days and Counting*, p. 110.

unending highway — the "Westward" route, as though these car-caged families are lighting out for the territories, when all evidence suggests they are merely circumnavigating a single highway, in a circle which has no end. This endless ribbon of road is only slightly more comprehensible than that of the equatorial wall circling the planet of Robinson's *A Short Sharp Shock* (1990), and lacking only the gore of David R. Bunch's *Moderan* stories, which take gleeful delight in rendering humans into machines whose destinies are quite as pointless as those in Kessel's story.

Kessel's and Bunch's stories are written satirically, though with existential punch in the former and with murderous merriment in the latter, but when Sawyer writes about the wreckage humans have created of our planet, it is not only with satire but also with pain and poignancy.

In *Hominids*, over dinner with Mary, Louise, and Reuben, the Neanderthal from the adjacent universe admits that he is becoming a bit bored with beef, and asks whether, for a change, they might have mammoth for dinner instead. The humans are amazed, and then awfully embarassed when Ponter learns that mammoths have become extinct.

> "All over the world. They've been extinct for thousands of years."
>
> "Why?" asked Ponter. "Was it illness?"
>
> Everyone fell silent. Mary slowly exhaled the air in her lungs, trying to decide how to present this. "No, that's not why," she said, at last. "Umm, you see, we — our kind, our ancestors — we hunted mammoths to extinction."
>
> Ponter's eyes went wide. "You did what?"
>
> Mary felt nauseous; she hated having her version of humanity come up so short. "We killed them for food, and, well, we kept on killing them until there were none left."
>
> "Oh," said Ponter, softly. He looked out the window, at the large backyard to Reuben's house. "I am fond of mammoths," he

said. "Not just their meat — which is delicious — but as animals, as part of the landscape. There is a small herd of them that lives near my home. I enjoy seeing them."

"We have their skeletons," said Mary, "and their tusks, and every once in a while a frozen one is found in Siberia, but ..."

"All of them," said Ponter, shaking his head back and forth slowly, sadly. "You killed all of them ..."

Mary felt like protesting, "Not me personally," but that would be disingenuous; the blood of the mammoths was indeed on her house. Still, she needed to make some defense, feeble though it was: "It happened a long time ago."

Ponter looked queasy. "I am almost afraid to ask," said Ponter, "but there are other large animals I am used to seeing in this part of the world on my version of Earth. Again, I had assumed they were just avoiding this city of yours, but ..."

Reuben shook his shaven head. "No, that's not it."

Mary closed her eyes briefly. "I'm sorry, Ponter. We wiped out just about all the megafauna — here, and in Europe ... and in Australia" — she felt a knot in her stomach as the litany grew — "and in New Zealand, and in South America. The only continent that has many really big animals left is Africa, and most of those are endangered."

Bleep.

"On the verge of extinction," said Louise.

Ponter's tone was one of betrayal. "But you said this had all happened long ago."

Mary looked down at her empty plate. "We stopped killing mammoths long ago, because, well, we ran out of mammoths to kill. And we stopped killing Irish elk, and the big cats that used to populate North America, and woolly rhinoceroses, and all the others, because there were none left to kill."

"To kill every member of a species ..." said Ponter. He shook his massive head slowly back and forth.

...

Mary thought about protesting that it wasn't all the result of hunting; much of it had to do with the destruction by humans of the natural habitats of these creatures — but somehow that didn't seem any better. [60]

Sawyer's last phrase speaks a world of condemnation.

Ponter's horror only grows when he hears about the endangered species of panda bears, whales, many more animals — including chimpanzees, our own closest cousins in the primate world, for both *Homo sapiens* and *Homo neandertalensis*. He takes the logical step:

"And, on this world, my kind is extinct."

"Yes," said Mary, very softly. [61]

What neither Ponter nor Sawyer suggests is that the *next* step might be the extinction of humans, and, in the third novel of the trilogy, *Hybrids*, several characters unwittingly take steps that will bring us all in that direction. Sawyer has often quoted a dictum that Canadian authors prefer tragic endings, while Americans prefer happy endings; in *Hybrids*, he creates (to paraphrase Mark Twain) a conclusion that can satisfy some and exasperate the rest.

As early as his first novel, *Golden Fleece*, Sawyer had evoked the possibility that humans might not be the best judges of our own decisions. That novel opens with the sinister line (again, one of the Great First Sentences of science fiction), narrated by the ship-manipulating Artificial Intelligence, "I love that they trusted me blindly." However, it ends with many proofs that the AI is right, and that humans cannot be expected during circum-

60   Sawyer, *Hominids*. New York: Tor, 2002, p. 333-334.
61   Sawyer, *Hominids*, p. 335.

stances of blind panic to choose correctly — and Sawyer makes it clear that wrong decisions *are* made under bad circumstances, and that sometimes an impartial judge is best. As Raymond Williams wrote, "The losses are real and heartbreaking because the desires were real, the shared work was real, the unsatisfied impulses were real ... People choose wrongly but under terrible pressures."[62]

And Sawyer, and the other authors in this volume, excel at putting their people under terrible pressures.

These Rationalist authors use drama and disaster, a heady mix of the sublime and a vigorous kaleidoscope of ideas whose facets shine different, and differently fractured, colors on the glow of first-time meetings and on the shadows of unpleasant memories. Variously, my authors dramatize an invigorating mixture of pumping exaltation and breathless humility to put on display their varied ideas about the desperate choices humanity now faces.

Despite the sheer entertainment value that disaster novels provide us — after all, there is inherent drama in the spectacle of human degradation, especially when characters are portrayed as political foes, alien enemies, or simply lousy humans — I insist that all of the Savage Humanists must be taken as didacts and as entertainers in equal measure.

These writers, who agree or disagree to self-identify as Savage Humanists, are undoubtedly the most daring writers we have today, as I write this in the censorious age of the George W. Bush presidency. They are fearless, they are funny, and as experts of the "If this goes on ..." school, they continue to excel and to push boundaries that frighten the sorts of folks who affix ratings on films coming to theaters near you. A century from now, they will be recognized as the ten percent rising above what Theodore Sturgeon referred to as the crud, just as J.R.R. Tolkien will be recognized as our greatest contributor to epic adventure/quest fiction and Sheri Tepper and Jack McDevitt among will be recognized as our greatest creators of what

62   Raymond Williams, *The Country and the City*. New York, Oxford University Press, 1973, p. 213.

used to be called "space opera" but which I call the SF Interplanetary Sublime. They exult in the sense of wonder and assault those who would censor or stifle it.

When reading the Savage Humanists, we do not read only satire. We encounter great vistas, we read of enormous possibilities stretching out infinitely in every direction, we encounter humans who can become gods and goddesses. These writers stimulate us with the ideas of exploration that push not out only of Earth's gravity well but also that push at the edges of reality, forcing our own ideas to challenge those of stupid earthly political ideas as well as the reaches of cosmology. They ground us in the social realities of our own times, the late 20th century and the early 21st, but they give us a tantalizing and tortured view of tomorrow. This view is not delivered from the back seat of a limousine, nor from the saddle of a domesticated dragon, but is an honest view of the future they expect to occur.

Among their concerns, these writers deal with the fact that our environment has become increasingly artificial and information-rich, and they present the variety of ways in which characters may react to and mediate it. They also see, in the modern awareness of escalating threat and anxiety, the irony that TV news stations and programs, video games, paperbacks and movies compete to keep the audience's attention by presenting the most graphic and horrifying events available. Part of this almost absurdist view of the modern world as a hellhole of noise is the suspicion that the variety of ways in which information may be received and interpreted is explicitly linked with the variety of ways in which real and fictional people cope with threatened or actual catastrophe. Perhaps this is why so many of these writers have a gift for comic invention in which they reveal their angers in comedic and realistic descriptions of disaster, placed in real-world geographical settings. They may hope that their prescriptions for real-world problem-solving will be heard, but may wryly expect them to be ignored. In the case of each of these authors, many of their expectations and prognostications have proven to be soundly founded, to become sad facts. Yet, to borrow William Faulkner's dictum from *The Sound and the Fury*, they endure — and they persevere. (Granted: Our world still has to catch up with the weird wonders of the worlds that Jim Kelly and Jonathan Lethem offer.)

I've been bold in choosing to identify a literary movement, yet I've identified it by means of the scientific method. There are other authors whom I would include under my rubric; I've chosen the best for this volume. I'm not alone in recognizing their quality: only seven writers in history have won all three of the world's top awards for best novel of the year, the Hugo, the Nebula, and the John W. Campbell Memorial Award; three of them are represented here (Robinson, Sawyer, and Willis), and all of the authors in this book have been nominated for the Hugo, the Nebula, or both.

Although I've affixed the words "disaster" or "catastrophe" to many of the novels and stories described here, each one has suffused me with a feeling of that expansive joy we feel when we see a way to improve the world, at both the personal and the political levels. These authors are not afraid to meet the challenge of the frenzied, irrational, and no longer banal evils they see in the world. I am proud of the Savage Humanists, because they do not simply complain. On the contrary.

Their novels and stories guide us on a progressive and preservationist path to the best possible future, for humans and for our fellow creatures who share this precious planet with us ... and for the Neanderthals, extra-terrestrials, or other peoples who might one day join us. ▮

MADONNA OF THE MAQUILADORA

BY GREGORY FROST

Gregory Frost (born 1951, in Des Moines, Iowa) has published seven novels, including *The Pure Cold Light* (1993), the World Fantasy Award nominee *Fitcher's Brides* (2002), and *Shadowbridge* and *Lord Tophet* (2008); a collection, *Attack of the Jazz Giants and Other Stories* (2005); and 39 short stories, including "How Meersh the Bedeviler Lost His Toes" (1998), a nominee for the Theodore Sturgeon Short Fiction Award. He graduated from Clarion Workshop in 1975 and has since taught there several times. "Madonna of the Maquiladora" was a finalist for the James Tiptree Award, the Nebula Award, the Theodore Sturgeon Memorial Award, and the Hugo Award. His website is at gregoryfrost.com.

In an interview with Victoria McManus (*Strange Horizons* online, December 2002), Frost asserted that his science fiction is not of the "hard" or "technical problem solving" variety: "If I'm going to read science fiction, it'll be Richard Russo, Molly Gloss, Michael Swanwick, James Patrick Kelly, John Kessel. Writers whose people are well-wrought and whose stories emerge from those people interacting with each other or their world." Nevertheless, notice how the science is crucial to this novelette. Consider also the implications of the fact that, in this story, the factory workers create "motion controller systems."

When Frost workshopped this story at Sycamore Hill, award-winning author Andy Duncan began his critique by saying, "This is an angry sf story. We need more angry stories in this field." I agree.

MADONNA OF THE MAQUILADORA

YOU FIRST HEAR OF GABRIEL PEREA AND THE VIRGIN WHILE covering the latest fire at the Chevron refinery in El Paso. The blaze is under control, the water cannon hoses still shooting white arches into the scorched sky.

You've collected some decent shots, but you would still like to capture something unique even though you know most of it won't get used. The *Herald* needs only one all-inclusive shot of this fire, and you got that hours ago. The rest is out of love. You like to think there's a piece of W. Eugene Smith in you, an aperture in your soul always seeking the perfect image.

The two firemen leaning against one of the trucks is a good natural composition. Their plastic clothes are grease-smeared; their faces, with the hoods off, are pristine. Both the men are Hispanic, but the soot all around them makes them seem pallid and angelic and strange. And both of them are smoking. It's really too good to ignore. You set up the shot without them knowing, without seeming to pay them much attention, and that's when you catch the snippet of their conversation.

"I'm telling you, *cholo*, the Virgin told Perea this explosion would happen. Mrs. Delgado knew all about it."

"She tells him everything. She's telling us all. The time is coming, I think."

Click. "What time is that?" you ask, capping the camera.

The two men stare at you a moment. You spoke in Spanish — part of the reason the paper hired you. Just by your inflection, though, they know you're not a native. You may understand all right, but you are an outsider.

The closest fireman smiles. His teeth are perfect, whiter than the white bar of the Chevron insignia beside him. Mexicans have good tooth genes, you think. His smile is his answer: He's not going to say more.

"All right, then. Who's Gabriel Perea?"

"Oh, he's a prophet. The prophet, man."

"A seer."

"He knows things. The Virgin tells him."

"The Virgin Mary?" Your disbelief is all too plain.

The first fireman nods and flicks away his cigarette butt, the gesture transforming into a cross — "Bless me, father …"

"Does he work for Chevron?"

The firemen look at each other and laugh. "You kidding, man? They'd never hire him, even if he made it across the Rio Bravo with a green card between his teeth."

Rio Bravo is what they call the Rio Grande. You turn and look, out past the refinery towers, past the scrub and sand and the Whataburger stand, out across the river banks to the brown speckled bluffs, the shapes that glitter and ripple like a mirage in the distance.

Juarez.

"He's over there?"

"*Un esclavo de la maquiladora.*"

A factory slave. Already you're imagining the photo essay. "The Man Who Speaks to the Virgin," imagining it in *The Smithsonian, The National Geographic.* An essay on Juarez, hell on earth, and smack in the middle of hell, the Virgin Mary and her disciple. It assembles as if it's been waiting for you to find it.

"How about," you say, "I buy you guys a few beers when you're finished and you tell me more about him."

The second guy stands up, grinning. "Hey, we're finished now, *amigo*."

"Yeah, that fire's drowning. Nothing gonna blow today. The Virgin said so."

You follow them, then, with a sky black and roiling on all sides like a Biblical plague settling in for a prolonged stay.

— • —

You don't believe in her. You haven't since long ago, decades, childhood. Lapsed Catholics adopt the faith of opposition. The Church lied to you all the time you were growing up. Manipulated your fears and guilts. You don't plan to forgive them for this. The ones who stay believers are the ones who didn't ask questions, who accepted the rules, the restrictions, on faith. Faith, you contend, is all about not asking the most important questions. Most people don't think; most people follow in their hymnals. It takes no more than a fingernail to scrape the gilt from the statues and see the rot below. Virgin Mary didn't exist for hundreds of years after the death of Jesus. She was fashioned by an edict, by a not very bright emperor. She had a cult following and they gained influence and the ear of Constantine. It was all politics. Quid pro quo. Bullshit. This is not what you tell the firemen, but it does make the Virgin the perfect queen for Juarez: that place is all politics and bullshit, too. Reality wrapped in a shroud of the fantastic and the grotesque. Just like the Church itself.

You went across the first time two years ago, right after arriving. The managing editor, a burly, bearded radical in a sportcoat and tie named Joe Baum took you in. He knew how you felt about the power of photography, and after all you're the deputy art director. One afternoon he just walked over to your desk and said, "Come on, we're gonna take the afternoon, go visit some people you need to see." You didn't understand until later that he was talking about the ones on film. Most of them were dead.

Baum covered El Paso cultural events, which meant he mingled with managers and owners of the *maquiladoras*. "We'll have to get you into the loop. Always need pictures of the overlords in their tuxes to biff up the society pages." He didn't like them too much.

In his green Ford you crossed over on the Puente Libre, all concrete and barbed wire. He talked the whole time he drove. "What you're gonna see here is George Bush's New World Order, and don't kid yourself that it isn't. Probably you won't want to see it. Hell, I don't want to see it, and America doesn't want to see it with a vengeance."

He took you to the apartment of a man named Jaime Pollamano. Baum calls him the Chicken Man. Mustache, dark hair, tattoos. A face like a young Charles Bronson. Chicken Man is a street photographer. "We buy some of his photos, and we buy some from the others." There were six or seven in the little apartment that day, one of them, unexpectedly, a woman. The windows were covered, and an old sheet had been stuck up on the wall. They'd been expecting you. Baum had arranged in advance for your edification. "What you're gonna see today," he promised, "is the photos we don't buy."

The slide show began. Pictures splashed across the sheet on the wall.

First there were the female corpses, all in various states of decay and decomposition. Most were nude, but they weren't really bodies as much as sculptures now in leather and wood. The photographers had made them strange and haunting and terrifying, all at the same time. In the projector light you can see their eyes — squinting, hard, glancing down, here and there a look of pride, something almost feral. The woman is different. She stares straight at death.

"Teenage girls," Baum told you while the images kept coming. "They get up at like 4 a.m. to walk for miles to catch a bus to take them to a factory by six. They live in *colonias*, little squatter villages made of pallet wood and trash. Most of these girls here were kidnapped on the way to work. Tortured, raped, murdered. Nobody goes looking for them much. Employee turnover in the *maquiladoras* is between fifty and a hundred and fifty percent annually, so they're viewed as just another runaway *chica* who has to be replaced. The *pandillas*, the local gangs, get them, or *federales* on patrol, or even the occasional serial murderer. Who knows who? No one's looking for her anyway, save maybe her family."

All you could think to say was, "They've lost their breadwinner."

Baum snorted. "That's right. She worked a forty-eight hour week, six days, for about twenty-five dollars."

"A day?"

"A week. Per day they make about four dollars and fifty cents. Not just these girls, you understand. All of 'em. All the workers."

You tried to work that out, how they live on so little money. Finally you suggested, "The cost of living here is cheaper?" The handsome woman photographer's eyes shifted to you, cold with disgust.

The pictures never stopped coming. You finally passed the gauntlet of dead women. Now it was a man dangling like a piñata from a power line. He'd been electrocuted while trying to run a line from a transformer to his home. Then other dead men. Some dying in the street with people all around them. Others dead like the women, executed, tortured, burned alive. You tried to look elsewhere as the images just kept slamming the wall. How many deaths could there be? Baum suddenly said, "Let me put the cost of living thing in perspective for you. You're seventeen, you live in El Paso, you work six days a week all day and you buy your groceries and pay your bills on your thirty-five dollar paycheck. That's adjusted gross to compensate for the differences in cost on our side of the river.

"On this side along the river there are over three hundred factories. Big names you know: RCA, Motorola, Westinghouse, GE. We use their products, we all do. They employ almost 200,000 workers, mostly female, living crammed into the *colonias*, altogether about two million people. That's eighty percent unemployment, by the way."

Between the images and the facts, you're lost and grasping for some sort of reality. This is what a series of smiling presidents promised the world? Even as you flounder, the photos change course. A severed arm dangles from the big face of Mickey Mouse, both nailed to a wall; a clown head tops a barbed wire fence post, with laundry drying on the wire; a six-year-old holds a Coca-Cola can, only the straw's going up his nose, and you can tell by his slack face that whatever's in that can is fucking him up severely. The power of these images is in their simplicity: This isn't art, it just is. All you could do was repeat the mantra that this is what art is supposed to do — shake you up, make you think differently. Make you sweat. Doing its job. God, yes.

Afterwards Baum introduced you to the photographers but the room stayed dark. You walked through the line, shaking hands, nodding, dazed. One man was drunk. Another, the feral one, had the jittery sheen of an addict. The woman hung back. Reality after that onslaught barely touched you.

Baum bought some of the pictures in spite of what he'd told you, paying far too much for them. Maybe he collected them — you were sure they weren't going to get into the paper. You know what the paper will print. He walked you out, across the street, past his car and through the *Plaza de Armas*, the main square. It was a Friday night and there must have been a thousand people milling about. The ghosts of all those photos tagged along, bleeding into the world. The cathedral across the plaza was lit in neon reds, greens and golds, looking more like a casino than a church. Everywhere, people were selling something. Most of it was trash collected and reassembled into trinkets, earrings, belts, whatever their skill allowed. There were clowns on stilts wandering around. A man selling flavored ice chips. Baum bought two. Others sold tortillas, drugs, themselves. All of it smelled desperate. A lot of the crowd, Baum told you as you drove home after, were actually Americans. "They come across the border on Friday nights for a little action. The factory girls sell themselves for whatever extra dollars they can get from the party boys."

You remember at some point in the drive asking him why the workers don't unionize, and provoking the biggest laugh of all. "No union organizer would have a job by day's end, is why. Some of them don't make it home alive, either, although you can't tie anything to the corporations that fire them. Just as likely they pissed off their co-workers by threatening the status quo. It's happened before — whole shifts have been fired, everyone blamed for the actions of one or two. When you're an ant, it doesn't take a very big rock to squash you. My, what a glorious testament to American greed — and we've even kept it from crossing the border, too. So far."

— • —

That conversation comes back to you now, driving away from your drinks with the firemen. Gabriel Perea was an activist. In Baum's terms, he was a dangerous man to himself and anyone who knew him. The Virgin turned him, saved him. She's protecting him for something important. The firemen expect something between Armageddon and Rapture. Transcendence. All you know is that you want to get there before the Kingdom of Heaven opens for business.

— • —

"*Pura guasa*," Baum says when you tell him what you want to do. "Just a lot of superstitious chatter. Nonsense. I've heard about this guy before. He's like an urban legend over there. They need for him to exist, just like her."

Nevertheless, you say, it's a great story — the kind of thing that could garner attention. Awards. The human spirit finding the means to survive in the *maquiladora* even if that means is a fantasy. Baum concedes it could be terrific.

"If there's anything to it."

There's only one way to find that out. In *c. de Juarez,* all roads lead to the Chicken Man.

— • —

On the outside of his apartment someone has sprayed the words "*Dios Está Aquí.*" Chicken Man has moved three times since you first met him. Most of the street photographers move routinely, just to stay alive, to stay ahead of the *narcotraficantes,* or the cops, or anyone else they've pissed off with their pictures. Of the six you met that first day, only five are still living. Now Pollamano's holed up just off the *Pasea Triunfa de la República.* And holed up is the right term. The cinder block building has chicken wire over the windows and black plastic trash bags on the inside of them. You knock once and slide your business card under the door.

After a while the door opens slightly and you go in. It's hot inside, and the air smells like chemicals, like fixer and developer. The only light on is a single red bulb. Chicken Man wears a Los Lobos tank top, shorts and sandals. He's been breathing this air forever. He should have mutated by now. "*¿Quiubo,* Deputy?" Deputy is the street photographers' name for you. Titles are better than names here anyway. They call Joe Baum "La Bamba."

He invites you to sit. You tell him what the firemen told you. What you want to do with it.

"*El Hombre de la Madonna.* I know the stories. A lot of 'em circulating round."

"So, what's the truth? He isn't real? Doesn't see her?"

"Oh, he's real. And he maybe sees her." He crosses to the shelves made of cinder blocks and boards, rummages around in one of thirty or so cardboard boxes, returns with a 4x5 print. In the red light, it's difficult to see. Chicken Man turns on a maglight and hands it to you.

You're looking at a man in dark coveralls. He's standing at a crazy, Elvis Presley kind of angle, feet splayed and legs twisted. His hands are up in front of him, the fingers curled. There are big protective goggles over his eyes. He has a long square jaw and a mustache. Behind him other figures in goggles and coveralls stand, out of focus. They're co-workers and this is inside a factory someplace. Fluorescent lights overhead are just greenish smears. The expression on his face is fierce — wide-eyed, damn near cross-eyed.

"He was seein' her right then," says the Chicken Man.

"You took this?"

"Me? I don't set foot in the *maquilas*. Factory owners don't like us, don't want us taking pictures in there. Some of the young ones get in for a day, shoot and get out. I'm too old to try that kind of crap."

"Who, then?"

"*Doncella loca.*"

He holds out his hand, takes the photo back. When he hands it back, there's writing on it in grease pencil. A name, Margarita Espinada, and the words "*Colonia Universidad.*" He describes how to drive there. "You met her," he says, "the very first time La Bamba brought you over. She lives in her car mostly. *Auto loco.* I let her use my chemicals when she needs to. And the sink. She's shooting the Tarahumara kids now. Indians. They don't trust nobody, but they trust her. Same with the *maquilas*. Most of the workers are women. She gets in where I can't. She's kinda like you, Deputy. Only smart." He grins.

You grin back and hand him a twenty and three rolls of film. He slides the money into his pocket but kisses the plastic canisters. "*Gracias, amigo.*"

— • —

Colonia Universidad is easy to find because half of it has just burned to the ground and the remains are still smoking. Blackened oil drums, charcoal that had defined shacks the day before, naked bed springs and a few bicycle frames twisted into Salvador Dali forms. Margarita Espinada is easy to find, too. She wears a camera around her neck, and black jeans, boots, and a blue work shirt. The jeans are dirty, the shirt stained dark under the arms and down the back. Her black hair is short. The other women around her are wearing dresses and have long hair, and scarves on their heads. At a quick glance you might mistake her for a man.

They're all watching you before the car even stops. When you stride toward them, the women all back up, spread apart, move away. Margarita stands her ground. She raises her camera and takes your picture, as though in an act of defiance. From a distance she looks to be about twenty, but up close you can see the lines around the eyes and mouth. More like early thirties. Lean. There's a thin scar across the bridge of her nose and one cheek.

If she remembers you from the Chicken Man's, there's no sign of it in her eyes. You hand her the photo. She looks at it, at her name on the back, then wipes it down her thigh. "You want a drink, Deputy?" There's the tiniest suggestion of amusement in the question.

"I'm not really a deputy, you know. It's just a nickname."

"Hey, at least they don't call you *pendejo*."

"I don't know that they don't."

She laughs, and for a moment that resolute, defiant face becomes just beautiful.

The shack she takes you to is barely outside the fire line. The frame is held together by nails driven through bottle caps. The walls are cut up shipping cartons for Three Musketeers candy bars. No floor, only dirt. There's an old, rust-stained mattress and a couple of beat-up suitcases. She comes up with a bottle of tequila from God knows where, apologizes for the lack of ice and glasses. Then she takes a long swig from the mouth of the bottle. Her eyes are watering as she passes it to you. You smell her then, the odor of a woman mixed in with the smoke smell, sweat and flesh and dirt. You almost want to ask her why she does this, lives this way, but you haven't any right. Instead you say his name as a question.

She lays down the photo. "Gabriel Perea is real, he exists. He's what they call an assembler, on a production line. The *maquila* is about twenty miles from here. The story of him grows as it travels. All around."

You recite the firemen's version: great prophet, seer who will lead them into the kingdom of Heaven.

"*Pura guasa,*" is her answer. Pure foolishness — exactly what Baum said.

"But the picture. He is seeing the Virgin?"

She shrugs. "Yes, I know. From your eyes — how could I take the picture and not say it's true?" She pushes her thumb against the image, covering the face. "This says it's real. Not true. I know that he tells everyone what the Virgin wants them to know."

"And what's that?"

"To be patient. To wait. To endure their hardships. To remember that they will all find Grace in Heaven more beautiful than anything they can imagine."

"That wouldn't take much of a heaven. Has anyone else seen her?"

"No one in the factory now."

"But someone else?"

Again, she shrugs. "Maybe. There are stories. Someone saw her in a bathroom. In a mirror. There are always stories once it starts. People who don't want to be left out, who need to hear from her. That can be a lot of people.

"In *Colonia El Mirador*, a Sacred Heart shrine begins to bleed. It's a cheap little cardboard picture, and they say it bleeds, so I go and take its picture."

"Does it? Does it bleed?"

"I look in the picture I take, at how this piece of cardboard is nailed up, and I think, ah, the nailhead has rusted, the rust has run down the picture. That's all. But I don't say so."

"So, you lied to them, the people who made the claims about it?"

She snatches back the bottle. Her nostrils are flared in defiance, anger; but she laughs at your judgment, dismissing it. "I take the picture and it says what is what. If you don't see, then what good is there in telling you how to see?"

The anger, contained, burns off her like radiation. You flip open your Minox and take her picture. She stares at you in the aftermath of the flash, as if in disbelief.

Breaking the tension, you ask, "Is he crazy?"

She squats down in the dirt, her back pressed against the far wall, takes off the camera and sets it on the mattress. "Listen, I got a job in a factory because I heard there was a dangerous man there. A Zapatista brother, someone of the Reality. He had workers stirred up.

"And I thought, I want to be there when they have him killed. I want to document it. The bosses there will pay workers to turn in their co-workers. Pay them more money than they can earn in a month, so it's for sure someone will turn him in. But this Perea, he sought out those people and he convinced them not to do this. He offered hope. 'The Dream we can all dream, so that when we awaken it will remain with us.' That's what he promised. When I learned that, then I knew I had to photograph him. And his murder."

"Except the Virgin showed up."

She grins. "I hadn't even gotten my first exciting twenty dollar paycheck. The rumor circulated that he was going to confront the managers. Everyone was breathing this air of excitement. And I have my camera, I'm ready. Only all of a sudden, right on the factory floor, Gabriel Perea has a vision. He points and he cries, 'Oh, Mother of God! See her? Can you see her? Can you hear her, good people?' Of course we can't. No one can. They try, they look all around, but you know they don't see. He has to tell it. She says, 'Wait.' She says, 'There will be a sign.' She'll come again and talk to us."

"Did she? Did she come back?"

"About once every week. She came in and spoke to him when he was working. People started crowding around him, waiting for the moment. It's always when he doesn't expect. Pretty soon there are people clustering outside the factory and following Gabriel Perea home. The managers in their glass booths just watch and watch."

"They didn't try to stop it?"

"No. And no one got into trouble for leaving their position, or for trespassing. Trying to see him. To hear his message. And I begin to think, these men are at least afraid of God. There is something greater and more powerful than these *norteamericanos*."

"Yet you don't believe it?"

In answer, she gets up and takes the larger suitcase and throws it open on the mattress. Inside are photos, some in sleeves, some loose, some in folders. You see a color shot of a mural of a Mayan head surrounded by temples, photos of women like those you scared off outside, one of a man lying peacefully sleeping on a mattress in a shack like this one. She glances at it and says, "He's dead. His heater malfunctioned and carbon monoxide killed him. Or maybe he did it on purpose."

She pulls out a manila folder and opens it. There's a picture of an assembly line — a dozen women in hairnets and surgical gowns and rubber gloves, seated along an assembly line.

"What's this place make?"

"Motion controller systems." You stare at a photo sticking out from the pack, of Gabriel Perea head-on, preaching, in that twisted martial arts pose of his. This time she has crouched behind equipment to get this shot, but in the background you can see the managers all gathered. Most of them are grainy shadows, but the three faces that are visible are clearly not frightened of what's happening here.

"They look almost bored."

She nods.

"You think he's a fake. Comes in as an agitator to catch workers who'd be inclined to organize, and then he catches them in a big net, a phony appearance by the Virgin Mary, promising them a wonderful afterlife if they just grind themselves down like good little girls and boys in this one."

She glances at you oddly, then says, "Maybe they don't call you names, Deputy."

You meet her eyes, smile, thinking that you'd be willing to fall in love with this other photographer; but the idea fades almost as fast as it arrives. She lives with nothing and takes all the risks while you have everything and take no risks at all. Her dreams are all of her people. Yours are of awards and recognition.

She offers you the bottle again and you drink and wheeze and wonder why it is you can't have both dreams. Why yours seems petty and cheap. You don't believe in the Virgin, either. The two of you should be able to support each other. Ignoring the delusions of a few people over their rusting shrine is a far cry from ignoring this kind of scam.

She agrees to get you an interview with Gabriel Perea. It will take some days. He is a very reluctant holy man, more shy than the Tarahumara.

"Come back in three days." To this *colonia*, to this shack, to wait for her. All right, you think, that's good. It gives you time to get information.

You give her five film canisters and she kisses you on the cheek for it. You can feel her lips all the way home.

— • —

When you tell Baum what you've found, he sends you down to see Andy Jardin. Andy's a walking encyclopedia of corporate factology — if it's listed on the DJI, Nasdaq or the S&P 500, he's got a profile in his computer if not in his head.

He barely acknowledges you when you show up. The two of you had one conversation on the day you were hired — Baum introduced you. Andy said, "Hey." You take pictures, he babbles in stocks — two languages that don't recognize each other without a translator. He has carrot-colored hair that might have been in dreadlocks the last time it was mowed, and wears black plastic frame glasses through which he peers myopically at his computer screen.

You clear your throat, ask him if he knows of the company. Immediately you get his undivided attention. He reels off everything — no one has ever accused this kid of trying to hold back.

They manufacture control systems, have government contracts, probably fall into someone's black budget, like most of the military manufacturers. Their stock is hot, a good investment, sound and steady. They don't actually manufacture anything in the *maquiladora*, which is a common story. They just assemble parts, which are shipped up to Iowa, where the company's based. That's where the controllers are made. He says they're developing what are called genetic algorithms. When you look blank, he happily sketches in the details: genetic algorithms are the basis for lots of artificial intelligence research. Of course, he adds, there is no such thing currently as AI — not in the evil, computer mind bent on world domination sense. It's all about learning circuits, routines that adjust when conditions change, that can refine themselves based on past experience. Not brains, not thinking — a kind of mathematical awareness.

Before you leave, he invites you to buy some of their stock. This is a really good time for them, he says.

Later on, Baum tells you that Andy's never invested a cent in his life, he just loves to watch, the ultimate investment voyeur. "And you can expect to get every article that even mentions your company from now on. He'll probably forward you their S&P daily, too.

"You're into something here?" he asks, as if that's the last thing that concerned him. The real question he's asking is "How long is this going to take?"

All you can do is shrug and say, "I really don't know. This woman — this photographer — she has a notion he's a ringer, someone the company threw in to manipulate the workers, keep them docile. I want to interview him, take his picture, get inside the factory and get some pictures there, too. You know, get what I can before they know that I'm looking at him specifically."

"Is it a Catholic thing — I mean, your interest?"

"It's not about me."

Whether or not he believes you, he doesn't say.

As you're leaving he adds, "You've seen enough to know that weird and bizarre are the norms over there, right?" Again, he's not saying it outright. Beneath his camaraderie lies the real edginess: He's worried about you and this story — how you fit together.

"I won't forget. Hecho in Mexico is Hecho in Hell."

Baum laughs. It's his saying, after all.

— • —

Perea speaks so quietly and so fast that you can't catch half of it. He sits in the corner away from the lantern, on the ground. He bows his head when he speaks as if he's ashamed to admit what's happening to him. This is not, to your thinking, the behavior of a man who is playing a role. Still, how could anyone be certain? You take pictures of him bathed in lantern light, looking like a medieval pilgrim who has made his journey, found his God.

Margarita kneels beside you, leaning forward to hear clearly, translating his murmured Spanish. "'I don't know why the Virgin picked me. I'm just a Chamula.' That's an Indian from Chiapas, Deputy," she explains. "'I believe that things need to change. People need their dignity as much as their income. I thought I could do this on my own — change things in this factory, I mean. The other workers would trust me and together we would break the cycle in which the neoliberals keep us.'"

"What does she look like?"

"'She has blue robes, a cloth over her head. I can sort of see through her, too. And her voice, it fills my head like a bell ringing. But it's soft, like she's whispering to me. No one else sees her. No one else hears her.'" He looks up at you, his eyes pleading for understanding. "'She stopped me from doing a terrible thing. If we had protested as I planned, many people would have been killed. They would bring in the *federales* and the *federales* would beat us. There would be people waiting for us when we got home — people the *federales* won't see. Some of us would have been tortured and killed. It might have been me. But I was willing to take that risk, to make this change.'"

"She stopped you."

He nods. "'Someone said my very first day that the factory is built on a sacred place. In the San Cristóbals we have these places. Maybe she heard our fear. There is a shrine nearby there where a picture of Jesus weeps. And another with tears of blood.'" Margarita glances sharply at you as she repeats this. You nod.

"'She tells us to live. To endure what life gives us, no matter how hard. She knew what was in my heart. She said that the greatest dignity could be found in the grace of God. To us finally the kingdom will be opened for all we suffer. It will be closed to those who oppress us.'" He is seeing her again as he speaks, his eyes looking at a memory instead of at you.

Afterwards, you ride in your car alone — Margarita insists on driving her own, an old Chevy Impala that rumbles without a muffler. She won't ride with anyone; it's one of those things about her that makes it clear she's crazy. Your tape recorder plays, Margarita's translation fills the night.

Perea's telling the truth so far as he knows it. In a moment of extreme danger, the Virgin appeared. That's happened before — in fact, she usually manifests where the climate's explosive, people are strained, fragmented, minds desperate for escape. It's religion to some, mental meltdown to you. So why do you resist even that explanation now? "A Catholic thing?" Baum asked. That's not it, though. You recollect something you once heard Carl Sagan say in an interview: Extraordinary events require extraordinary proof. "So, Carl," you ask the dark interior, "how do you pull proof out of a funhouse mirror?"

— • —

By the time Margarita returns, you know what you're going to do. You tell her to see what she thinks. She sits back on the mattress. You can hear her pulling off her boots. "You might get away with it," she answers, and there's anger in her voice. "If they don't pay too much attention to your very Castilian Español. You still talk like a *gringo*. And you still think like one, too. You listen to what he says, and you see it all in black and white, Norte Americano versus us. La Bamba's the same way. You guys see what most of your people won't, but you see it with old eyes."

"How are we — I don't understand. The Zapatistas you mean? What—?"

She makes a noise to dismiss you, and there's the sound of the bottle being opened. Not sharing. Then suddenly she's talking, close enough now you can almost feel the heat of her breath.

"It's not north against south anymore, rich whites against poor Mexicans. That's only a thing, a speck. It's the whole world, Deputy. The *maquiladora* is the whole world now. Japan is here, Korea is here, anyone who wants to make things without being watched, without having to answer to anyone, without having to pay fairly. They're here and everywhere else, too. *Ya, basta!* You understand? Enough! It's not about NAFTA, about whose treaty promises what. Whoever's treaty, it will be just the same. Here right now in Mexico the drug dealers invest, buy factories, take their money and grind their own people to make more money, clean money. Clean! And it's no different here than anywhere else, it's even, *Dios mio*, better here than some places. It's a new century and the countries bleed together, and the only borders, the only fences, are all made of bodies. All the pictures you've seen, but if you don't see this in all of them, then you're seeing nothing!"

Clearly it's time to leave. "I'm sorry," is all you can think to say, and you turn to go. And suddenly she's blocking your way. Her hands close on your arms. For all your fantasies you didn't see this coming. Here in a shack with a cardboard door is not where you'd have chosen. Only this isn't your choice, it's entirely hers. Anybody could come by, but no one does. She works your clothes off, at the same time tugging at her own in hasty, angry, near-violent action. Sex out of anger. You keep thinking, she's as crazy as they said she was, she's furious with you for your stupidity, how can she possibly want to fuck you, too? For all of which, you don't fight, of course you don't, it's your fantasy however unexpected and inexplicable.

You fall asleep with your arms around her, her breasts warm against you, almost unsure that any of it happened.

— • —

The Virgin visits Perea only in the factory. That's where you get a job. Driving a fork lift. It's something you used to do, so at least you don't look like an idiot even if they're suspicious of your accent. If they are, they say nothing. They're hiring — from what Baum said, they're always hiring.

You get assigned a small locker. In it are your work things — coveralls and safety glasses. There are signs up in every room in bright red Spanish: "Protective Gear Must Be Worn At All Times!" and "Wear Your Goggle. Protect Your Eyes." Your guide points to one of these and says, "Don't think they're kidding. They'll fire you on the spot if they catch you not wearing the correct apparel."

The lift is articulated. It can take you almost to the ceiling with a full pallet. It has control buttons for your left hand like those found on computer game devices. Working it is actually a pleasure at first.

The day is long and dull. Breaks are almost non-existent. One in the morning, one in the afternoon, both about as long as it takes to smoke a cigarette. The other workers ask where you're from, how you got here.

Margarita helped you work out a semi-plausible story about being fired from dock work in Veracruz when you got caught drunk. At least you've been to Veracruz. A few people laugh at the story and commiserate. Drunk, yeah. Nobody pries — there's hardly time for questions, even over lunch, which is the only place you get to take off the safety glasses and relax — but you see suspicion in a few eyes. You can tell any story you want, but you can't hide the way you tell it. Your voice isn't from Veracruz. Nevertheless, no one challenges you. Maybe they think you're a company ringer, a spy. That would give them good reason to steer clear of you. Whatever you are, they don't want trouble — that's what Baum said. This job is all they've got. And at week's end, just like them, you'll collect your $22.50, too.

— • —

The second day you're there, the Virgin appears to Gabriel Perea.

You're unloading a shipment of circuit boards and components off the back of a semi, when suddenly you find yourself all alone. It's too strange. You climb down and wander out of the loading bay and into the warehouse itself. Everyone's gathered there. A circle of hundreds. Right in the middle Perea stands at that crazy angle like a man with displaced hips. His hands are out, palms wide, and he's repeating her words for everyone: "She loves us all. We are all her children. We are all of us saved and our children are saved. Our blood is His blood!" The atmosphere practically crackles. Every eye is riveted to him. You move around the outside perimeter, looking for the masters. There are two up on a catwalk. One looks at you as if you're a bigger spectacle than Perea. You turn away quickly and stare like the others are doing, trying to make like you were looking for a better view of the event. From somewhere in the crowd comes the clicking of a shutter. Someone is taking shots. You could take out your tiny Minox now and shoot a couple yourself, but there's nothing to see that Margarita didn't capture already. Nothing worth drawing any more attention to yourself.

Nada que ver, the words echo in your head.

For a long time you stare at him. "The *niño* loves us all. His is the pure love of a child. Care for Him, for it's all He asks of you." People murmur, "Amen," and "Yes."

Eventually you chance another look at the two on the catwalk. One of them seems to be talking, but not to the other. You think: He's either schizophrenic or he's got a microphone.

— • —

In a matter of minutes the spectacle is over. She had nothing remarkable to say; she was just dropping in to remind everyone of her love for them and theirs for her. Now she won't come again for days, another week.

Except for the first two nights you eat alone in the shack. Margarita is somewhere else, living out of her car, photographing things, capturing moments. How does she do this? How does she live forever on the edge, capturing death, surrounded, drenched in it? How can anybody live this way? It's hopeless. The end of the world.

You lie alone in the shack, as cold at night as you are scalding in the afternoon when you walk down the dirt path from the bus drop. You'd like to fall into a swimming pool and just float. The closest you can come is communal rain barrels outside — which were once chemical barrels and God knows whether there's benzene or something worse floating in them, death in the water. Little kids are splashing it over themselves, drinking from it. Watching makes you yearn for a cold drink but you wouldn't dare. Margarita's friends there cook you dinner on their makeshift stoves, for which you gladly pay. By week's end, they've made more from the dinners than you'll take home from the factory.

Friday you drive home for the weekend, exhausted.

You flop down on your bed, so tired that your eyes ache. All you can think about is Margarita. Gabriel Perea's Virgin has melted into a mad photographer who is using you for sex. That's how it feels, that's how it is, too. A part of her clings to you, drowns with you in that dark and dirty shack, at the same time as she dismisses your simplistic comprehension of the complexities of life where she lives. A week now and you've begun maybe to understand it better — at least, you've begun taking pictures around the *colonia* — it's as though she's given you permission to participate. It would be hard not to find strange images: the dead ground outside a shack where someone has stuck one little, pathetic plant in a coffee can; another plywood shack with a sign dangling beside the door proclaiming "*Siempre Coke!*" The factory, too. A couple of rolls of film so far, as surreptitiously as possible. The machinery is too interesting not to photograph, even though you feel somehow complicitous in making it seem beautiful and exotic. Even in ugliness and cruelty, there is beauty. Even in the words of an apparition there are lies and deceit. You finally drift off on the thought that the reason you despise the Virgin is that she sells accommodation. It's always been her message and it's the message of the elite, the rich, a recommendation that no one who actually endures the misery would make.

The phone wakes you at noon. Baum has an invitation to a reception for a Republican Senator on the stump. "All our best people will be there. I could use a good photographer and you can use the contacts."

"Sure," you say.

"You'll need a tux."

"Got one."

"You'll need a shower, too."

How he figured that out over the phone, you can't imagine; but he's right, you do smell bad, and it's been only a week. When you get up, your whole body seems to be knitted of broken joints. It's a test of will to stand up to the spray. Being pummeled by water feels like the Rapture, pleasure meeting pain.

— • —

It's an outdoor patio party with three Weber Platinum grills big enough to feed the Dallas Cowboys, half a dozen chefs and one waiter for every three people. Everybody wants to have their picture taken with the Senator, who is wearing tan makeup to cover the fact that he looks like he's been stumping for two weeks without sleep, much less sunlight, and you're glad it's not your job to make him look good.

As it is, you end up taking dozens of pictures anyway. Baum calls most of the shots, who he wants with the Senator, whose faces will grace the paper in the morning. He introduces you to too many people for you to keep track of them — all the corporate executives and spouses have turned out for this gala event. When he introduces you to the head of the Texas Republican Party, just the way he says it makes it sound as if you are beholding a specifically Texan variety of Republican. For a week you've been living in a shack with dirt floors among people who cook their food on stoves made from bricks and flat hunks of iron, and here you are in a bow tie and cummerbund, hobnobbing with the richest stratum of society in El Paso and munching on shrimp bigger than your thumb, a spread that would feed an entire *colonia* for days. It's not just the disparity, it's the displacement, the fragmentation of reality into razor-edged jigsaw puzzle pieces.

And then Baum hauls you before a thin, balding man wearing glasses too small for his face, the kind that have no frames, just pins to hold the earpieces on. "This is Stuart Coopersmith." He beams at you — a knowing smile if ever there was one. To Coopersmith, he says, "He's the guy I told you about who's into image manipulation." He withdraws before he has to explain anything to either of you.

"So, you're Joe's new photo essayist," he says.

A smile to hide your panic. "I like that title better than the one they gave me at the paper. Mind if I use it?"

"Be my guest." If he recognizes you, he shows no indication.

"So, what do you do that I should consider taking your picture, Mr. Coopersmith?"

He touches his tie as he names his company. It seems to be a habit. "Across the river?"

"*La maquiladora.* You guys make what —"

"Control devices. We're all about control." There's a nice, harmless word for someone in the big black budget of government bureaucracy, flying under the public radar.

"It's more than that, though, right? Someone told me, your devices actually learn."

"Pattern recognition is not quite learning, not like most people think of it. Something occurs, our circuit notices, and predicts the likelihood of it recurring, and then if it does as predicted, the circuit loops, and the more often the event occurs when it's supposed to, the more certain the circuit becomes, the more reliable the information and, ah, the more it seems like there's an intelligence at work. What we know to be feedback looks like behavior, which is where people start saying that the things are alive and thinking."

"I'm not sure I —"

"Well, it's no matter, is it? You can still take pictures without understanding something this complex." Coopersmith says this so offhandedly, you can't be certain whether you've been put down. He flutters his hand through the air as if brushing the subject away. "We just manufacture parts down here. We do employ lots of people — we're very popular in the *maquiladora.* Like to help out the folks over there."

You nod. "So, what's on deck now?"

He looks at his champagne glass, then glances sidelong, like Cassius conspiring to kill Caesar. "Oh, some work for NASA. For a Mars flight they're talking about. Using GAs to predict stress, breakdown — things they can't afford in the middle of the solar system. The software will actually measure the individual's stress from moment to moment, and weigh in with a protective environment if that stress jumps at all. It's still pattern recognition, you know, but not the same as on an assembly line. I suppose it's really very exciting."

"Amazing." It's probably even important work.

"In fact, you all should do a story on it — I mean, not right this second, but in a few months, maybe, when the program's a little further along and NASA's happy, you and Joe should come over to the factory, shoot some pictures. Write this thing up. I'd give you the exclusive. You guys beat out all the other papers, get a little glory. We'd sure love the PR. That never hurts. You come and I'll give you the guided tour of the place, how's that?"

He adjusts his tie again on the way to reaching into his coat and coming up with a business card. The card has a spinning globe on it, with tiny lights flashing here and there as the world spins. Coopersmith smiles. "Cool, isn't it? The engine's embedded in the card. Doesn't take much to drive a little animation. You be sure and have Joe give me a call real soon."

He turns his back, striking up another conversation almost immediately. You've been dismissed. Heading over to where Joe stands balancing a plate of ribs, you glance back.

Coopersmith with eyes downcast listens to another man talk, his hand fiddling with the knot on his tie again.

You might not have been sure at first, but you are now: He was the one on the catwalk, watching as you edged around the factory floor while the Virgin paid her visit.

Joe says, "So?"

"He offered us the exclusive on their new program for NASA."

"You have been blessed, my son. An overlord has smiled upon you." He tips his glass.

— • —

When you tell Margarita what you suspected, she isn't surprised so much as hurt. Even though she'd been certain of the fraud, the fact of it stings her. By association, you're part of her pain. Although she welcomed you back with a kiss, after the news she doesn't want to touch at all. She withdraws into smoke and drink, and finally wanders off with her cold black camera into the *colonia*, disgusted, she says, with the human race and God Himself. You begin to realize that despite her tough cynical skin, there's at least a kernel of Margarita that wanted the miracle in all its glory. Beneath your rejection, does some part of you want it, too? Once in a while in seeking for truth it would be nice to find something better than truth.

Later, in the dark, she comes back, slides down beside you on the mattress and starts to cry. From her that's an impossible sound, so terrifying that it paralyzes you. It's the sound of betrayal, the very last crumb of purity floating away.

You reach over to hold her, and she pushes your hand away. So you lie there, unable to take back the knowledge, the doubt, the truth, and knowing that the betrayal will always be tied to you. There's nothing you can do.

— • —

The first opportunity you have, you swap your goggles with Gabriel Perea. The only place you can do this is at lunch. You have to wait for a day when he carries the goggles off the assembly line straight to the lunch area. You sit with him, listening to other workers ask him things about the Virgin. He looks at you edgily. He knows he's supposed to pretend that you've never met, but you're making this impossible by sitting there beside him. Making the switch is child's play. Everyone's staring at him, hanging on his every word. You set your goggles beside his, and then pick up the wrong pair a minute later and walk away.

Close up, you can see that his goggles have a slight refractive coating. He's going to know immediately what's happened, but with luck he won't be able to do anything about it. He won't want to be seen talking to you in the middle of the factory.

If Perea remotely shares your suspicions, he hasn't admitted it even to himself. This makes you think of Margarita, and your face burns with still more betrayal. It's too late, you tell yourself. This is what you came here to do.

Two days later, ten feet up in the forklift, you get what you wanted: The Virgin Mary appears to you.

It's a bare wall, concrete brick and metal conduits, and suddenly there she is. She floats in the air and when you look through the cage front of the forklift she is floating beyond it. The cage actually cuts her off. It's incredible. Wherever you look, she has a fixed location, an anchored spot in space. If you look up, her image remains fixed, sliding down the glasses. Somehow the circuit monitors your vision, tracks the turn of your head. "Feedback loops" — wasn't that what Coopersmith said? It must be automatic, though. She may recognize the geometry, but not the receiver, because the first thing out of her mouth is: "*Te amo*, Gabriel, *mi profeta*." So much for divinity. She doesn't know you've swapped goggles even if the goggles themselves do.

She is beautiful. Her hair, peeking out beneath a white wimple, is black. The blue of her robes is almost painful to see. No sky could match it. Her oval face is serene, a distillation of a million tender mothers. Oh, they're good, whoever created her. Who wouldn't want to believe in this Mary? Gabriel couldn't help but succumb.

The camera in your pocket is useless.

She reminds you of your duty to your flock. She promises that you will all live in glory and comfort in Heaven after this life of misery and toil, and not to blame —

In the middle of her speech, she vanishes.

It's so quick that you almost keel forward out of your seat, thank God for the harness.

You can guess what happened. Management came out for their afternoon show, and things were wrong. Gabriel Perea, the poor bastard, didn't respond. He's still somewhere, attaching diodes to little green boards, unaware that divinity has dropped by to see him again.

You lower the forklift, and get out, unable to help one last glance up into the air, looking for her. A mere scintilla, a Tinkerbell of light would do, but there is nothing. Nothing.

The last hour and a half you go about your business as usual. Nothing has changed, nothing can have changed. Your hope is they think their circuits or the goggles malfunctioned, something failed to project. Who knows what sort of feedback system was at work there — it has to be sophisticated to have dodged every solid shape in front of you. They'll want to see his goggles at the end of his shift. No one seems to be watching you yet. No one calls you in off the floor. So at the end of the day you drop the goggles in the trash and leave with the others in your shift. Everyone's talking about going home, how hot it is, how much they'd like a bath or a beer. Everything's so normal it sets your teeth on edge. You ride the bus down the highway and get off with a dozen others at your *colonia* and head for home.

It's on the dusty cowpath of a road, on foot, that they grab you. Three of them. They know who they're looking for, and everyone else knows to stay out of it. These guys are *las pandillas*, the kind who'd kill someone for standing too close to you. A dozen people are all moving away, down the road, and the looks they give you are looks of farewell. *Adios, amigo.* Won't be seeing you again. They know it and so do you. You've seen the photos. The thousand merciless ways people don't come home, and you're about to become one.

The first guy walks straight up as if he's going to walk by, but suddenly his elbow swings right up into your nose, and the sky goes black and shiny at the same time, and time must have jumped because you're on your knees, blood flowing out between your fingers, but you don't remember getting there. And then you're on your back, looking at the sky, and still it seems no one's said a word to you, but your head is ringing, blood roaring like a waterfall. Someone laid you out. Each pose is a snapshot of pain. Each time there's less of you to shoot. They'll compress you, maybe for hours, maybe for days — that's how it works, isn't it? How long before gasoline and a match? Will you feel anything by then?

You stare up at the sky, at the first few stars, and wait for the inevitable continuation. The bodies get buried in the Lote Bravo. At least you know where you're going. In a couple of months someone might find you. Will Joe come looking?

Someone yells, "¡Aguila!" and a door slams. Or is that in your head, too?

Footsteps approach. Here it comes, you think. Is there anything you can do to prepare for the pain? Probably not, no.

The face that peers down at you doesn't help. Hispanic, handsome, well-groomed. This could be any businessman in Mexico, but you know it isn't, and you remember someone telling you about the *narcotraficantes* investing in the *maquiladora*, taking their drug money and buying into international trade. Silent partners.

"Not going to hurt you, keemo sabe," he's saying with a sly grin, as though your broken nose and battered skull don't exist. "Couldn't do that. No, no. Questions would be asked about you — you're not just some factory cunt, are you?" His grin becomes a sneer — you've never actually seen anyone sneer before. This guy hates women for a hobby. "No, no," he says again, "you're a second rate wedding photographer who thought he was Dick fucking Tracy. What did you do, hang out with the Juarez photo-locos and get all righteous? Sure, of course you did." He kneels, clucking his tongue. You notice that he's holding your Minox. "Listen, *cholo*, you print what you've uncovered, and Señor Perea will die. You think that's a threat, hey? But it's not. You'll make him out a fool to his own people. They trust him, you know? It's all they got, so you go ahead and take it from them and see what you get. We care so much, we're lettin' you go home. Here." He tosses the camera into the dirt. "You're only a threat to the people who think like you do, man." Now he grabs your arm and pulls you upright. The world threatens to flip on you, and your stomach promises to go with it if it does. Close up, he smells of citrus cologne. He whispers to you, "Go home, *cholo*, go take pictures of little kids in swimming pools and cats caught in trees and armadillos squashed on the highway. Amateurs don't survive. Neither do the professionals, here. Next time, you gonna meet some of them." Then he just walks away. You're left wobbling on the road. The gang of three are gone, too. Nobody's around. Behind you, you hear a car door and the rev of an engine. A silver SUV shoots off down the dirt road, back to the pavement and away.

You stumble along the path to the *colonia*. Your head feels as tender as the skin of a plum. Your sinuses are clogged with blood and your nose creaks when you inhale. People watch in awe as you approach your shack. In that moment you're as much a miracle to them as Gabriel Perea. They probably think they're seeing a ghost. And they're right, aren't they? You aren't here any longer.

Margarita's not inside. Her camera's gone. There's no one to comfort you, no one to hear how you were written off. The heat inside is like the core of the sun. Back outside you walk to the water barrel, no longer concerned with what contaminants float in the water. You splash it on your face, over your head. Benzene? Who cares? You're dead anyway. You touch your nose and it's swollen up the size of a saguaro. Embarrassing how easily you've been persuaded to leave. It didn't take anything at all, did it? One whack and a simple "Go away, Señor, you're a fool." What, did you think you could change the world? Make a difference? Not a second rate wedding photographer like you. Not someone with an apartment and a bed and an office and a car. Compromised by the good life. Nobody who leads your life is going to make the difference over here. It takes a breed of insanity you can't even approach.

Baum was dead wrong about everything. He simplified the problems to fit, but they aren't simple. Answers aren't simple. You, you're simple.

Two little girls kneel not far from the barrel, cooking their meal in tin pans on top of an iron plate mounted over an open flame. There's a rusted electrical box beside them, with outlet holes like eyes and a wide slit for a switch. It's a robot face silently screaming. The girls watch you even when they're not looking.

Long after it gets dark you're still alone inside. Margarita must be off on some adventure, doing what she does best, what you can't do. You've had hours to build upon your inadequacy. Run your story and they'll tear Perea apart. He was doomed the moment he believed in the possibility of her. Just like the Church and the little Catholic boy you were once. When you see that, you don't want to see Margarita. You don't want to have to explain why you aren't going any further. All you can do is hurt her. Only a threat.

You pack up your few things, leaving the dozen film canisters you didn't use. Let the real photojournalist have them. "*Nada que ver*," you tell the empty room.

Back across the border before midnight, before your life turns back into a pumpkin — better she should think you're lying under three feet of dirt.

— · —

A month rolls by in a sort of fog. Booze, pain killers and the hell-bent desire to forget your own name. Your nose is healing. It's a little crooked, has a bluish bump in the middle. Baum keeps his distance and doesn't ask you anything about your story, though at first you're too busy to notice. Then one day you find out from the sports editor that Joe got a package while you were gone, and although nobody knows what was in it, when he opened it, he turned white as a ghost and just packed up his office and went home. Called in sick the next three days.

When you do try and talk to him about what happened, he interrupts with an angry "Don't think you're the first person who's been smashed on the rocks of old Juarez." Then he walks away. They got to him somehow. If they wanted to, they could get to both of you. Like the wind, this can blow across the river. That message was for you.

Then one day while you're placing ad graphics, Joe Baum comes over and sits beside you. He won't look you in the eye. Very softly he says, "Got a call from Chicken Man. Margarita Espinada's dead."

You stare at the page on the monitor so hard you're seeing the pixels. Finally, you ask him, "What happened?"

"Don't know. Don't know who did it. She's been gone for weeks and weeks, but he said that wasn't unusual. She lived mostly in her car."

"*Auto loco.*"

"Yeah." He starts to get up, but as if his weight is too much for him, he drops back onto the chair. "Um, he says she left a package for you. Addressed to him, so maybe whatever happened, she had some warning." With every word he puts more distance between himself and her death. "There's gonna be a funeral tomorrow."

"So soon?"

Baum makes a face, lips pressed tight. Defiantly he meets your gaze. "She was dumped in the Lote Bravo a while ago."

— • —

Pollamano nods sadly as he lets you in. "¿*Quiubo*, Deputy?" he asks, but not with any interest. His eyes are bloodshot, drunk or crying, maybe both. Some others are there inside. A few nod — some you remember. Most of them pretend you aren't there. Her body lies in *la Catedral*, three blocks from Chicken Man's current abode. You shouldn't see it. Their newest member took pictures. Ernesto. He was there, following the cops with his police band radio the way he always does, always trying to get to the scene before they do. He'd taken half a dozen shots before he saw the black boots and realized whose body he was photographing. They'd torn off most of her clothes but left the boots. You remember the one who warned you off. The boots were left on so everyone would know who she was.

Everyone drinks, toasting her memory. One of them begins weeping and someone else throws an arm around him and mutters. One of the others spits. None of them seems to suspect that you and she spent time together. In any case, you're an interloper on their private grief. Not one of them.

Margarita must have known you weren't dead — otherwise, why send a package for you?

Late in the afternoon, everyone has shown up, almost two dozen photographers, and some unseen sign passes among you all, and everyone rises up and goes out together. You move in a line through the crowds, between white buses in a traffic snarl and across the square to the neon cathedral. Orange lights bathe you all. Ernesto with his nothing mustache runs up to the door and snaps a picture. Even in this solemn moment, his instinct is for the image. A few glare at him, but no one chastises him. You gather in the front pews, kneel, pray, go up one by one and light your candles for her soul. Your hand is shaking so hard you can hardly ignite the wick.

— • —

After everyone else has left he gives you the package. It's nearly the size of a suitcase. He says, "She left it for you, and I don't violate her wishes. She was here a couple times when I wasn't around. Using the darkroom."

You pull out a folder of photos. On top is the picture of you she took the first day you arrived in *Colonia Universidad*. You look like you could take on anything. Just looking at it is humiliating.

Underneath is her collection of shots inside the factory. The top photo is Gabriel Perea standing all twisted and pointing. Foam on his mouth, eyes bugging out. The image is spoiled because of some fogging on the left side of it as if there was a light leak. Whatever caused it lit up Perea, too.

You almost miss the thing that's different: He's not wearing his goggles.

You go on to the next shot, but it's a picture of the crowd behind him, all staring, wide-eyed. She's not using a flash, but there's some kind of light source. In the third, fourth and fifth shots you see it. It shines straight at Perea. There are lens flares in each image. The light is peculiar, diffuse, as if a collection of small bulbs are firing off, making a sort of ring. The middle is hard to make out until the sixth picture. She must have slid on her knees between all the onlookers to get it. Perea's feet are close by and out of focus. The light is the center of the image, the light which is different in each shot.

"Jaime," you say, "do you have a loupe?"

"Of course." He gives it to you. You hold it over the image, over the light. Back in the lab at the *Herald*, you'll blow the image up poster size to see the detail without the lens — the outline, and at the top of it a bunch of smudges, a hint of eye sockets and mouth, a trace of nose and cheek. Can an AI break loose from its handlers? you wonder. Does it have a will? Or is this the next step in their plan?

You give the loupe back.

He says, "That Perea is gone. Disappeared. People are looking all over for him. They say he was called up to Heaven."

One way or another, that's probably true. If the Virgin can float on the air now, then they don't need an interpreter. Belief itself will do the work hereafter, hope used as a halter.

"That crazy girl, she went right back into that factory even after he was gone."

You wipe at your eyes, and a half-laugh escapes you. That crazy girl.

You close the folder. You can't let anyone have these. That's the ultimate, wrenching realization. Margarita died because of this and no one can see it. The story can't be told, because it's a lie. She knew it, too, but she went ahead.

This is your Sacred Heart. Your rusting nail. Gabriel Perea was called up to heaven or killed — for you it doesn't matter which. By revealing nothing you let him go on living.

Under the top folder there are others full of negatives, hundreds of inverted images of the world — black teeth and faces, black suns and black clouds. The world made new. Made hers. There is a way you can keep her alive.

Jaime pats you on the shoulder as you leave with your burden. "You go home, Deputy," he tells you. "Even the devil won't live here." ■

CIBOLA

BY CONNIE WILLIS

Connie Willis (born 1945 in Denver, Colorado) is one of
the most popular science fiction and cross-over writers
of the late 20th and early 21st centuries; she is beloved
for her gift for writing both humor and tragedy. These
talents often combine in tour-de-force tragicomedy, as in
Lincoln's Dreams (1987, a John W. Campbell Memorial
Award winner), "Fire Watch" (1983, a Hugo and Nebula
winner), *The Doomsday Book* (1993, a Hugo and Nebula
winner and a *New York Times* Notable Book), and
Passage (2002, Hugo and Nebula nominee). Her list of
awards and nominations, as of this writing, includes nine
Hugo Awards, six Nebula Awards, two World Fantasy
Award nominations, and 21 additional nominations for
the Hugo and the Nebula. Her website is at sftv.org/cw.

Willis is widely admired for focusing on the most
challenging of themes, including how humans confront

the fear of death or the end of the world; the eternal clash between reason and faith; the problems of loss, destruction of beauty, and the human condition. These themes are presented via a range of affects (always in dramatic conflict) from religious faith to guilt, grief, and expiation; from bureaucratic fussiness to truth-seeking rationality and scholarship; from helplessness to incredible heroism. *Passage* is admirable on many levels: epic in vision, it covers about a year in the lives of its characters; its relevance here is its fearless targeting of the evils that charlatans and hypocrites can create. Her Hugo-winning "Inside Job" (2006) is the best example of her hunt for such illogic-mongers at novella-length; here, in the shorter "Cibola," she combines the exasperations of a skeptical reporter, the certitude of a credulous believer, several painful facts about the history of the Spanish conquest of America, and a surprise-twist ending. Willis calls herself an optimist, though her narrative voice is that of a cheerful pessimist; pay attention to the transformation of a skeptic's cynicism to a sort of awe.

CIBOLA

"CARLA, YOU GREW UP IN DENVER," JAKE SAID. "HERE'S AN assignment that might interest you."

This is his standard opening line. It means he is about to dump another "local interest" piece on me.

"Come on, Jake," I said. "No more nutty Bronco fans who've spray-painted their kids orange and blue, okay? Give me a real story. Please?"

"Bronco season's over, and the NFL draft was last week," he said. "This isn't a local interest."

"You're right there," I said. "These stories you keep giving me are of no interest, local or otherwise. I did the time machine piece for you. And the psychic dentist. Give me a break. Let me cover something that doesn't involve nuttos."

"It's for the 'Our Living Western Heritage' series." He handed me a slip of paper. "You can interview her this morning and then cover the sky-scraper moratorium hearings this afternoon."

This was plainly a bribe, since the hearings were front page stuff right now, and "historical interests" could be almost as bad as locals — senile old women in nursing homes rambling on about the good old days. But at least they didn't crawl in their washing machines and tell you to push "rinse" so they could travel into the future. And they didn't try to perform psychic oral surgery on you.

"All right," I said, and took the slip of paper. "Rosa Turcorillo," it read and gave an address out on Santa Fe. "What's her phone number?"

She doesn't have a phone," Jake said. "You'll have to go out there." He started across the city room to his office. "The hearings are at one o'clock."

"What is she, one of Denver's first Chicano settlers?" I called after him.

He waited till he was just outside his office to answer me. "She says she's the great-granddaughter of Coronado," he said, and beat a hasty retreat into his office. "She says she knows where the Seven Cities of Cibola are."

— • —

I spent forty-five minutes researching Coronado and copying articles and then drove out to see his great-granddaughter. She lived out on south Santa Fe past Hampden, so I took I-25 and then was sorry. The morning rush hour was still crawling along at about ten miles an hour pumping carbon monoxide into the air. I read the whole article stopped behind a semi between Speer and Sixth Avenue.

Coronado trekked through the Southwest looking for the legendary Seven Cities of Gold in the 1540s, which poked a big hole in Rosa's story, since any great-granddaughter of his would have to be at least three hundred years old.

There wasn't any mystery about the Seven Cities of Cibola either. Coronado found them, near Gallup, New Mexico, and conquered them but they were nothing but mud-hut villages. Having been burned once, he promptly took off after another promise of gold in Quivira in Kansas someplace where there wasn't any gold either. He hadn't been in Colorado at all.

I pulled onto Santa Fe, cursing Jake for sending me on another wild-goose chase, and headed south. Denver is famous for traffic, air pollution, and neighborhoods that have seen better days. Santa Fe isn't one of those neighborhoods. It's been a decaying line of rusting railroad tracks, crummy bars, old motels, and waterbed stores for as long as I can remember, and I, as Jake continually reminds me, grew up in Denver.

Coronado's granddaughter lived clear south past Hampden, in a trailer park with a sign with "Olde West Motel" and a neon bison on it, and Rosa Turcorillo's old Airstream looked like it had been there since the days when the buffalo roamed. It was tiny, the kind of trailer I would call "Turcorillo's modest mobile home" in the article, no more than fifteen feet long and eight feet wide.

Rosa was nearly that wide herself. When she answered my knock, she barely fit in the door. She was wearing a voluminous turquoise housecoat, and had long black braids.

"What do you want?" she said, holding the metal door so she could slam it in case I was the police or a repo man.

"I'm Carla Johnson from the *Denver Record*," I said. "I'd like to interview you about Coronado." I fished in my bag for my press card. "We're doing a series on 'Our Living Western Heritage.'" I finally found the press card and handed it to her. "We're interviewing people who are part of our past."

She stared at the press card disinterestedly. This was not the way it was supposed to work. Nuttos usually drag you in the house and start babbling before you finish telling them who you are. She should already be halfway through her account of how she'd traced her ancestry to Coronado by means of the I Ching.

"I would have telephoned first, but you didn't have a phone," I said.

She handed me the card and started to shut the door.

"If this isn't a good time, I can come back," I babbled. "And we don't have to do the interview here if you'd rather not. We can go to the *Record* office or to a restaurant."

She opened the door and flashed a smile that had half of Cibola's missing gold in it. "I ain't dressed," she said. "It'll take me a couple of minutes. Come on in."

I climbed the metal steps and went inside. Rosa pointed at a flowered couch, told me to sit down and disappeared into the rear of the trailer.

I was glad I had suggested going out. The place was no messier than my desk, but it was only about six feet long and had the couch, a dinette set, and a recliner. There was no way it would hold me and Coronado's granddaughter, too. The place may have had a surplus of furniture but it didn't have any of the usual crazy stuff, no pyramids, no astrological charts, no crystals. A deck of cards was laid out like the tarot on the dinette table, but when I leaned across to look at them, I saw it was a half-finished game of solitaire. I put the red eight on the black nine.

Rosa came out, wearing orange polyester pants and a yellow print blouse and carrying a large black leather purse. I stood up and started to say, "Where would you like to go? Is there someplace close?" but I only got it half out.

"The Eldorado Café," she said and started out the door, moving pretty fast for somebody three hundred years old and three hundred pounds.

"I don't know where the Eldorado Café is," I said, unlocking the car door for her. "You'll have to tell me where it is."

"Turn right," she said. "They have good cinnamon rolls."

I wondered if it was the offer of the food or just the chance to go someplace that had made her consent to the interview. Whichever, I might as well get it over with. "So Coronado was your great-grandfather?" I said.

She looked at me as if I were out of my mind. "No. Who told you that?"

Jake, I thought, who I plan to tear limb from limb when I get back to the *Record*. "You aren't Coronado's great-granddaughter?"

She folded her arms over her stomach. "I am the descendant of El Turco."

El Turco. It sounded like something out of *Zorro*. "So it's this El Turco who's your great-grandfather?"

"Great-*great*. El Turco was Pawnee. Coronado captured him at Cicuye and put a collar around his neck so he could not run away. Turn right."

We were already halfway through the intersection. I jerked the steering wheel to the right and nearly skidded into a pickup.

Rosa seemed unperturbed. "Coronado wanted El Turco to guide him to Cibola," she said.

I wanted to ask if he had, but I didn't want to prevent Rosa from giving me directions. I drove slowly through the next intersection, alert to sudden instructions, but there weren't any. I drove on down the block.

"And did El Turco guide Coronado to Cibola?"

"Sure. You should have turned left back there," she said.

She apparently hadn't inherited her great-great-grandfather's scouting ability. I went around the block and turned left, and was overjoyed to see the Eldorado Café down the street. I pulled into the parking lot and we got out.

"They make their own cinnamon rolls," she said, looking at me hopefully as we went in. "With frosting."

We sat down in a booth. "Have anything you want," I said. "This is on the *Record*."

She ordered a cinnamon roll and a large Coke. I ordered coffee and began fishing in my bag for my tape recorder.

"You lived here in Denver a long time?" she asked.

"All my life. I grew up here."

She smiled her gold-toothed smile at me. "You like Denver?"

"Sure," I said. I found the pocket-sized recorder and laid it on the table. "Smog, oil refineries, traffic. What's not to like?"

"I like it too," she said.

The waitress set a cinnamon roll the size of Mile High Stadium in front of her and poured my coffee.

"You know what Coronado fed El Turco?" The waitress brought her large Coke. "Probably one tortilla a day. And he didn't have no shoes.

Coronado made him walk all that way to Colorado and no shoes."

I switched the tape recorder on. "You say Coronado came to Colorado," I said, "but what I've read says he traveled through New Mexico and Oklahoma and up into Kansas, but not Colorado."

"He was in Colorado." She jabbed her finger into the table. "He was *here*."

I wondered if she meant here in Colorado or here in the Eldorado Café.

"When was that? On his way to Quivira?"

"Quivira?" she said, looking blank. "I don't know nothing about Quivira."

"Quivira was a place where there was supposed to be gold," I said. "He went there after he found the Seven Cities of Cibola."

"He didn't find them," she said, chewing on a mouthful of cinnamon roll. "That's why he killed El Turco."

"Coronado killed El Turco?"

"Yeah. After he led him to Cibola."

This was even worse than talking to the psychic dentist.

"Coronado said El Turco made the whole thing up," Rosa said. "He said El Turco was going to lead Coronado into an ambush and kill him. He said the Seven Cities didn't exist."

"But they did?"

"Of course. El Turco led him to the place."

"But I thought you said Coronado didn't find them."

"He didn't."

I was hopelessly confused by now. "Why not?"

"Because they weren't there."

I was going to run Jake through his paper shredder an inch at a time. I had wasted a whole morning on this and I was not even going to be able to get a story out of it.

"You mean they were some sort of mirage?" I asked.

Rosa considered this through several bites of cinnamon roll. "No. A mirage is something that isn't there. These were there."

"But invisible?"

"No."

"Hidden."

"No."

"But Coronado couldn't see them?"

She shook her head. With her forefinger, she picked up a few stray pieces of frosting left on her plate and stuck them in her mouth. "How could he when they weren't there?"

The tape clicked off, and I didn't even bother to turn it over. I looked at my watch. If I took her back now I could make it to the hearings early and maybe interview some of the developers. I picked up the check and went over to the cash register.

"Do you want to see them?"

"What do you mean? See the Seven Cities of Cibola?"

"Yeah. I'll take you to them."

"You mean go to New Mexico?"

"No. I told you, Coronado came to Colorado."

"When?"

"When he was looking for the Seven Cities of Cibola."

"No, I mean when can *I* see them? Right now?"

"No," she said, with that 'how dumb can anyone be?' look. She reached for a copy of the *Rocky Mountain News* that was lying on the counter and looked inside the back page. "Tomorrow morning. Six o'clock."

— • —

One of my favorite things about Denver is that it's spread all over the place and takes you forever to get anywhere. The mountains finally put a stop to things twenty miles to the west, but in all three other directions it can sprawl all the way to the state line and apparently is trying to. Being a reporter here isn't so much a question of driving journalistic ambition as of driving, period.

The skyscraper moratorium hearings were out on Colorado Boulevard across from the Hotel Giorgio, one of the skyscrapers under discussion. It took me forty-five minutes to get there from the Olde West Trailer Park.

I was half an hour late, which meant the hearings had already gotten completely off the subject. "What about reflecting glass?" someone in the audience was saying. "I think it should be outlawed in skyscrapers. I was nearly blinded the other day on the way to work."

"Yeah," a middle-aged woman said. "If we're going to have skyscrapers, they should look like skyscrapers." She waved vaguely at the Hotel Giorgio, which looks like a giant black milk carton.

"And not like that United Bank building downtown!" someone else said. "It looks like a damned cash register!"

From there it was a short illogical jump to the impossibility of parking downtown, Denver's becoming too decentralized, and whether the new airport should be built or not. By five-thirty they were back on reflecting glass.

"Why don't they put glass you can see though in their skyscrapers?" an old man who looked a lot like the time machine inventor said. "I'll tell you why not. Because those big business executives are doing things they should be ashamed of, and they don't want us to see them."

— • —

I left at seven and went back to the *Record* to try to piece my notes together into some kind of story. Jake was there.

"How'd your interview with Coronado's granddaughter go?" he asked.

"The Seven Cities of Cibola are here in Denver only Coronado couldn't see them because they're not there." I looked around. "Is there a copy of the *News* someplace?"

"*Here?* In the *Record* building!" he said, clutching his chest in mock horror. "That bad, huh? You're going to go work for the *News*?" But he fished a copy out of the mess on somebody's desk and handed it to me. I opened it to the back page.

There was no "Best Time for Viewing Lost Cities of Gold" column. There were pictures and dates of the phases of the moon, road conditions, and "What's in the Stars: by Stella." My horoscope of the day read: "Any assignment you accept today will turn out differently than you expect." The rest of the page was devoted to the weather, which was supposed to be sunny and warm tomorrow.

The facing page had the crossword puzzle, "Today in History," and squibs about Princess Di and a Bronco fan who'd planted his garden in the shape of a Bronco quarterback. I was surprised Jake hadn't assigned me that story.

I went down to Research and looked up El Turco. He was an Indian slave, probably Pawnee, who had scouted for Coronado, but that was his nickname, not his name. The Spanish had called him "The Turk" because of his peculiar hair. He had been captured at Cicuye, *after* Coronado's foray into Cibola, and had promised to lead them to Quivira, tempting them with stories of golden streets and great stone palaces. When the stories didn't pan out, Coronado had had him executed. I could understand why.

Jake cornered me on my way home. "Look, don't quit," he said. "Tell you what, forget Coronado. There's a guy out in Lakewood who's planted his garden in the shape of John Elway's face. Daffodils for hair, blue hyacinths for eyes."

"Can't," I said, sidling past him. "I've got a date to see the Seven Cities of Gold."

— • —

Another delightful aspect of the Beautiful Mile-High City is that in the middle of April, after you've planted your favorite Bronco, you can get fifteen inches of snow. It had started getting cloudy by the time I left the paper, but fool that I was, I thought it was an afternoon thunderstorm. The *News*'s forecast had, after all, been for warm and sunny. When I woke up at four-thirty there was a foot and a half of snow on the ground and more tumbling down.

"Why are you going back if she's such a nut?" Jake had asked me when I told him I couldn't take the Elway garden. "You don't seriously think she's onto something, do you?" and I had had a hard time explaining to him why I was planning to get up at an ungodly hour and trek all the way out to Santa Fe again.

She was *not* El Turco's great-great-granddaughter. Two greats still left her at two hundred and fifty plus, and her history was as garbled as her math, but when I had gotten impatient she had said "Do you want to see them?" and when I had asked her when, she had consulted the *News*'s crossword puzzle and said, "Tomorrow morning."

I had gotten offers of proof before. The time machine inventor had proposed that I climb in his washing machine and be sent forward to "a glorious future, a time when everyone is rich," and the psychic dentist had offered to pull my wisdom teeth. But there's always a catch to these offers.

"Your teeth will have been extracted in another plane of reality," the dentist had said. "X-rays taken in this plane will show them as still being there," and the time machine guy had checked his soak cycle and the stars at the last minute and decided there wouldn't be another temporal agitation until August of 2158.

Rosa hadn't put any restrictions at all on her offer. "You want to see them?" she said, and there was no mention of reality planes or stellar-laundry connections, no mention of any catch. Which doesn't mean there won't be one, I thought, getting out the mittens and scarf I had just put away for the season and going out to scrape the windshield off. When I got there she would no doubt say the snow made it impossible to see the Cities or I could only see them if I believed in UFOs. Or maybe she'd point off somewhere in the general direction of Denver's brown cloud and say, "What do you mean, you can't see them?"

I-25 was a mess, cars off the road everywhere and snow driving into my headlights so I could barely see. I got behind a snowplow and stayed there, and it was nearly six o'clock by the time I made it to the trailer. Rosa took a good five minutes to come to the door, and when she finally got there she wasn't dressed. She stared blearily at me, her hair out of its braids and hanging tangled around her face.

"Remember me? Carla Johnson? You promised to show me the Seven Cities?"

"Cities?" she said blankly.

"The Seven Cities of Cibola."

"Oh, yeah," she said, and motioned for me to come inside. "There aren't seven. El Turco was a dumb Pawnee. He don't know how to count."

"How many are there?" I asked, thinking, this is the catch. There aren't seven and they aren't gold.

"Depends," she said. "More than seven. You still wanta go see them?"

"Yes."

She went into the bedroom and came out after a few minutes with her hair braided, the pants and the blouse of the day before and an enormous red carcoat, and we took off toward Cibola. We went south again, past more waterbed stores and rusting railroad tracks, and out to Belleview.

It was beginning to get fairly light out, thought it was impossible to tell if the sun was up or not. It was still snowing hard.

She had me turn onto Belleview, giving me at least ten yards' warning, and we headed east toward the Tech Center. Those people at the hearing who'd complained about Denver becoming too decentralized had a point. The Tech Center looked like another downtown as we headed toward it.

A multi-colored downtown, garish even through the veil of snow. The Metropoint building was pinkish-lavender, the one next to it was midnight blue, while the Hyatt Regency had gone in for turquoise and bronze, and there was an assortment of silver, sea-green, and taupe. There was an assortment of shapes, too: deranged trapezoids, overweight butterflies, giant beer cans. They were clearly moratorium material, each of them with its full complement of reflecting glass, and, presumably, executives with something to hide.

Rosa had me turn left onto Yosemite, and we headed north again. The snowplows hadn't made it out here yet, and it was heavy going. I leaned forward and peered through the windshield, and so did Rosa.

"Do you think we'll be able to see them?" I asked.

"Can't tell yet," she said. "Turn right."

I turned into a snow-filled street. "I've been reading about your great-grandfather."

"Great-*great*," she said.

"He confessed he'd lied about the cities, that there really wasn't any gold."

She shrugged. "He was scared. He thought Coronado was going to kill him."

"Coronado *did* kill him," I said. "He said El Turco was leading his army into a trap."

She shrugged again and wiped a space clear on the windshield to look through.

"If the Seven Cities existed, why didn't El Turco take Coronado to them? It would have saved his life."

"They weren't there." She leaned back.

"You mean they're not there all the time?" I said.

"You know the Grand Canyon?" she asked. "My great-great-grandfather discovered the Grand Canyon. He told Coronado he seen it. Nobody saw the Grand Canyon again for three hundred years. Just because nobody seen it don't mean it wasn't there. You was supposed to turn right back there at the light."

I could see why Coronado had strangled El Turco. If I hadn't been afraid I'd get stuck in the snow, I'd have stopped and throttled her right then. I turned around, slipping and sliding, and went back to the light.

"Left at the next corner and go down the block a little ways," she said, pointing. "Pull in there."

"There" was the parking lot of a donut shop. It had a giant neon donut in the middle of its steamed-up windows. I knew how Coronado felt when he rode into the huddle of mud huts that was supposed to have been the City of Gold.

"This is Cibola?" I said.

"No way," she said, heaving herself out of the car. "They're not there today."

"You *said* they were always there," I said.

"They are." She shut the car door, dislodging a clump of snow. "Just not all the time. I think they're in one of those time-things."

"Time-things? You mean a time warp?" I asked, trying to remember what the washing-machine guy had called it. "A temporal agitation?"

"How would I know? I'm not a scientist. They have good donuts here. Cream-filled."

— • —

The donuts were actually pretty good, and by the time we started home the snow had stopped and was already turning to slush, and I no longer wanted to strangle her on the spot. I figured in another hour the sun would be out, and John Elway's hyacinth-blue eyes would be poking through again. By the time we turned onto Hampden, I felt calm enough to ask when she thought the Seven Cities might put in another appearance.

She had bought a *Rocky Mountain News* and a box of cream-filled donuts to take home. She opened the box and contemplated them. "More than seven," she said. "You like to write?"

"What?" I said, wondering if Coronado had had this much trouble communicating with El Turco.

"That's why you're a reporter, because you like to write?"

"No," I said. "The writing's a real pain. When will this time-warp thing happen again?"

She bit into a donut. "That's Cinderella City," she said, gesturing to the mall on our right with it. "You ever been there?"

I nodded.

"I went there once. They got marble floors and this big fountain. They got lots of stores. You can buy just about anything you want there. Clothes, jewels, shoes."

If she wanted to do a little shopping now that she'd had breakfast, she could forget it. And she could forget about changing the subject. "When can we go see the Seven Cities again? Tomorrow?"

She licked cream filling off her fingers and turned the *News* over. "Not tomorrow," she said. "El Turco would have liked Cinderella City. He didn't have no shoes. He had to walk all the way to Colorado in his bare feet. Even in the snow."

I imagined my hands closing around her plump neck. "When are the Seven Cities going to be there again?" I demanded. "And don't tell me they're always there."

She consulted the celebrity squibs. "Not tomorrow," she said. "Day after tomorrow. Five o'clock. You must like people, then. That's why you wanted to be a reporter? To meet all kinds of people?"

"No," I said. "Believe it or not, I wanted to travel."

She grinned her golden smile at me. "Like Coronado," she said.

— • —

I spent the next two days interviewing developers, environmentalists, and council members, and pondering why Coronado had continued to follow El Turco, even after it was clear he was a pathological liar.

I had stopped at the first 7-Eleven I could find after letting Rosa and her donuts off and bought a copy of the *News*. I read the entire back section, including the comics. For all I knew, she was using *Doonesbury* for an oracle. Or *Nancy*.

I read the obits and worked the crossword puzzle and then went over the back page again. There was nothing remotely time-warp-related. The moon was at first quarter. Sunset would occur at 7:51 P.M. Road conditions for the Eisenhower Tunnel were snow-packed and blowing. Chains required. My horoscope read, "Don't get involved in wild goose chases. A good stay-at-home day."

Rosa no more knew where the Seven Cities of Gold were than her great-great-grandfather. According to the stuff I read in between moratorium jaunts, he had changed his story every fifteen minutes or so, depending on what Coronado wanted to hear.

The other Indian scouts had warned Coronado, told him there was nothing to the north but buffalo and a few teepees, but Coronado had gone blindly on. "El Turco seems to have exerted a Pied-Piperlike power over Coronado," one of the historians had written, "a power which none of Coronado's officers could understand."

"Are you still working on that crazy Coronado thing?" Jake asked me when I got back to the *Record*. "I thought you were covering the hearings."

"I am," I said, looking up the Grand Canyon. "They've been postponed because of the snow. I have an appointment with the United Coalition Against Uncontrolled Growth at eleven."

"Good," he said. "I don't need the Coronado piece, after all. We're running a series on 'Denver Today' instead."

He went back upstairs. I found the Grand Canyon. It had been discovered by Lopez de Cardeñas, one of Coronado's men. El Turco hadn't been with him.

I drove out to Aurora in a blinding snowstorm to interview the United

Coalition. They were united only in spirit, not in location. The president had his office in one of the Pavilion Towers off Havana, but the secretary, who had all the graphs and spreadsheets, was out at Fiddler's Green. I spent the whole afternoon shuttling back and forth between them through the snow, and wondering what had ever possessed me to become a journalist. I'd wanted to travel. I'd had the idea, gotten from TV, that journalists got to go all over the world, writing about exotic and amazing places. Like the UNIPAC building and the Plaza Towers.

They were sort of amazing, if you like Modern Corporate. Brass and chrome and Persian carpets. Atriums and palm trees and fountains splashing in marble pools. I wondered what Rosa, who had been so impressed with Cinderella City, would have thought of some of these places. El Turco would certainly have been impressed. Of course, he would probably have been impressed by the donut shop, and would no doubt have convinced Coronado to drag his whole army there with tales of fabulous, cream-filled wealth.

I finished up the United Coalition and went back to the *Record* to call some developers and builders and get their side. It was still snowing, and there weren't any signs of snow removal, creative or otherwise, that I could see. I set up some appointments for the next day, and then went back down to Research.

El Turco hadn't been the only person to tell tales of the fabulous Seven Cities of Gold. A Spanish explorer, Cabeza de Vaca, had reported them first, and his black slave Estevanico claimed to have seen them, too. Friar Marcos had gone with Estevanico to find them, and, according to him, Estevanico had actually entered Cibola.

They had made up a signal. Estevanico was to send back a small cross if he found a little village, a big cross if he found a city. Estevanico was killed in a battle with Indians, and Friar Marcos fled back to Coronado, but he said he'd seen the Seven Cities in the distance, and he clamed that Estevanico had sent back "a cross the size of a man."

There were all kinds of other tales, too, that the Navajos had gold and silver mines, that Montezuma had moved his treasure north to keep it from the Spanish, that there was a golden city on a lake, with canoes whose oarlocks were solid gold. If El Turco had been lying, he wasn't the only one.

I spent the next day interviewing pro-uncontrolled growth types. They were united, too. "Denver has to retain its central identity," they all told me from what it was hard to believe was not a pre-written script. "It's becoming split into a half-dozen sub-cities, each with its own separate goals."

They were in less agreement as to where the problem lay. One of the builders who'd developed the Tech Center thought the Plaza Tower out at Fiddler's Green was an eyesore, Fiddler's Green complained about Aurora, Aurora thought there was too much building going on around Colorado Boulevard. They were all united on one thing, however: downtown was completely out of control.

I logged several miles in the snow, which showed no signs of letting up, and went home to bed. I debated setting my alarm. Rosa didn't know where the Seven Cities of Gold were, the Living Western Heritage series had been cancelled, and Coronado would have saved everybody a lot of trouble if he had listened to his generals.

But Estevanico had sent back a giant cross, and there was the "time-thing" thing. I had not done enough stories on psychic peridontia yet to start believing their nutto theories, but I had done enough to know what they were supposed to sound like. Rosa's was all wrong.

"I don't know what it's called," she said, which was far too vague. Nutto theories may not make any sense, but they're all worked out, down to the last bit of pseudo-scientific jargon. The psychic dentist had told me all about transcendental maxillofacial extractile vibrations, and the time travel guy had showed me a hand-lettered chart showing how the partial load setting affected future events.

If Rosa's Seven Cities were just one more nutto theory, she would have been talking about morphogenetic temporal dislocation and simultaneous reality modes. She would at least know what the "time-thing" was called.

I compromised by setting the alarm on "music" and went to bed.

— • —

I overslept. The station I'd set the alarm to wasn't on the air at four-thirty in the morning. I raced into my clothes, dragged a brush through my hair, and took off. There was almost no traffic — who in their right mind is up at four-thirty? — and it had stopped snowing. By the time I pulled onto Santa Fe I was only running ten minutes late. Not that it mattered. She would probably take half an hour to drag herself to the door and tell me the Seven Cities of Cibola had cancelled again.

I was wrong. She was standing outside waiting in her red carcoat and a pair of orange Bronco earmuffs. "You're late," she said, squeezing herself in beside me. "Got to go."

"Where?"

She pointed. "Turn left."

"Why don't you just tell me where we're going?" I said, "and that way I'll have a little advance warning."

"Turn right," she said.

We turned onto Hampden and started up past Cinderella City. Hampden is never free of traffic, no matter what time of day it is. There were dozens of cars on the road. I got in the center lane, hoping she'd give me at least a few feet of warning for the next turn, but she leaned back and folded her arms across her massive bosom.

"You're sure the Seven Cities will appear this morning?" I asked.

She leaned forward and peered through the windshield at the slowly lightening sky, looking for who knows what. "Good chance. Can't tell for sure."

I felt like Coronado, dragged from pillar to post. Just a little farther, just a little farther. I wondered if this could be not only a scam but a set-up, if we would end up pulling up next to a black van in some dark parking lot, and I would find myself on the cover of the *Record* as a robbery victim or worse. She was certainly anxious enough. She kept holding up her arm so she could read her watch in the lights of the cars behind us. More likely, we were heading for some bakery that opened at the crack of dawn, and she wanted to be there when the fried cinnamon rolls came out of the oven.

"Turn right!" she said. "Can't you go no faster?"

I went faster. We were out in Cherry Creek now, and it was starting to get really light. The snowstorm was apparently over. The sky was turning a faint lavender-blue.

"Now right, up there," she said, and I saw where we were going. This road led past Cherry Creek High School and then up along the top of a dam. A nice isolated place for a robbery.

We went past the last houses and pulled onto the dam road. Rosa turned in her seat to peer out my window and the back, obviously looking for something. There wasn't much to see. The water wasn't visible from this point, and she was looking the wrong direction, out towards Denver. There were still a few lights, the early-bird traffic down on I-225 and the last few orangish street lights that hadn't gone off automatically. The snow had taken on the bluish lavender of the sky.

I stopped the car.

"What are you doing?" she demanded. "Go all the way up."

"I can't," I said, pointing ahead. "The road's closed."

She peered at the chain strung across the road as if she couldn't figure out what it was, and then opened the door and got out.

Now it was my turn to say, "What are you doing?"

"We gotta walk," she said. "We'll miss it otherwise."

"Miss what? Are you telling me there's going to be a time warp up there on top of the dam?"

She looked at me like I was crazy. "Time warp?" she said. Her grin glittered in my headlights. "No. Come on."

Even Coronado had finally said, "All right, enough," and ordered his men to strangle El Turco. But not until he'd been lured all the way up to Kansas. And, according to Rosa, Colorado. The Seven Cities of Cibola were *not* going to be up on top of Cherry Creek dam, no matter what Rosa said, and I wasn't even going to get a story out of this, but I switched off my lights and got out of the car and climbed over the chain.

It was almost fully light now, and the shadowy dimnesses below were sorting themselves out into decentralized Denver. The black *2001* towers off Havana were right below us, and past them the peculiar Mayan-pyramid shape of the National Farmer's Union. The Tech Center rose in a jumble off to the left, beer cans and trapezoids, and then there was a long curve of isolated buildings all the way to downtown, an island of sky-scraping towers obviously in need of a moratorium.

"Come on," Rosa said. She started walking faster, panting along the road ahead of me and looking anxiously toward the east, where at least a black van wasn't parked. "Coronado shouldn't have killed El Turco. It wasn't his fault."

"What wasn't his fault?"

"It was one of those time-things, what did you call it?" she said, breathing hard.

"A temporal agitation?"

"Yeah, only he didn't know it. He thought it was there all the time, and when he brought Coronado there it wasn't there, and he didn't know what had happened."

She looked anxiously to the east again, where a band of clouds extending about an inch above the horizon was beginning to turn pinkish-gray, and broke into an ungainly run. I trotted after her, trying to remember the procedure for CPR.

She ran into the pullout at the top of the dam and stopped, panting hard. She put her hand up to her heaving chest and looked out across the snow at Denver.

"So you're saying the cities existed in some other time? In the future?"

She glanced over her shoulder at the horizon. The sun was nearly up. The narrow cloud turned pale pink, and the snow on Mt. Evans went the kind of fuchsia we use in Sunday supplements. "And you think there's going to be another time-warp this morning?" I said.

She gave me that "how can one person be so stupid" look. "Of course not," she said, and the sun cleared the cloud. "There they are," she said.

There they were. The reflecting glass in the curved towers of Fiddler's Green caught first, and then the Tech Center and the Silverado Building and the Plaza Towers, blazing pinnacles and turrets and towers.

"You didn't believe me, did you?" Rosa said.

"No," I said, unwilling to take my eyes off them. "I didn't."

There were more than seven. Far out to the west of the Federal Center ignited, and off to the north the angled lines of grain elevators gleamed. Downtown blazed, blinding building moratorium advocates on their way to work. In between, the Career Development Institute and the United Bank Building and the Hyatt Regency burned gold, standing out from the snow like citadels, like cities. No wonder El Turco had dragged Coronado all the way to Colorado. Marble palaces and golden streets.

"I told you they were there all the time," she said.

It was over in another minute, the fires going out one by one in the panes of reflecting glass, downtown first and then the Cigna building and the Belleview Place, fading to their everyday silver and onyx and emerald. The Pavilion Towers below us darkened and the last of the sodium street lights went out.

"There all the time," Rosa said solemnly.

"Yeah," I said. I would have to get Jake up here to see this. I'd have to buy a *News* on the way home and check on the time of sunrise for tomorrow. And the weather.

I turned around. The sun glittered off the water of the reservoir. There was an aluminum rowboat out in the middle of it. It had golden oarlocks.

Rosa had started back down the road to the car. I caught up with her. "I'll buy you a pecan roll," I said. "Do you know of any good places around here?"

She grinned. Her gold teeth gleamed in the last light of Cibola. "The best," she said. ■

INVADERS

BY JOHN KESSEL

John Kessel (born 1950 in Buffalo, New York) received a B.A. in English and Physics from the University of Rochester in 1972, an M.A. in English from the University of Kansas in 1974, and a Ph.D. in English from the University of Kansas in 1981. Since 1982 he has taught American literature, science fiction, fantasy, and creative writing at North Carolina State University. Kessel's first published short fiction appeared in 1978, and he has since become a frequent contributor to *Asimov's Science Fiction* and *The Magazine of Fantasy and Science Fiction*, as well as to many other magazines and anthologies. His acclaimed 1982 novella "Another Orphan" received the Nebula Award. He later won the 1992 Theodore Sturgeon Memorial Award for his short story "Buffalo" (also a winner of the *Locus* Award that year); he won a Paul Green Playwright's prize in 1994 for his play "Faustfeathers"; and his one-act play "A Clean Escape" was produced by the Allowance Theater in Raleigh in 1986. His novella "Stories for Men" earned the 2002 James Tiptree Jr. Award for science fiction dealing with gender issues.

Kessel co-authored *Freedom Beach* (1985) with James Patrick Kelly. His later works include the millenialist satire *Good News From Outer Space* (1989, a Nebula finalist) and the screwball comedy / time-travel adventure *Corrupting Dr. Nice* (1997), plus the collections *Meeting in Infinity* (1992, nominated for the World Fantasy Award and named a Notable Book by the *New York Times Book Review*), *The Pure Product* (1997), and *The Baum Plan for Financial Independence and Other Stories* (2008). He edited an anthology of stories from the Sycamore Hill Writers' Workshop (which he also helps to run), called *Intersections* (1996), with Mark L. Van Name and Richard Butner. With Kelly, he edited *Feeling Very Strange: The Slipstream Anthology* (2006) and *Rewired: The Post-Cyberpunk Anthology* (2007). His website is at www4.ncsu.edu/~tenshi.

In a 1993 interview with me ("An Interview with John Kessel," *Science Fiction Studies* online), he discussed his works which deal with alien invasions and with humans' reactions to the whole notion (both in reality and in fiction). He said that " ... if enough people believe in a stupid thing, then it becomes a stupid fact ... And they will order their lives so as to react in response to this delusion ... And some of these may be originated by people consciously plotting out some nefarious plan or purpose ... But I don't tend to ascribe to conspiracy what can more easily be ascribed to incompetence. If there are Aliens out there planning everything, I have a feeling that what they're planning is not what we might imagine they're planning." In "Invaders," "they come and all they want is cocaine. They're not out to do anything in particular; all they want to do is score some cocaine. That's more amusing and perhaps more real to me than the idea of a vast conspiracy ... I'm not a writer who comes up with ideas that have never been done before in science fiction. If I have a virtue, it's a matter of doing these old things in a new way, or adding another wrinkle on an old thing." Besides the alien invasion, his new wrinkles here include the alternate history and the meta-referential "breaking of the fourth wall."

INVADERS

15 NOVEMBER 1532: THAT NIGHT NO ONE SLEPT. ON THE HILLS outside Cajamarca, the campfires of the Inca's army shone like so many stars in the sky. De Soto had reported that Atahualpa had perhaps forty thousand troops under arms, but looking at the myriad lights spread out across those hills, de Candia realized that estimate was, if anything, low.

Against them, Pizarro could throw one hundred foot soldiers, sixty horses, eight muskets, and four harquebuses. Pizarro, his brother Hernando, de Soto, and Benalcázar laid out plans for an ambush. They would invite the Inca to a parlay. De Candia and his artillery would be hidden in the building along one side of the square, the cavalry and infantry along the others. De Candia watched Pizarro prowl through the camp that night, checking the men's armor, joking with them, reminding them of the treasure they would have, and the women. The men laughed nervously and whetted their swords.

They might sharpen them until their hands fell off; when morning dawned, they would be slaughtered. De Candia breathed deeply of the thin air and turned from the wall.

Ruiz de Arce, an infantryman with a face like a clenched fist, hailed him as he passed. "Are those guns of yours ready for some work tomorrow?"

"We need prayers more than guns."

"I'm not afraid of these brownies," de Arce said.

"Then you're a half-wit."

"Soto says they have no swords."

The man was probably just trying to reassure himself, but de Candia couldn't abide it. "Will you shut your stinking fool's trap! They don't need swords! If they all only spit at once, we'll be drowned."

Pizarro overheard him. He stormed over, grabbed de Candia's arm, and shook him. "Have they ever seen a horse, Candia? Have they ever felt steel? When you fired the harquebus on the seashore, didn't the town chief pour beer down its barrel as if it were a thirsty god? Pull up your balls and show me you're a man!"

His face was inches away. "Mark me! Tomorrow, Saint James sits on your shoulder, and we win a victory that will cover us in glory for five hundred years."

— • —

2 December 2001: "DEE-fense! DEE-fense!" the crowd screamed. During the two-minute warning, Norwood Delacroix limped over to the Redskins' special conditioning coach.

"My knee's about gone," said Delacroix, an outside linebacker with eyebrows that ran together and all the musculature that modern pharmacology could load onto his six-foot-five frame. "I need something."

"You need the power of prayer, my friend. Stoner's eating your lunch."

"Just do it."

The coach selected a popgun from his rack, pressed the muzzle against Delacroix's knee, and pulled the trigger. A flood of well-being rushed up Delacroix's leg. He flexed it tentatively. It felt better than the other one now.

Delacroix jogged back onto the field. "DEE-fense!" the fans roared. The overcast sky began to spit frozen rain. The ref blew the whistle, and the Bills broke huddle.

Delacroix looked across at Stoner, the Bills' tight end. The air throbbed with electricity. The quarterback called the signals; the ball was snapped; Stoner surged forward. As Delacroix back-pedaled furiously, sudden sunlight flooded the field. His ears buzzed. Stoner jerked left and went right, twisting Delacroix around like a cork in a bottle. His knee popped. Stoner had two steps on him. TD for sure. Delacroix pulled his head down and charged after him.

But instead of continuing downfield, Stoner slowed. He looked straight up into the air. Delacroix hit him at the knees, and they both went down. He'd caught him! The crowed screamed louder, a scream edged with hysteria.

Then Delacroix realized the buzzing wasn't just in his ears. Elation fading, he lifted his head and looked toward the sidelines. The coaches and players were running for the tunnels. The crowd boiled toward the exits, shedding Thermoses and beer cups and radios. The sunlight was harshly bright. Delacroix looked up. A huge disk hovered no more than fifty feet above, pinning them in its spotlight. Stoner untangled himself from Delacroix, stumbled to his feet, and ran off the field.

Holy Jesus and the Virgin Mary on toast, Delacroix thought.

He scrambled toward the end zone. The stadium was emptying fast, except for the ones who were getting trampled. The throbbing in the air increased in volume, lowered in pitch, and the flying saucer settled onto the NFL logo on the forty-yard line. The sound stopped as abruptly as if it had been sucked into a sponge.

Out of the corner of his eye, Delacroix saw an NBC cameraman come up next to him, focusing on the ship. Its side divided, and a ramp extended itself to the ground. The cameraman fell back a few steps, but Delacroix held his ground. The inside glowed with the bluish light of a UV lamp.

A shape moved there. It lurched forward to the top of the ramp. A large manlike thing, it advanced with a rolling stagger, like a college freshman at a beer blast. It wore a body-tight red stretchsuit, a white circle on its chest with a lightning bolt through it, some sort of flexible mask over its face. Blond hair covered its head in a kind of brush cut, and two cup-shaped ears poked comically out of the sides of its head. The creature stepped off onto the field, nudging aside the football that lay there. Delacroix, who had majored in public relations at Michigan State, went forward to greet it. This could be the beginning of an entirely new career. His knee felt great.

He extended his hand. "Welcome," he said. "I greet you in the name of humanity and the United States of America."

"Cocaine," the alien said. "We need cocaine."

— • —

Today: I sit at my desk writing a science-fiction story, a tall, thin man wearing jeans, a white T-shirt with the abstract face of a man printed on it, white high-top basketball shoes, and gold-plated wire-rimmed glasses.

In the morning I drink coffee to get me up for the day, and at night I have a gin and tonic to help me relax.

— • —

16 November 1532: "What are they waiting for, the shitting dogs!" the man next to de Arce said. "Are they trying to make us suffer?"

"Shut up, will you?" De Arce shifted his armor. Wedged into the stone building on the side of the square, sweating, they had been waiting since dawn, in silence for the most part except for the creak of leather, the uneasy jingle of cascabels on the horses' trappings. The men stank worse than the restless horses. Some had pissed themselves. A common foot soldier like de Arce was lucky to get a space near enough to the door to see out.

As noon came and went with still no sign of Atahualpa and his retinue, the mood of the men went from impatience to near panic. Then, late in the day, word came that the Indians again were moving toward the town.

An hour later, six thousand brilliantly costumed attendants entered the plaza. They were unarmed. Atahualpa, borne on a golden litter by eight men in cloaks of green feathers that glistened like emeralds in the sunset, rose above them. De Arce heard a slight rattling, looked down, and found that his hand, gripping the sword so tightly the knuckles stood out white, was shaking uncontrollably. He unknotted his fist from the hilt, rubbed the cramped fingers, and crossed himself.

"Quiet now, my brave ones," Pizarro said.

Father Valverde and Felipillo strode out to the center of the plaza, right through the sea of attendants. The priest had guts. He stopped before the litter of the Inca, short and steady as a fence post. "Greetings, my lord, in the name of Pope Clement VII, His Majesty the Emperor Charles V, and Our Lord and Savior Jesus Christ."

Atahualpa spoke and Felipillo translated: "Where is this new god?"

Valverde held up the crucifix. "Our God died on the cross many years ago and rose again to Heaven. He appointed the Pope as His viceroy on earth, and the Pope has commanded King Charles to subdue the peoples of the world and convert them to the true faith. The king sent us here to command your obedience and to teach you and your people in this faith."

"By what authority does this pope give away lands that aren't his?"

Valverde held up his Bible. "By the authority of the word of God."

The Inca took the Bible. When Valverde reached out to help him get the cover unclasped, Atahualpa cuffed his arm away. He opened the book and leafed through the pages. After a moment he threw it to the ground. "I heard no words," he said.

Valverde snatched up the book and stalked back toward Pizarro's hiding place. "What are you waiting for?" he shouted. "The saints and the Blessed Virgin, the bleeding wounds of Christ himself, cry vengeance!

Attack, and I'll absolve you!"

Pizarro had already stridden into the plaza. He waved his kerchief. "Santiago, and at them!"

On the far side, the harquebuses exploded in an enfilade. The lines of Indians jerked like startled cats. Bells jingling, de Soto's and Hernando's cavalry burst from the lines of doorways on the adjoining side. De Arce clutched his sword and rushed out with the others from the third side. He felt the power of God in his arm. "Santiago!" he roared at the top of his lungs, and hacked halfway through the neck of his first Indian. Bright blood spurted. He put his boot to the brown man's shoulder and yanked free, lunged for the belly of another wearing a kilt of bright red-and-white checks. The man turned, and the sword caught between his ribs. The hilt was almost twisted from de Arce's grasp as the Indian went down. He pulled free, shrugged another man off his back, and daggered him in the side.

After the first flush of glory, it turned to filthy, hard work, an hour's wade through an ocean of butchery in the twilight, bodies heaped waist-high, boots skidding on the bloody stones. De Arce alone must have killed forty. Only after they'd slaughtered them all and captured the Sapa Inca did it end. A silence settled, broken only by the moans of dying Indians and distant shouts of the cavalry chasing the ones who had managed to break through the plaza wall to escape.

Saint James had indeed sat on their shoulders. Six thousand dead Indians, and not one Spaniard nicked. It was a pure demonstration of the power of prayer.

— • —

31 January 2002: It was Colonel Zipp's third session interrogating the alien. So far the thing had kept a consistent story, but not a credible one. The only consideration that kept Zipp from panic at the thought of how his career would suffer if this continued was the rumor that his fellow case officers weren't doing any better with any of the others. That, and the fact that the Krel possessed technology that would reestablish American superiority for another two hundred years. He took a drag on his cigarette, the first of his third pack of the day.

"Your name?" Zipp asked.

"You may call me Flash."

Zipp studied the red union suit, the lightning bolt. With the flat chest, the rounded shoulders, pointed upper lip, and pronounced underbite, the alien looked like a cross between Wally Cleaver and the Mock Turtle. "Is this some kind of joke?"

"What is a joke?"

"Never mind." Zipp consulted his notes. "Where are you from?"

"God has ceded us an empire extending over sixteen solar systems in the Orion arm of the galaxy, including the systems around the stars you know as Tau Ceti, Epsilon Eridani, Alpha Centauri, and the red dwarf Bernard's star."

"God gave you an empire?"

"Yes. We were hoping He'd give us your world, but all He kept talking about was your cocaine."

The alien's translating device had to be malfunctioning. "You're telling me that God sent you for cocaine?"

"No. He just told us about it. We collect chemical compounds for their aesthetic interest. These alkaloids do not exist on our world. Like the music you humans value so highly, they combine familiar elements — carbon, hydrogen, nitrogen, oxygen — in pleasing new ways."

The colonel leaned back, exhaled a cloud of smoke. "You consider cocaine like — like a symphony?"

"Yes. Understand, Colonel, no material commodity alone could justify the difficulties of interstellar travel. We come here for aesthetic reasons."

"You seem to know what cocaine is already. Why don't you just synthesize it yourself?"

"If you valued a unique work of aboriginal art, would you be satisfied with a mass-produced duplicate manufactured in your hometown? Of course not. And we are prepared to pay you well, in a coin you can use."

"We don't need any coins. If you want cocaine, tell us how your ships work."

"That is one of the coins we had in mind. Our ships operate according to a principle of basic physics. Certain fundamental physical reactions are subject to the belief system of the beings promoting them. If I believe that X is true, then X is more probably true than if I did not believe so."

The colonel leaned forward again. "We know that already. We call it the 'observer effect.' Our great physicist Werner Heisenberg —"

"Yes. I'm afraid we carry this principle a little further than that."

"What do you mean?"

Flash smirked. "I mean that our ships move through interstellar space by the power of prayer."

— • —

13 May 1533: Atahualpa offered to fill a room twenty-two feet long and seventeen feet wide with gold up to a line as high as a man could reach, if the Spaniards would let him go. They were skeptical. How long would this take? Pizarro asked. Two months, Atahualpa said.

Pizarro allowed the word to be sent out, and over the next several months, bearers, chewing the coca leaf in order to negotiate the mountain roads under such burdens, brought in tons of gold artifacts. They brought plates and vessels, life-sized statues of women and men, gold lobsters and spiders and alpacas, intricately fashioned ears of maize, every kernel reproduced, with leaves of gold and tassels of spun silver.

Martin Bueno was one of the advance scouts sent with the Indians to Cuzco, the capital of the empire. They found it to be the legendary city of gold. The Incas, having no money, valued precious metals only as ornament. In Cuzco the very walls of the Sun Temple, Coricancha, were plated with gold. Adjoining the temple was a ritual garden where gold maize plants supported gold butterflies, gold bees pollinated gold flowers.

"Enough loot that you'll shit in a different gold pot every day for the rest of your life," Bueno told his friend Diego Leguizano upon his return to Cajamarca.

They ripped the plating off the temple walls and had it carried to Cajamarca. There they melted it down into ingots.

The huge influx of gold into Europe was to cause an economic catastrophe. In Peru, at the height of the conquest, a pair of shoes cost $850, and a bottle of wine $1,700. When their old horseshoes were worn out, iron being unavailable, the cavalry shod their horses with silver.

— • —

21 April 2003: In the executive washroom of Bellingham, Winston, and McNeese, Jason Prescott snorted a couple of lines and was ready for the afternoon. He returned to the brokerage to find the place in a whispering uproar. In his office sat one of the Krel. Prescott's secretary was about to piss himself. "It asked specifically for you," he said.

What would Attila the Hun do in this situation? Prescott thought. He went into the office. "Jason Prescott," he said. "What can I do for you, Mr. …?"

The alien's bloodshot eyes surveyed him. "Flash. I wish to make an investment."

"Investments are our business." Rumors had flown around the New York Merc for a month that the Krel were interested in investing. They had earned vast sums selling information to various computer, environmental, and biotech firms. Several of the aliens had come to observe trading in the currencies pit last week, and only yesterday Jason had heard from a reliable source that they were considering opening an account with Merrill Lynch. "What brings you to our brokerage?"

"Not the brokerage. You. We heard that you are the most ruthless currencies trader in this city. We worship efficiency. You are efficient."

Right. Maybe there was a hallucinogen in the toot. "I'll call in some of our foreign-exchange experts. We can work up an investment plan for your consideration in a week."

"We already have an investment plan. We are, as you say in the markets, 'long' in dollars. We want you to sell dollars and buy francs for us."

"The franc is pretty strong right now. It's likely to hold for the next six months. We'd suggest —"

"We wish to buy fifty billion dollars worth of francs."

Prescott stared. "That's not a very good investment." Flash said nothing. The silence grew uncomfortable. "I suppose if we stretch it out over a few months, and hit the exchanges in Hong Kong and London at the same time —"

"We want these francs bought in the next week. For the week after that, a second fifty billion dollars. Fifty billion a week until we tell you to stop."

Hallucinogens for sure. "That doesn't make any sense."

"We can take our business elsewhere."

Prescott thought about it. It would take every trick he knew — and he'd have to invent some new ones — to carry this off. The dollar was going to drop through the floor, while the franc would punch through the sell-stops of every trader on ten world markets. The exchanges would scream bloody murder. The repercussions would auger holes in every economy north of Antarctica. Governments would intervene. It would make the historic Hunt silver squeeze look like a game of Monopoly.

Besides, it made no sense. Not only was it criminally irresponsible, it was stupid. The Krel would squander every dime they'd earned.

Then he thought about the commission on $50 billion a week.

Prescott looked across at the alien. From the right point of view, Flash resembled a barrel-chested college undergraduate from Special Effects U. He felt an urge to giggle, a euphoric feeling of power. "When do we start?"

— • —

19 May 1533: In the fields the *purics*, singing praise to Atahualpa, son of the sun, harvested the maize. At night they celebrated by getting drunk on *chicha*. It was, they said, the most festive month of the year.

Pedro Sancho did his drinking in the dark of the treasure room, in the smoke of the smelter's fire. For months he had been troubled by nightmares of the heaped bodies lying in the plaza. He tried to ignore the abuse of the Indian women, the brutality toward the men. He worked hard. As Pizarro's squire, it was his job to record daily the tally of Atahualpa's ransom. When he ran low on ink, he taught the *purics* to make it for him from soot and the juice of berries. They learned readily.

Atahualpa heard about the ink and one day came to him. "What are you doing with those marks?" he said, pointing to the scribe's tally book.

"I'm writing the list of gold objects to be melted down."

"What is this 'writing'?"

Sancho was nonplussed. Over the months of Atahualpa's captivity, Sancho had become impressed by the sophistication of the Incas. Yet they were also queerly backward. They had no money. It was not beyond belief that they should not know how to read and write.

"By means of these marks, I can record the words that people speak. That's writing. Later other men can look at these marks and see what was said. That's reading."

"Then this is a kind of quipu?" Atahualpa's servants had demonstrated for Sancho the quipu, a system of knotted strings by which the Incas kept tallies. "Show me how it works," Atahualpa said.

Sancho wrote on the page: *God have mercy on us.* He pointed. "This, my lord, is a representation of the word 'God.'"

Atahualpa looked skeptical. "Mark it here." He held out his hand, thumbnail extended.

Sancho wrote "God" on the Inca's thumbnail.

"Say nothing now." Atahualpa advanced to one of the guards, held out his thumbnail. "What does this mean?" he asked.

"God," the man replied.

Sancho could tell the Inca was impressed, but he barely showed it. That the Sapa Inca had maintained such dignity throughout his captivity tore at Sancho's heart.

"This writing is truly a magical accomplishment," Atahualpa told him. "You must teach my *amautas* this art."

Later, when the viceroy Estete, Father Valverde, and Pizarro came to chide him for the slow pace of the gold shipments, Atahualpa tested each of them separately. Estete and Valverde each said the word "God." Atahualpa held his thumbnail out to the conquistador.

Estete chuckled. For the first time in his experience, Sancho saw Pizarro flush. He turned away. "I don't waste my time on the games of children," Pizarro said.

Atahualpa stared at him. "But your common soldiers have this art."

"Well, I don't."

"Why not?"

"I was a swineherd. Swineherds don't need to read."

"You are not a swineherd now."

Pizarro glared at the Inca. "I don't need to read to order you put to death." He marched out of the room.

After the others had left, Sancho told Atahualpa, "You ought not to humiliate the governor in front of his men."

"He humiliates himself," Atahualpa said. "There is no skill in which a leader ought to let himself stand behind his followers."

— • —

Today: The part of this story about the Incas is as historically accurate as I could make it, but this Krel business is science fiction. I even stole the name "Krel" from a 1950s SF flick. I've been addicted to SF for years. In the evening my wife and I wash the bad taste of the news out of our mouths by watching old movies on videotape.

A scientist, asked why he read SF, replied, "Because in science fiction the experiments always work." Things in SF stories work out more neatly than in reality. Nothing is impossible. Spaceships move faster than light. Atomic weapons are neutralized. Disease is abolished. People travel in time. Why, Isaac Asimov even wrote a story once that ended with the reversal of entropy!

The descendants of the Incas, living in grinding poverty, find their most lucrative crop in coca, which they refine into cocaine and sell in vast quantities to North Americans.

— • —

23 August 2008: "Catalog number 208," said John Bostock. "Georges Seurat, *Bathers*."

FRENCH GOVERNMENT FALLS, the morning *Times* had announced. JAPAN BANS U.S. IMPORTS. FOOD RIOTS IN MADRID. But Bostock had barely glanced at the newspaper over his coffee; he was buzzed on caffeine and adrenaline, and it was too late to stop the auction, the biggest day of his career. The lot list would make an art historian faint. *Guernica*. *The Potato Eaters*. *The Scream*. Miró, Rembrandt, Vermeer, Gauguin, Matisse, Constable, Magritte, Pollock, Mondrian. Six desperate governments had contributed to the sale. And rumor had it the Krel would be among the bidders.

The rumor proved true. In the front row, beside the solicitor Patrick McClannahan, sat one of the unlikely aliens, wearing red tights and a light-ning-bolt insignia. The famous Flash. The creature leaned back lazily while

McClannahan did the bidding with a discreetly raised forefinger.

Bidding on the Seurat started at ten million and went orbital. It soon became clear that the main bidders were Flash and the U.S. government. The American campaign against cultural imperialism was getting a lot of press, ironic since the Yanks could afford to challenge the Krel only because of the technology the Krel had lavished on them. The probability suppressor that prevented the detonation of atomic weapons. The autodidactic antivirus that cured most diseases. There was talk of an immortality drug. Of a time machine. So what if the European Community was in the sixth month of an economic crisis that threatened to dissolve the unifying efforts of the past twenty years? So what if Krel meddling destroyed humans' capacity to run the world? The Americans were making money, and the Krel were richer than Croesus.

The bidding reached $1.2 billion, at which point the American ambassador gave up. Bostock tapped his gavel. "Sold," he said in his most cultured voice, nodding toward the alien.

The crowd murmured. The American stood. "If you can't see what they're doing to us, then you don't deserve our help!"

For a minute Bostock thought the auction was going to turn into a riot. Then the new owner of the pointillist masterpiece stood, smiled. Ingenuous, clumsy. "We know that there has been considerable disquiet over our purchase of these historic works of art," Flash said. "Let me promise you, they will be displayed where all humans — not just those who can afford to visit the great museums — can see them."

The crowd's murmur turned into applause. Bostock put down his gavel and joined in. The American ambassador and his aides stalked out. Thank God, Bostock thought. The attendants brought out the next item.

"Catalog number 209," Bostock said. "Leonardo da Vinci, *Mona Lisa*."

— • —

26 July 1533: The soldiers, seeing the heaps of gold grow, became anxious. They consumed stores of coca meant for the Inca messengers. They fought over women. They grumbled over the airs of Atahualpa. "Who does he think he is? The governor treats him like a hidalgo."

Father Valverde cursed Pizarro's inaction. That morning, after matins, he spoke with Estete. "The governor has agreed to meet and decide what to do," Estete said.

"It's about time. What about Soto?" De Soto was against harming Atahualpa. He maintained that, since the Inca had paid the ransom, he should be set free, no matter what danger this would present. Pizarro had stalled. Last week he had sent de Soto away to check out rumors that the Tahuantinsuyans were massing for an attack to free the Sapa Inca.

Estete smiled. "Soto's not back yet."

They went to the building Pizarro had claimed as his, and found the others already gathered. The Incas had no tables or proper chairs, so the Spaniards were forced to sit in a circle on mats as the Indians did. Pizarro, only a few years short of three-score, sat on a low stool of the sort that Atahualpa used when he held court. His left leg, whose battle wound still pained him at times, was stretched out before him. His loose white shirt had been cleaned by some *puric*'s wife. Valverde sat beside him. Gathered were Estete, Benalcázar, Almagro, de Candia, Riquelme, Pizarro's young cousin Pedro, the scribe Pedro Sancho, Valverde, and the governor himself.

As Valverde and Estete had agreed, the viceroy went first. "The men are jumpy, governor," Estete said. "The longer we stay cooped up here, the longer we give these savages the chance to plot against us."

"We should wait until Soto returns," de Candia said, already looking guilty as a dog. "We've got nothing but rumors so far. I won't kill a man on a rumor."

Silence. Trust de Candia to speak aloud what they were all thinking but were not ready to say. The man had no political judgment — but maybe it was just as well to face it directly. Valverde seized the opportunity.

"Atahualpa plots against us even as we speak," he told Pizarro. "As governor, you are responsible for our safety. Any court would convict him of treason, and execute him."

"He's a king," de Candia said. Face flushed, he spat out a cud of leaves. "We don't have authority to try him. We should ship him back to Spain and let the emperor decide what to do."

"This is not a king," Valverde said. "It isn't even a man. It is a creature that worships demons, that weaves spells about half-wits like Candia. You saw him discard the Bible. Even after my months of teaching, after the extraordinary mercies we've shown him, he doesn't acknowledge the primacy of Christ! He cares only for his wives and his pagan gods. Yet he's satanically clever. Don't think we can let him go. If we do, the day will come when he'll have our hearts for dinner."

"We can take him with us to Cuzco," Benalcázar said. "We don't know the country. His presence would guarantee our safe conduct."

"We'll be traveling over rough terrain, carrying tons of gold, with not enough horses," Almagro said. "If we take him with us, we'll be ripe for ambush at every pass."

"They won't attack if we have him."

"He could escape. We can't trust the rebel Indians to stay loyal to us. If they turned to our side, they can just as easily turn back to his."

"And remember, he escaped before, during the civil war," Valverde said. "Huascar, his brother, lived to regret that. If Atahualpa didn't hesitate to murder his own brother, do you think he'll stop for us?"

"He's given us his word," Candia said.

"What good is the word of a pagan?"

Pizarro, silent until now, spoke. "He has no reason to think the word of a Christian much better."

Valverde felt his blood rise. Pizarro knew as well as any of them what was necessary. What was he waiting for? "He keeps a hundred wives! He betrayed his brother! He worships the sun!" The priest grabbed Pizarro's hand, held it up between them so they could both see the scar there, where Pizarro had gotten cut preventing one of his own men from killing Atahualpa. "He isn't worth an ounce of the blood you spilled to save him."

"He's proved worth twenty-four tons of gold." Pizarro's eyes were hard and calm.

"There is no alternative!" Valverde insisted. "He serves the Antichrist! God demands his death."

At last Pizarro seemed to have gotten what he wanted. He smiled. "Far be it from me to ignore the command of God," he said. "Since God forces us to it, let's discuss how He wants it done."

— • —

5 October 2009: "What a lovely country Chile is from the air. You should be proud of it."

"I'm from Los Angeles," Leon Sepulveda said. "And as soon as we close this deal, I'm going back."

"The mountains are impressive."

"Nothing but earthquakes and slag. You can have Chile."

"Is it for sale?"

Sepulveda stared at the Krel. "I was just kidding."

They sat at midnight in the arbor, away from the main buildings of Iguassu Microelectronics of Santiago. The night was cold and the arbor was overgrown and the bench needed a paint job — but then, a lot of things had been getting neglected in the past couple of years. All the more reason to put yourself in a financial situation where you didn't have to worry. Though Sepulveda had to admit that, since the advent of the Krel, such positions were harder to come by, and less secure once you had them.

Flash's earnestness aroused a kind of horror in him. It had something to do with Sepulveda's suspicion that this thing next to him was as superior to him as he was to a guinea pig, plus the alien's aura of drunken adolescence, plus his own willingness, despite the feeling that the situation was out of control, to make a deal with it. He took another Valium and tried to calm down.

"What assurance do I have that this time-travel method will work?" he asked.

"It will work. If you don't like it in Chile, or back in Los Angeles, you can use it to go into the past."

Sepulveda swallowed. "Okay. You need to read and sign these papers."

"We don't read."

"You don't read Spanish? How about English?"

"We don't read at all. We used to, but we gave it up. Once you start reading, it gets out of control. You tell yourself you're just going to stick to nonfiction — but pretty soon you graduate to fiction. After that, you can't kick the habit. And then there's the oppression."

"Oppression?"

"Sure. I mean, I like a story as much as the next Krel, but any pharmacologist can show that arbitrary cultural, sexual, and economic assumptions determine every significant aspect of a story. Literature is a political tool used by ruling elites to ensure their hegemony. Anyone who denies that is a fish who can't see the water it swims in. Or the fascist who tells you, as he beats you, that those blows you feel are your own delusion."

"Right. Look, can we settle this? I've got things to do."

"This is, of course, the key to temporal translation. The past is another arbitrary construct. Language creates reality. Reality is smoke."

"Well, this time machine better not be smoke. We're going to find out the truth about the past. Then we'll change it."

"By all means. Find the truth." Flash turned to the last page of the contract, pricked his thumb, and marked a thumbprint on the signature line.

After they sealed the agreement, Sepulveda walked the alien back to the courtyard. A Krel flying pod with Vermeer's *The Letter* varnished onto its door sat at the focus of three spotlights. The painting was scorched almost into unrecognizability by atmospheric friction. The door peeled downward from the top, became a canvas-surfaced ramp.

"I saw some interesting lines inscribed on the coastal desert on the way here," Flash said. "A bird, a tree, a big spider. In the sunset, it looked beautiful. I didn't think you humans were capable of such art. Is it for sale?"

"I don't think so. That was done by some old Indians a long time ago. If you're really interested, though, I can look into it."

"Not necessary." Flash waggled his ears, wiped his feet on Mark Rothko's *Earth and Green*, and staggered into the pod.

— • —

26 July 1533: Atahualpa looked out of the window of the stone room in which he was kept, across the plaza where the priest Valverde stood outside his chapel after his morning prayers. Valverde's chapel had been the house of the virgins; the women of the house had long since been raped by the Spanish soldiers, as the house had been by the Spanish god. Valverde spoke with Estete. They were getting ready to kill him, Atahualpa knew. He had known ever since the ransom had been paid.

He looked beyond the thatched roofs of the town to the crest of the mountains, where the sun was about to break in his tireless circuit of Tahuantinsuyu. The cold morning air raised dew on the metal of the chains that bound him hand and foot. The metal was queer, different from the bronze the *purics* worked or the gold and silver Atahualpa was used to wearing. If gold was the sweat of the sun, and silver the tears of the moon, what was this metal, dull and hard like the men who held him captive, yet strong, too — stronger, he had come to realize, than the Inca. It, like the men who brought it, was beyond his experience. It gave evidence that Tahuantinsuyu, the Four Quarters of the World, was not all the world after all. Atahualpa had thought none but savages lived beyond their lands. He'd imagined no man readier to face ruthless necessity than himself. He had ordered the death of Huascar, his own brother. But he was learning that these men were capable of enormities against which the Inca civil war would seem a minor discomfort.

That evening they took him out of the building to the plaza. In the plaza's center, the soldiers had piled a great heap of wood on flagstones, some of which were still stained with the blood of the six thousand slaughtered attendants. They bound him to a stake amid the heaped fagots, and Valverde appealed one last time for the Inca to renounce Satan and be baptized. He promised that if Atahualpa would do so, he would earn God's mercy: they would strangle him rather than burn him to death.

The rough wood pressed against his spine. Atahualpa looked at the priest, and the men gathered around, and the women weeping beyond the circle of soldiers. The moon, his mother, rode high above. Firelight flickered on the breastplates of the Spaniards, and from the waiting torches drifted the smell of pitch. The men shifted nervously. Creak of leather, clink of metal. Men on horses shod with silver. Sweat shining on Valverde's forehead. Valverde stared at Atahualpa as if he desired something, but was prepared to destroy him without getting it if need be. The priest thought he was showing Atahualpa resolve, but Atahualpa saw that beneath Valverde's face he was a dead man. Pizarro stood aside, with the Spanish viceroy Estete and the scribe. Pizarro was an old man. He ought to be sitting quietly in some village, outside the violence of life, giving advice and teaching the children. What kind of world did he come from, that sent men into old age still charged with the lusts and bitterness of the young?

Pizarro, too, looked as if he wanted this to end.

Atahualpa knew that it would not end. This was only the beginning. These men would suffer for this moment as they had already suffered for it all their lives, seeking the pain blindly over oceans, jungles, deserts, probing it like a sore tooth until they'd found and grasped it in this plaza of Cajamarca, thinking they sought gold. They'd come all this way to create a moment that would reveal to them their own incurable disease. Now they had it. In a few minutes, they thought, it would at last be over, that once he was gone, they would be free — but Atahualpa knew it would be with them ever after, and with their children and grandchildren and the million others of their race in times to come, whether they knew of this hour in the plaza or not, because they were sick and would pass the sickness on with their breath and semen. They could not burn out the sickness so easily as they could burn the Son of God to ash. This was a great tragedy, but it contained a huge jest. They were caught in a wheel of the sky and could not get out. They must destroy themselves.

"Have your way, priest," Atahualpa said. "Then strangle me, and bear my body to Cuzco, to be laid with my ancestors." He knew they would not do it, and so would add an additional curse to their faithlessness.

He had one final curse. He turned to Pizarro. "You will have responsibility for my children."

Pizarro looked at the pavement. They put up the torch and took Atahualpa from the pyre. Valverde poured water on his head and spoke words in the tongue of his god. Then they sat him upon a stool, bound him to another stake, set the loop of cord around his neck, slid the rod through the cord, and turned it. His women knelt at his side and wept. Valverde spoke more words. Atahualpa felt the cord, woven by the hands of some faithful *puric* of Cajamarca, tighten. The cord was well made. It cut his access to the night air; Atahualpa's lungs fought, he felt his body spasm, and then the plaza became cloudy and he heard the voice of the moon.

— • —

12 January 2011: Israel Lamont was holding big-time when a Krel monitor zipped over the alley. A minute later one of the aliens lurched around the corner and approached him. Lamont was ready.

"I need to achieve an altered state of consciousness," the alien said. It wore a red suit, a lightning bolt on its chest.

"I'm your man," Lamont said. "You just try this. Best stuff on the street." He held the vial out in the palm of his hand. "Go ahead, try it." The Krel took it.

"How much?"

"One million."

The Krel gave him a couple hundred thousand. "Down payment," it said. "How does one administer this?"

"What, you don't know? I thought you guys were hip."

"I have been working hard, and am unacquainted."

This was ripe. "You burn it," Lamont said.

The Krel started toward the trash-barrel fire. Before he could empty the vial into it, Lamont stopped him. "Wait up, homes! You use a pipe. Here, I'll show you."

Lamont pulled a pipe from his pocket, torched up, and inhaled. The Krel watched him. Brown eyes like a dog's. Goofy honkie face. The rush took him, and Lamont saw in the alien's face a peculiar need. The thing was hungry. Desperate.

"I may try?" The alien reached out. Its hand trembled.

Lamont handed over the pipe. Clumsily, the creature shook a block of crack into the bowl. Its beaklike upper lip, however, prevented it from getting its mouth tight against the stem. It fumbled with the pipe, from somewhere producing a book of matches. "Shit, I'll light it," Lamont said.

The Krel waited while Lamont held his Bic over the bowl. Nothing happened. "Inhale, man."

The creature inhaled. The blue flame played over the crack; smoke boiled through the bowl. The creature drew in steadily for what seemed to be minutes. Serious capacity. The crack burned totally through. Finally the Krel exhaled.

It looked at Lamont. Its eyes were bright.

"Good shit?" Lamont said.

"A remarkable stimulant effect."

"Right." Lamont looked over his shoulder toward the alley's entrance. It was getting dark. Yet he hesitated to ask for the rest of the money.

"Will you talk with me?" the Krel asked, swaying slightly.

Surprised, Lamont said, "Okay. Come with me."

Lamont led the Krel back to a deserted store that abutted the alley. They went inside and sat down on some crates against the wall.

"Something I been wondering about you," Lamont said. "You guys are coming to own the world. You fly across the planets, Mars and that shit. What you want with crack?"

"We seek to broaden our minds."

Lamont snorted. "Right. You might as well hit yourself in the head with a hammer."

"We seek escape," the alien said.

"I don't buy that, neither. What you got to escape from?"

The Krel looked at him. "Nothing."

They smoked another pipe. The Krel leaned back against the wall, arms at its side like a limp doll. It started a queer coughing sound, chest spasming. Lamont thought it was choking and tried to slap it on the back. "Don't do that," it said. "I'm laughing."

"Laughing? What's so funny?"

"I lied to Colonel Zipp," it said. "We want cocaine for kicks."

Lamont relaxed a little. "I hear you now."

"We do everything for kicks."

"Makes for hard living."

"Better than maintaining consciousness continuously without interruption."

"You said it."

"Human beings cannot stand too much reality," the Krel said. "We don't blame you. Human beings! Disgust, horror, shame. Nothing personal."

"No problem."

"Nonbeing penetrates that in which there is no space."

"Uh-huh."

The alien laughed again. "I lied to Sepulveda, too. Our time machines take people to the past they believe in. There is no other past. You can't change it."

"Who the fuck's Sepulveda?"

"Let's do some more," it said.

They smoked one more. "Good shit," it said. "Just what I wanted."

The Krel slid off the crate. Its head lolled. "Here is the rest of your payment," it whispered, and died.

Lamont's heart raced. He looked at the Krel's hand, lying open on the floor. In it was a full-sized ear of corn, fashioned of gold, with tassels of finely spun silver wire.

— • —

Today: It's not just physical laws that science-fiction readers want to escape. Just as commonly, they want to escape human nature. In pursuit of this, SF offers comforting alternatives to the real world. For instance, if you start reading an SF story about some abused wimp, you can be pretty sure that by chapter two he's going to discover he has secret powers unavailable to those tormenting him, and by the end of the book, he's going to save the universe. SF is full of this sort of thing, from the power fantasy of the alienated child to the alternative history where Hitler is strangled in his cradle and the Library of Alexandria is saved from the torch.

Science fiction may in this way be considered as much an evasion of reality as any mind-distorting drug. I know that sounds a little harsh, but think about it. An alkaloid like cocaine or morphine invades the central nervous system. It reduces pain, produces euphoria, enhances our perceptions. Under its influence we imagine we have supernormal abilities. Limits dissolve. Soon, hardly aware of what's happened to us, we're addicted.

Science fiction has many of the same qualities. The typical reader comes to SF at a time of suffering. He seizes on it as a way to deal with his pain. It's bigger than his life. It's astounding. Amazing. Fantastic. Some grow out of it; many don't. Anyone who's been around SF for a while can cite examples of longtime readers as hooked and deluded as crack addicts.

Like any drug addict, the SF reader finds desperate justifications for his habit. SF teaches him science. SF helps him avoid "future shock." SF changes the world for the better. Right. So does cocaine.

Having been an SF user myself, however, I have to say that, living in a world of cruelty, immersed in a culture that grinds people into fish meal like some brutal machine, with histories of destruction stretching behind us back to the Pleistocene, I find it hard to sneer at the desire to escape. Even if escape is delusion.

— • —

18 October 1527: Timu drove the foot plow into the ground, leaned back to break the crust, drew out the pointed pole, and backed up a step to let his wife, Collyur, turn the earth with her hoe. To his left was his brother, Okya; and to his right, his cousin, Tupa; before them, their wives planting the seed. Most of the *purics* of Cajamarca were there, strung out in a line across the terrace, the men wielding the foot plows, and the women or children carrying the sacks of seed potatoes.

As he looked up past Collyur's shoulders to the edge of the terrace, he saw a strange man approach from the post road. The man stumbled into the next terrace up from them, climbed down steps to their level. He was plainly excited.

Collyur was waiting for Timu to break the next row; she looked up at him questioningly.

"Who is that?" Timu said, pointing past her to the man.

She stood up straight and looked over her shoulder. The other men had noticed, too, and stopped their work.

"A *chasqui* come from the next town," said Okya.

"A *chasqui* would go to the *curaca*," said Tupa.

"He's not dressed like a *chasqui*," Timu said.

The man came up to them. Instead of a cape, loincloth, and flowing *onka*, the man wore uncouth clothing: cylinders of fabric that bound his legs tightly, a white short-sleeved shirt that bore on its front the face of a man, and flexible white sandals that covered all his foot to the ankle. He shivered in the spring cold.

He was extraordinarily tall. His face, paler than a normal man's, was long, his nose too straight, mouth too small, and lips too thin. Upon his face he wore a device of gold wire that, hooking over his ears, held disks of crystal before his eyes. The man's hands were large, his limbs long and spiderlike. He moved suddenly, awkwardly.

Gasping for air, the stranger spoke rapidly the most abominable Quechua Timu had ever heard.

"Slow down," Timu said. "I don't understand."

"What year is this?" the man asked.

"What do you mean?"

"I mean, what is the year?"

"It is the thirty-fourth year of the reign of the Sapa Inca Huayna Capac."

The man spoke some foreign word. "Goddamn," he said in a language foreign to Timu, but which you or I would recognize as English. "I made it."

Timu went to the *curaca*, and the *curaca* told Timu to take the stranger in. The stranger told them that his name was "Chuan." But Timu's three-year-old daughter, Curi, reacting to the man's sudden gestures, unearthly thinness, and piping speech, laughed and called him "the Bird." So he was ever after to be known in that town.

There he lived a long and happy life, earned trust and respect, and brought great good fortune. He repaid them well for their kindness, alerting the people of the Tahuantinsuyu to the coming of the invaders. When the first Spaniards landed on their shores a few years later, they were slaughtered to the last man, and everyone lived happily ever after. ■

ZEKE

BY TIM SULLIVAN

Tim Sullivan (born 1948) grew up in Bangor, Maine, but has lived in many cities around the country, including several years in South Florida, Philadelphia (where he roomed with Gregory Frost), the Washington, D.C., area, and Los Angeles. He has published seven novels, including the acclaimed *Destiny's End* (1988), *The Parasite War* (1989), *The Martian Viking* (1991), and *Lords of Creation* (1992); has edited two anthologies; and has published more than thirty short stories and novelettes, including "The Nocturnal Adventures of Dr. O and Mr. D" (*Fantasy and Science Fiction*, 2008), "Planetesimal Dawn" (*F&SF*, 2008), and "Way Down East" (*Asimov's*, 2008). His film credentials include *Twilight of the Dogs* (1995), which he wrote and starred in; this post-apocalyptic movie suggests that the U.S. government, upon hearing of a new viral version of AIDS, would send out a fighter pilot to bomb areas of "concentrated homosexuality," thereby wiping out nearly all of humanity. His disgust and impatience with this and other forms of intolerance shows up in many of his works.

"Zeke," which was nominated for the Nebula Award, is revelatory for its implication that, in the Deep South, albinos will be regarded with suspicion, yet an alien from outer space is given genuinely affectionate hospitality by the "regional hicks." While reading this, note the ways in which both narrator and alien regard their different approaches toward true societal alienation, and consider its implicit critique of the movie *E.T.: The Extra-Terrestrial* (1982), which glibly romanticizes the plight of the stranger in a strange land.

ZEKE

ALONG ROUTE 31, FROM THE GEORGIA BORDER TO KEY WEST, much of the old Florida remains. There one can still spend the night in a roach-infested "motor court," visit a roadside spiritualist, or marvel at the lethargic denizens of an alligator farm. This is the Florida of Indian-head coconuts, cracked swimming pools, and concrete fountains claimed by their exhibitors to be the very ones for which Ponce de León searched.

It was the third time I had traversed old Highway 31, though I'd never done it alone before. After spending a childhood of miserable solitude, I had discovered in my teens that I could exploit my freakishness, that I could even use it to get girls. Down that sultry road I went, in a busload of freewheelin' hippie "freaks" back in the smoky days of fall 1968. The "family" was smaller on my second trip down Route 31 in 1974; a blue Toyota carried me and Joannie, a girl who saw in me all the weird and wonderful things she'd never dared to do herself. The results of that romantic interlude were pregnancy, marriage, and a boy we named Danny. A real family.

So, for masochism's sake, I was heading a third time — all by myself, just like when I was a kid — down that seldom-traveled road before long-distance driving became too exorbitant. Besides, I had an expense account; I'd been attending an exporters' convention in Atlanta, and had left a day early, on a Thursday morning. That way I could make a leisurely, bittersweet trek down memory lane. I wasn't planning to get back to work until Monday morning, so I had called to clear it with my boss. Okay, he had said, take your time, George. Not a bad guy, Mr. Noloff, but twenty-five years of selling heavy road equipment to banana republics had instilled in him a certain dictatorial air. I often dreamed, when he was being particularly imperious, of telling him off and chucking my job at Coastal Trading, Inc ... but there were always the rent, the payments on my year-old Plymouth Horizon, the alimony, and of course the child support, at a time when the price of a loaf of bread approached a buck.

Through a loose tweeter, the grinding white blues guitar of Johnny Winter vibrated. I turned it up anyway, cruising over the rolling hills of central Florida, orange groves sliding by on either side of the potholed two-lane blacktop. A curved damask strip of late afternoon sunlight melted into the treetops as I passed a tattered sign announcing MONSTERS, BEASTS, FREAKS OF NATURE JUST AHEAD, SR 74, in pastel colors that had once been lurid.

"This," I said over Johnny's melodic growls, "has got to be the world's sleaziest roadside attraction."

My tank was almost empty, and there weren't any open gas stations in sight, but I wasn't worried. There hadn't been a lit neon NO in front of VACANCY on any of these fleabags' signs in years; they were all dying for business. I would spend the night in this next town — whatever town it was — and search for fuel in the morning.

The Horizon turned easily into the parking lot of the Azalea Motel, a low pink building with rust stains bleeding through the walls from the reinforcing steel rods beneath the concrete.

Such establishments rarely have lobbies, and the Azalea was no exception. Inside the cramped manager's office, a fat woman sat in the arctic gale of a Fedders air conditioner, watching "Hee-Haw." She couldn't hear me over the AC's ceaseless exhalations and the laugh track, but soon subdued strains of sweet country music replaced the canned yuks, making conversation barely possible. I negotiated a room key, but she didn't let it go at that.

"You look like the type might wanna see the freak show," she said.

It had been some time since an adult had made such a reference to my albinism. I always explain to children about the lack of pigmentation that makes my skin so white, but this woman was no child. I glared at her ... and she glared right back until I lowered my eyes to the guest book.

"I'm Mrs. Nickerson," she said as I signed my name. "Bump — that's my husband — ain't here right now." She eyed my suitcase as if it were a dangerous animal.

"Oh." I assumed she was trying to tell me she wasn't taking my bag to my room for me. "Just point me in the right direction."

"Ain't but one direction." She gestured to her left.

"Uh ... thank you, Mrs. Nickerson." I hefted my bag, key dangling from my free hand, and went back out into the still considerable heat like a good boy. Sunset had now created a peach-colored world, except for blood-red ixora, yellow hibiscus, and purple bougainvillea, whose roots snaked into the broken walk alongside the motel. I didn't see any azaleas.

The room wasn't as bad as I'd expected: plasterboard walls; a reasonably unlumpy mattress sheathed in fresh linen; a lampshade emblazoned with a horse's head, the animal's sensitive eyes gazing longingly toward the alcove harboring the sink (why don't motels ever have sinks in the bathroom?); clean white towels; a color TV with a sick tube, making the actors look a little bilious; a slightly musty smell; and a shower, which I promptly tried out.

After cleaning up, I decided to go for a walk. There were three vehicles besides mine in the parking lot. One was a green Ford pickup loaded with sacks of peat moss. A big man, fat, fiftyish, and sunburned, was finishing the loading. He wore a white undershirt, the kind with shoulder straps, and his few remaining hairs were plastered to his creased skull with hair cream. Once he noticed me and nodded, I asked him if he was by any chance Bump Nickerson.

"None other," he replied, wiping sweat from his brow. He shook my hand, and then leaned against the tailgate while I asked him what went on in these parts.

"Florabella Tavern's closed for renovations. There's a movie in Apopka, but that's twenty-five mile. Ain't much in Boca Blanca nowadays."

"I guess there wouldn't be." So that was the name of this burg: Boca Blanca, or White Mouth, if my rudimentary Spanish didn't fail me. Funny, I thought, Boca, or "mouth," always refers to a bay or inlet, but this Boca is nowhere near the Atlantic or Gulf coasts ...

"No, sir," Bump agreed. "No, sir."

"Apopka's got the closest entertainment, huh?" No place to lose myself here, like there was in Miami when my loneliness became intolerable. "What about the freak show?"

"'Ats the on'y thing till the Florabella opens up agin." Bump shrugged. "Course, it's a little off the beaten path."

"Oh, yeah?" I'd always had a penchant for the bizarre, and this seemed a sufficiently mysterious diversion to cure my melancholy. "How do I get there?"

"South two mile, then a left, jis past the canal bridge. She's down the job road there another mile or so."

I thanked Bump and got into the Horizon. Smacked the gas gauge a couple of times and decided six miles wouldn't drain it dry. So, off to see the Fat Lady, the Dog-Faced Boy, or whatever exotic creatures might infest Boca Blanca's version of the Big Top. Odd that it was located off the main road, I thought. As the stars brightened over the darkening orange groves, I expected to hear the *pizzicato* guitar that used to preface "The Twilight Zone."

"George Hallahan," Rod Serling's gravelly voice intoned inside my skull, "thirty-two years old. A rather peculiar-looking idealist who once foolishly thought he could help fashion a better world out of a cloud of cannabis smoke. George found that he couldn't even hold his own life together, much less an ailing society. Now, driving on a back road in Florida, the disillusioned albino ex-hippie exporter is headed straight toward ... " Straight toward a tacky freak show. Appropriate.

The stigma of albinism hadn't been quite so bad in the New England town where I spent the first eight years of my life. A bout of rheumatic fever had made me unable to tolerate the cold weather, however, and my father, a civil servant, took a job in Miami at my mom's instigation. So, for my sake, the family went south, and I grew up a ghostly exile among the bronzed gods and goddesses.

Then came the Summer of Love. I grew my white hair long, and wasted people thought I was far out. There wasn't a cynical bone in my body the first time I dropped acid, at a rock festival near Orlando — even after I recovered from the severe case of sun poisoning I got from dancing naked under the blazing sun — but reality soon reared its ugly head during my radical college days. The tear gas and truncheons the cops wielded at the political conventions at Miami Beach in '72 taught me a valuable lesson about the way things *are*, as opposed to the way I thought they ought to be.

Then there had been the courtship of Joannie, culminating at the Saturn Motor Lodge on good ol' Route 31. Love? I don't know; looking back, I think I just had to have her because she was such a nice girl. Cute, brunette, upper-middle-class background; what more could I have asked for? Not that she was guiltless in this bizarre misalliance of woman and freak. How neat it must have seemed to her murky sense of developing social consciousness to miscegenate with a misfit. Danny's birth had shortly thereafter squelched that particular living fantasy, forcing my capitulation to the ogre of capitalism in the bargain.

Every single one of these misadventures had been a failure in some painfully essential way, each taking a bigger chunk of my soul than the last.

By the time I got to the canal bridge, I couldn't stop thinking of Danny. I hadn't wanted a child, judging the two of us far too immature for such a responsibility, but Joannie had refused to consider abortion. I never told her how scared I was that the child would be a freak like me. But when I saw that normal, beautiful baby, I was happy for the one and only time in my life. At first Danny was kind of a novelty, but when he got a little older and we started to get to know each other, I think we were more than father and son. We were friends.

Still, the bickering between Joannie and me got worse — and, oh, she always had a sharp tongue. When we finally decided to split, there was never any doubt about who was better suited to bring up Danny. I was an aging albino hippie earning a shaky income from the exporting trade. She, on the other hand, was solidly establishment; she'd never touched a drug, never even smoked a cigarette. I knew it was only right, and yet I resented her for the way things had turned out.

A year had passed since she took my son away from me. He was only five when his home fell apart. On Sunday he'd be celebrating his sixth birthday, and his father was too scared of a verbal whipping — "Why don't you get a job where you can make enough money to provide the things Danny needs?" — to be where he could help Danny blow out the candles. I'd have to mail him a present in the morning. Would it get to Miami in time?

The jog road was dusty and bumpy as the night descended. On the other side of the canal there were no orange groves, just palmetto clumps and Florida pines. Down the road was a house made of cinder blocks, one story high, with no windows in the front, like a porn parlor. The house was flanked by two sago palms in the terminal stages of "lethal yellowing disease," their drooping fronds like black spiders' legs in the deepening gloom.

I parked in front of the house, and the Horizon bogged down in the sugary sand. I wondered if its wheels would be able to spin free, and, if not, whether Boca Blanca had a wrecker. As I walked toward the house, I reflected that mine had not always been such a defeatist attitude.

"Whatever happened to the Woodstock Generation?" I muttered, recalling a more innocent time when I could toke up and consider obliterating war, racism, and injustice. Particularly the injustice that I suffered because I happened to be born a "whiter shade of pale," to borrow a phrase from the old Procol Harum song.

A light around the side of the little house threw a patch of amber on the sand. There was a screen door, and what looked like the kitchen on the other side of it. I took a whiff of jasmine-scented air and rapped.

From within came a stirring, a rustling of paper, the creaking of a chair sliding across the floor, footsteps; there was no television or radio to dilute these intimate sounds, only the chirruping of crickets. A shadow appeared on the screen, followed by a thin, stooped old man, wearing baggy pants and smiling.

"I've, uh, come to see the freak show," I said.

He nodded and unhooked the screen door. "Through here," he said, leading me through a room filled with books and magazines, literary and scientific journals in a state of disarray on tables, sofa, and floor. Curiouser and curiouser.

The back door opened into a dark shed, and the old man pulled a dangling string, illuminating a naked hundred-watt bulb that cast swinging shadows on four small cages and something draped with a greasy cloth. The cages were made of pine and chicken wire. In them were four unfortunate animals — not the usual circus freaks, but strange enough in their various ways.

How do you define a freak, anyway? The word is used to hurt more often than to inform or amuse. At least these creatures would never know what people called them.

The most striking of the animals was a two-headed calf. One of the heads was a shrunken, lolling appendage with dead eyes and flaccid lips, but the rest of the calf seemed healthy enough.

In spite of the terrible stench, I moved closer to the cages. Next to the calf, so help me, was a snake with legs. Spindly little useless things, but four limbs nevertheless. It was asleep on a pile of hay inside its two-foot-square prison.

Then there was a "giant lizard," as the old man called it — nothing but an iguana.

The fourth cage held a featherless chicken, its hideously pocked flesh a repulsive sight. In its nakedness, the fowl resembled a scrawny old man. It stared at me so murderously that it must have thought I'd plucked it myself.

"Donations appreciated," my affable host said as he shuffled toward the door.

"Uh, fine. But I don't think I've seen everything yet, have I?" I turned toward the thing under the greasy cloth, in a cage that appeared to be circular at the top, unlike the others.

Hitching up his trousers, the old man looked from me to the covered object and back again. "Well ... "

I waited. The old man clearly didn't want to show me what was under that cloth, which naturally made me want to see it all the more.

"He's asleep, I think."

"He?"

The old man didn't seem to hear me. He lifted a corner of the cloth and peeked under it. "No, it's all right ... if you're sure you want to see him."

"Yes."

Without ceremony, he undraped a large glass terrarium, standing back with the greasy cloth in his gnarled farmer's hands.

I don't know how long I stood there with my mouth open, staring at that incredible sight. I remember the old man speaking to me as if in a dream: "That's the way most folks act when they see him."

The thing was an albino monkey ... no ... the white fur was flesh ... bald, like the chicken ... arms and legs bent at ridiculous angles ... as stooped as the old man ...

No, not stooped. The impossible thing stood erect on a bed of dark chips. Its joints suggested a Rube Goldberg cartoon in their complexity. With delicate, hinged hands much too large for its eighteen-inch body, it grasped the lip of the terrarium, gazing at me from between its pipestem arms with crimson eyes.

It was a mockery, an image from a funhouse mirror in a nightmare. As if to imitate my gape, the creature opened its mouth, revealing a ribbed whiteness inside, a furrowed snowfield here in the stifling Florida summer. No discernible sound came from that virginal cavity.

The chicken clucked, the sound bringing me a little closer to reality. Without taking my eyes off the creature, I whispered, "What is it?"

"He," the old man corrected me. "He's a person. Might look and act a little different, but he's folks. Just like me ... just like you."

"What?" I glanced at him to see if he were goading me as Mrs. Nickerson had at the motel. But there was no malice in his weather-beaten face. He nodded at the strange creature.

"Ain't he sum'p'n?"

"Where did you get him?"

"Well, he's been livin' with me since I was, let's see ... twenty-six. Before that he stayed with ol' Bo Wadley till Bo passed away, and Bo told me his daddy kept him 'fore Bo was born. Claimed he was livin' around here 'fore white men ever came to Florida."

"Boca Blanca," I said. A revelation. The Spanish must have named their settlement for this creature perhaps four centuries ago. "But how could he have been around so long?"

The old man sucked on his false teeth. "Jis longer-lived than us, I guess."

"What does he eat?"

"Dead plants, rotten wood, peat moss. Takes a little water with it."

I could make out the baroque pattern of the ribs, a surrealist sculpture beneath striated bands of muscle and smooth, milky flesh. The physique was vaguely humanoid, and the gleaming red eyes were unfathomable. These features were grotesque enough, but that mouth twisted the ridged skull into a painful prognathous expression that opened like a funnel — a scream of silence that touched an empathic chord inside me.

"Why do you keep him in this shed with these deformed animals?" I demanded.

"Why, it was his idea," the old man said reproachfully. "We got to have money to git along on, so he came up with the idea of a freak show some years back. After a while, he got in the habit of sleepin' out here, sorta keepin' an eye on things."

"His idea? Did I hear you right?"

"Yup. He's smart as a whip. Showed me where to find these critters — cept for the lizard. Him we bought from a pet shop in Orlando."

"This is beyond belief." I shook my head. "He's ... "

"Sum'p'n, ain't he?" It was Bump, carrying a sack of peat moss through the shed door.

"You're in on this, too?" I asked.

"In on what?" Bump said. "I run a garden s'ply ever since the interstate highway and Disneyworld pulled the rug out from under the motel bidness. Oncet a week I bring Zeke out some peat moss."

"Zeke!" I laughed, remembering the old gospel song about Ezekiel's "dry bones," an image that perfectly suggested the creature in the terrarium.

"Got to call him sum'p'n," Bump said, and he laughed too. "Never did tell us what his right name is."

"Prob'ly where he come from," the old man said, "they don't have names same as we do."

"Where he comes from ... " The thought inspired awe, wonder.

"A long ways away," Bump said softly. "A long ways."

"Another world," I said, even more quietly.

The old man was grave, and none of us spoke while we considered the implications of what we had just said.

After a while, Bump tore open the sack, scooping out some peat moss with a meaty hand and dropping it into the snifter-shaped terrarium. Zeke's twig-like fingers, catching the offering, were nearly as long as Bump's. Instead of eating in front of us, Zeke set the peat moss chips among those already spread on the floor of his terrarium.

"Not ever'body knows what they seein' when they come in here," the old man said, frowning. "Bump's wife, now, she don't care for things that are ... different."

"So I noticed," I said.

"She thinks to this day he's jis some kinda hairless monkey."

"Hell, Levon," Bump said, "she never stuck around long enough to see him read and write, and she never would believe me. Rayette can't hardly read, herself, and she don't want to nohow. It's all she can do to set in front of that damn TV all day long." Having vented his spleen, Bump stuck his hand inside the terrarium. Grasping two fingers, Zeke allowed himself to be lifted out of the terrarium and set on the straw-covered shed floor. He was wearing a tiny pair of beige shorts.

It seemed wrong for Zeke to be here. My fitful sense of social morality awakened briefly as I considered our Duty to Mankind. "Kennedy Space Center's not far," I said. "Why don't you let somebody over there look at Zeke?"

"Let him 'splain about things himself," Levon said.

The diminutive alien led us inside the house in a jerkily articulated walk, the calf lowing as Levon closed the shed door. The adjoining room was littered with reading material. Next to a battered old sofa, a slate leaned against one of the cinder-block walls. Zeke picked up a piece of chalk and wrote, "I have no desire to go anywhere."

"Maybe they could get you back home someday," I said.

"By the time your spacecraft are able to go that far," he wrote in carefully blocked-in letters, "I will no longer be living."

"But the things you must know!" I protested. "Don't you want to share them with us? Help us?"

Zeke bowed, showing two pinpricks on top of his snowy skull that I took to be his ears. The chalk squeaked in the still room as he wrote, "My technological expertise is limited, but even if it weren't, there would be difficulties."

"Difficulties?"

"In bypassing so many levels of technical sophistication."

"I see." I had skipped third grade. Adjusting to life in fourth grade was hell, intellectually and emotionally. At least the kids my age were used to "Whitey," as I came to be called. The bigger kids really put me through the meat grinder, and I had trouble with my math, too. So you might say I had found it difficult to bypass only one level of sophistication.

Zeke wiped the slate clean with a chalk-dust-caked eraser, and then wrote, "How well does the average human being understand the principle behind a machine he or she uses every day?"

"Like television?" I was amused to think of Rayette Nickerson contributing to our discussion.

"Yes, television," Zeke wrote, "or even an automobile? Our machines were autonomous. They built themselves, maintained themselves, but were still slaves to do our bidding. I couldn't begin to show you how to make even the simplest of them."

So much for saviors from the stars. Still, there was wonder enough here, even without miracles. "But how did you end up on Earth?" I asked. "Where did you come from?"

Instead of answering, Zeke beckoned for me to follow him through the kitchen. With both hands, he pushed open the groaning screen door and went outside. The stars gleamed like ice and the night breeze was cool, quickly drying the sweat on my forehead. It took me a moment to identity a pungent odor wafting over the jasmine as Zeke. I hadn't noticed his exotic smell inside the house because of the animals, whose odor persisted even into the living room. His aroma surprised me because I had already come to regard him as human, perhaps more like me than anyone I'd ever known. It was not unpleasant, it was just ... different.

With a little flourish, Zeke indicated the heavens. Overhead were Venus and Mars, and in the west was brilliant Jupiter. The Pleiades were peripherally visible, hard to see when I looked directly at them. Just to the north were Perseus and Cassiopeia, frozen in an eternal marital spat, like Joannie and me. Happiness seemed as unattainable as Zeke's planet.

"He never tells how he come here," Levon said, "or why. And you can ask him till you're blue in the face. When he don't want to talk about sum'p'n, he jis don't talk."

We stood in the moonlight by two sickly palms. Zeke's unaccountably graceful figure was as immobile as his crimson eyes were dispassionate. Had my initial impression of anguish been nothing more than a distorted projection of my own pain?

Then Zeke's mouth jutted forward, widening once again into that terrible, silent scream. As though in sympathetic reaction, the night sounds of insects and hoot owls quieted. Zeke lifted a hand, opening his fingers as if to grasp the stars and pull them to Earth. His entire body trembled while he stretched onto the tips of his splayed feet. And then he slumped so close to the sand I thought he would fall. He managed to stay off his feet, though, staring down at the crabgrass.

My face felt flushed, and a drop of perspiration rolled down my forehead in spite of the cool breeze. I was embarrassed — this vision of pain was like a distorted reflection of my own soul — and had to look away.

So I said good-bye to Bump and Levon, their homely faces showing the depth of their emotion of their friend's anguish. Taking a five-dollar bill from my wallet, I slipped it to Levon as a donation.

"He gits tired," Levon said.

I nodded and, without turning back, walked the few yards to my car.

I felt, rather than heard, Zeke behind me. My hand on the open car door, I turned to him. I squatted so that we were more or less on the same eye level.

In the dim illumination shed by the car's dome light, Zeke raised his fragile hands to touch mine. I stretched out my fingers and their tips met his. His fingers were warm and emotion seemed to emanate from them, entering me. Something went out of me, too. Something sour and ugly I had been carrying around for far too long. Zeke absorbed it like dirty water in a sponge.

I won't say that I was suddenly whole, as the laying on of hand is supposed to make you; I was just relieved. Not a revelation or a cleansing, but an exchange, a sharing. Zeke shared my pain ... and I shared his.

It took only an instant, and then our fingertips parted. I stood, still transfixed by Zeke's ruby eyes. They no longer seemed dispassionate; I had, in a sense, seen with them. There was no sudden Fujicolor image of an alien world, only the feeling of a loss so great that acceptance had been the only alternative to death. My problems seemed so insignificant next to Zeke's that I felt ashamed of myself for wallowing in self-pity.

"So long, Zeke," I said, "and thanks." As I got in the car and shut the door, the dome light winked out, leaving a vague, pale shape outside in place of Zeke. I started up the motor and backed out of the sand with no problem. As I headed back toward Route 31, there were three shrinking silhouettes in the rearview mirror, two men and the small figure of a being from another world. Was he an exile, a fugitive, a lost traveler? He would die on this planet, but even so, he had made the best of things.

Next morning, as I walked down to the office to pay my bill, I noticed that Bump's pickup wasn't in the parking lot. Maybe he had spent the night at Levon's or maybe he was just out early, delivering garden supplies to some of his more conventional customers.

Mrs. Nickerson's manners hadn't improved. She was watching "Bowling for Dollars," but turned grudgingly away to take my money. While I signed my check, she asked, "So you seen the freak?"

I looked straight at her, masking my hostility. "Yes, I did. Don't you think we look a lot alike?"

The smirk vanished from her puffy face, and she turned stiffly back to her television program. I smiled. The question had freaked her out, but it wasn't really a joke. Especially for Zeke. Coming from so far away, living so long with no chance of getting home, he had to be Earth's greatest expert on alienation.

It was already sweltering and muggy at half past eight, but I walked out of that air-conditioned office whistling. After all, I still had plenty of time to make it back for Danny's birthday party. ■

THINK LIKE A DINOSAUR

BY JAMES PATRICK KELLY

James Patrick Kelly (born 1951 in Mineola, New York) has had an eclectic writing career. He has written novels, short stories, essays, reviews, poetry, plays and planetarium shows. His most recent publication is a collection, *The Wreck of the Goodspeed*. His short novel *Burn* won the Nebula Award in 2007. He has won the Hugo Award twice: in 1996, for this novelette, "Think Like A Dinosaur," and in 2000, for his novelette "Ten to the Sixteenth to One." His fiction has been translated into eighteen languages. With John Kessel he is co-editor of *Feeling Very Strange: The Slipstream Anthology* and *Rewired: The Post Cyberpunk Anthology*. He writes a column on the internet for *Asimov's Science Fiction* and is on the faculty of the Stonecoast Creative Writing MFA

Program at the University of Southern Maine and the Board of Directors of the Clarion Foundation. He produces two podcasts: James Patrick Kelly's StoryPod for Audible.com, which features him reading fifty-two of his own stories, and the Free Reads Podcast where he most recently finished podcasting his novel *Look Into The Sun*. His website is at jimkelly.net.

"Think Like A Dinosaur" has also been adapted as an audioplay for Scifi.com's *Seeing Ear Theater* and as an episode of television's *The Outer Limits*. The question of identity that is at the center of this story is one that appears as a theme throughout his work, from *Look Into The Sun* and *Burn* to stories like "The Wreck of the Godspeed" and "The Edge of Nowhere." "Think Like A Dinosaur" holds its own power, yet, as discussed in the Introduction, is best understood as a response to Tom Godwin's 1954 "The Cold Equations." Those equations are, under Kelly's forensic (and far more poetically written) analysis, severely flawed.

THINK LIKE A DINOSAUR

KAMALA SHASTRI CAME BACK TO THIS WORLD AS SHE HAD LEFT it — naked. She tottered out of the assembler, trying to balance in Tuulen Station's delicate gravity. I caught her and bundled her into a robe with one motion, then eased her onto the float. Three years on another planet had transformed Kamala. She was leaner, more muscular. Her fingernails were now a couple of centimeters long and there were four parallel scars incised on her left cheek, perhaps some Gendian's idea of beautification. But what struck me most was the darting strangeness in her eyes. This place, so familiar to me, seemed almost to shock her. It was as though she doubted the walls and was skeptical of air. She had learned to think like an alien.

"Welcome back." The float's whisper rose to a *whoosh* as I walked it down the hallway. She swallowed hard and I thought she might cry. Three years ago, she would have. Lots of migrators are devastated when they come out of the assembler; it's because there is no transition. A few seconds ago Kamala was on Gend, fourth planet of the star we call Epsilon Leo, and now she was here in lunar orbit. She was almost home; her life's greatest adventure was over.

"Matthew?" she said.

"Michael." I couldn't help but be pleased that she remembered me. After all, she had changed my life.

— • —

I've guided maybe three hundred migrations — comings and goings — since I first came to Tuulen to study the dinos. Kamala Shastri's is the only quantum scan I've ever pirated. I doubt that the dinos care; I suspect this is a trespass they occasionally allow themselves. I know more about her — at least, as she was three years ago — than I know about myself. When the dinos sent her to Gend, she massed 50,391.72 grams and her red cell count was 4.81 million per mm^3. She could play the *nagasvaram*, a kind of bamboo flute. Her father came from Thana, near Bombay, and her favorite flavor of chewyfrute was watermelon and she'd had five lovers and when she was eleven she'd wanted to be a gymnast but instead she had become a biomaterials engineer who at age twenty-nine had volunteered to go to the stars to learn how to grow artificial eyes. It took her two years to go through migrator training; she knew she could have backed out at any time, right up until the moment Silloin translated her into a superluminal signal. She understood what it meant to balance the equation.

I first met her on June 22, 2069. She shuttled over from Lunex's L1 port and came through our airlock at promptly 10:15, a small roundish woman with black hair parted in the middle and drawn tight against her skull. They had darkened her skin against Epsilon Leo's UV; it was the deep blue-black of twilight. She was wearing a striped clingy and Velcro slippers to help her get around for the short time she'd be navigating our .2 micrograv.

"Welcome to Tuulen Station." I smiled and offered my hand. "My name is Michael." We shook. "I'm supposed to be a sapientologist, but I also moonlight as the local guide."

"Guide?" She nodded distractedly. "Okay." She peered past me, as if expecting someone else.

"Oh, don't worry," I said, "the dinos are in their cages."

Her eyes got wide as she let her hand slip from mine. "You call the Hanen dinos?"

"Why not?" I laughed. "They call us babies. The weeps, among other things."

She shook her head in amazement. People who've never met a dino tended to romanticize them: the wise and noble reptiles who had mastered superluminal physics and introduced Earth to the wonders of galactic civilization. I doubt Kamala had ever seen a dino play poker or gobble down a screaming rabbit. And she had never argued with Linna, who still wasn't convinced that humans were psychologically ready to go to the stars.

"Have you eaten?" I gestured down the corridor to the reception rooms.

"Yes ... I mean, no." She didn't move. "I am not hungry."

"Let me guess. You're too nervous to eat. You're too nervous to talk, even. You wish I'd just shut up, pop you into the marble, and beam you out. Let's just get this part the hell over with, eh?"

"I don't mind the conversation, actually."

"There you go. Well, Kamala, it is my solemn duty to advise you that there are no peanut butter and jelly sandwiches on Gend. And no chicken vindaloo. What's my name again?"

"Michael?"

"See, you're not *that* nervous. Not one taco, or a single slice of eggplant pizza. This is your last chance to eat like a human."

"Okay." She did not actually smile — she was too busy being brave — but a corner of her mouth twitched. "Actually, I would not mind a cup of tea."

"Now, tea they've got." She let me guide her toward Reception D; her slippers *snicked* at the velcro carpet. "Of course, they brew it from lawn clippings."

"The Gendians don't keep lawns. They live underground."

"Refresh my memory." I kept my hand on her shoulder; beneath the clingy, her muscles were rigid. "Are they the ferrets or the things with the orange bumps?"

"They look nothing like ferrets."

We popped through the door bubble into Reception D, a compact rectangular space with a scatter of low unthreatening furniture. There was a kitchen station at one end, a closet with a vacuum toilet at the other. The ceiling was blue sky; the long wall showed a live view of the Charles River and the Boston skyline, baking in the late June sun. Kamala had just finished her doctorate at M.I.T.

I opaqued the door. She perched on the edge of a couch like a wren, ready to flit away.

While I was making her tea, my fingernail screen flashed. I answered it, and a tiny Silloin came up in discreet mode. She didn't look at me; she was too busy watching arrays in the control room. =A problem,= her voice buzzed in my earstone, =most negligible, really. But we will have to void the last two from today's schedule. Save them at Lunex until first shift tomorrow. Can this one be kept for an hour?=

"Sure," I said. "Kamala, would you like to meet a Hanen?" I transferred Silloin to a dino-sized window on the wall. "Silloin, this is Kamala Shastri. Silloin is the one who actually runs things. I'm just the doorman."

Silloin looked through the window with her near eye, then swung around and peered at Kamala with her other. She was short for a dino, just over a meter tall, but she had an enormous head that teetered on her neck like a watermelon balancing on a grapefruit. She must have just oiled herself because her silver scales shone. =Kamala, you will accept my happiest intentions for you?= She raised her left hand, spreading the skinny digits to expose dark crescents of vestigial webbing.

"Of course, I ..."

=And you will permit us to render you this translation?=

She straightened. "Yes."

=Have you questions?=

I'm sure she had several hundred, but at this point was probably too scared to ask. While she hesitated, I broke in. "Which came first, the lizard or the egg?"

Silloin ignored me. =It will be excellent for you to begin when?=

"She's just having a little tea," I said, handing her the cup. "I'll bring her along when she's done. Say, an hour?"

Kamala squirmed on the couch. "No, really, it will not take me ... "

Silloin showed us her teeth, several of which were as long as piano keys. =That would be most appropriate, Michael.= She closed; a gull flew through the space where her window had been.

"Why did you do that?" Kamala's voice was sharp.

"Because it says here that you have to wait your turn. You're not the only migrator we're sending this morning." This was a lie, of course; we had had to cut the schedule because Jodi Latchaw, the other sapientologist assigned to Tuulen, was at the University of Hipparchus presenting our paper on the Hanen concept of identity. "Don't worry, I'll make the time fly."

For a moment, we looked at each other. I could have laid down an hour's worth of patter; I'd done that often enough. Or I could have drawn her out on why she was going: no doubt she had a blind grandma or second cousin just waiting for her to bring home those artificial eyes, not to mention potential spin-offs that could well end tuberculosis, famine, and premature ejaculation, *blah, blah, blah*. Or I could have just left her alone in the room to read the wall. The trick was guessing how spooked she really was.

"Tell me a secret," I said.

"What?"

"A secret, you know, something no one else knows."

She stared as if I'd just fallen off Mars.

"Look, in a little while you're going some place that's what ... three hundred and ten light-years away? You're scheduled to stay for three years. By the time you come back, I could easily be rich, famous, and elsewhere; we'll probably never see each other again. So what have you got to lose? I promise not to tell."

She leaned back on the couch, and settled the cup in her lap. "This is another test, right? After everything they have put me through, they still have not decided whether to send me."

"Oh no, in a couple of hours you'll be cracking nuts with ferrets in some dark Gendian burrow. This is just me, talking."

"You are crazy."

"Actually, I believe the technical term is logomaniac. It's from the Greek: *logos* meaning word, *mania* meaning two bits short of a byte. I just love to chat is all. Tell you what, I'll go first. If my secret isn't juicy enough, you don't have to tell me anything."

Her eyes were slits as she sipped her tea. I was fairly sure that whatever she was worrying about at the moment, it wasn't being swallowed by the big blue marble.

"I was brought up Catholic," I said, settling onto a chair in front of her. "I'm not anymore, but that's not the secret. My parents sent me to Mary, Mother of God High School; we called it Moogoo. It was run by a couple of old priests, Father Thomas and his wife, Mother Jennifer. Father Tom taught physics, which I got a D in, mostly because he talked like he had walnuts in his mouth. Mother Jennifer taught theology and had all the warmth of a marble pew; her nickname was Mama Moogoo.

"One night, just two weeks before my graduation, Father Tom and Mama Moogoo went out in their Chevy Minimus for ice cream. On the way home, Mama Moogoo pushed a yellow light and got broadsided by an ambulance. Like I said, she was old, a hundred and twenty something; they should've lifted her license back in the fifties. She was killed instantly. Father Tom died in the hospital.

"Of course, we were all supposed to feel sorry for them and I guess I did a little, but I never really liked either of them and I resented the way their deaths had screwed things up for my class. So I was more annoyed than sorry, but then I also had this edge of guilt for being so uncharitable. Maybe you'd have to grow up Catholic to understand that. Anyway, the day after it happened they called an assembly in the gym and we were all there squirming on the bleachers and the cardinal himself tele-presented a sermon. He kept trying to comfort us, like it had been our *parents* that had died. When I made a joke about it to the kid next to me, I got caught and spent the last week of my senior year with an in-school suspension."

Kamala had finished her tea. She slid the empty cup into one of the holders built into the table.

"Want some more?" I said.

She stirred restlessly. "Why are you telling me this?"

"It's part of the secret." I leaned forward in my chair. "See, my family lived down the street from Holy Spirit Cemetery and in order to get the carryvan line on McKinley Ave., I had to cut through. Now this happened a couple of days after I got in trouble at the assembly. It was around midnight and I was coming home from a graduation party where I had taken a couple of pokes of insight, so I was feeling sly as a philosopher-king. As I walked through the cemetery, I stumbled across two dirt mounds right next to each other. At first I thought they were flower beds, then I saw the wooden crosses. Fresh graves: here lies Father Tom and Mama Moogoo. There wasn't much to the crosses: they were basically just stakes with cross-pieces, painted white and hammered into the ground. The names were hand-printed on them. The way I figured it, they were there to mark the graves until the stones got delivered. I didn't need any insight to recognize a once-in-a-lifetime opportunity. If I switched them, what were the chances anyone was going to notice? It was no problem sliding them out of their holes. I smoothed the dirt with my hands and then ran like hell."

Until that moment, she'd seemed bemused by my story and slightly condescending toward me. Now there was a glint of alarm in her eyes.

"That was a terrible thing to do," she said.

"Absolutely," I said, "although the dinos think that the whole idea of planting bodies in graveyards and marking them with carved rocks is weepy. They say there is no identity in dead meat, so why get so sentimental about it? Linna keeps asking how come we don't put markers over our shit. But that's not the secret. See, it'd been a warmish night in the middle of June, only as I ran, the air turned cold. Freezing, I could see my breath. And my shoes got heavier and heavier, like they had turned to stone. As I got closer to the back gate, it felt like I was fighting a strong wind, except my clothes weren't flapping. I slowed to a walk. I know I could have pushed through, but my heart was thumping and then I heard this whispery seashell noise and I panicked. So the secret is, I'm a coward. I switched the crosses back, and I never went near that cemetery again. As a matter of fact," I nodded at the walls of Reception D on Tuulen Station, "when I grew up, I got about as far away from it as I could."

She stared as I settled back in my chair. "True story," I said, and raised my right hand. She seemed so astonished that I started laughing. A smile bloomed on her dark face, and suddenly she was giggling too. It was a soft liquid sound, like a brook bubbling over smooth stones; it made me laugh even harder. Her lips were full and her teeth were very white.

"Your turn," I said, finally.

"Oh no, I could not." She waved me off. "I don't have anything so good ... " She paused, then frowned. "You have told that before?"

"Once," I said. "To the Hanen, during the psych screening for this job. Only I didn't tell them the last part. I know how dinos think, so I ended it when I switched the crosses. The rest is baby stuff." I waggled a finger at her. "Don't forget, you promised to keep my secret."

"Did I?"

"Tell me about when you were young. Where did you grow up?"

"Toronto." She glanced at me, appraisingly. "There *was* something, but not funny. Sad."

I nodded encouragement and changed the wall to Toronto's skyline dominated by the CN Tower, Toronto-Dominion Centre, Commerce Court, and the King's Needle.

She twisted to take in the view and spoke over her shoulder. "When I was ten we moved to an apartment, right downtown on Bloor Street so my mother could be close to work." She pointed at the wall and turned back to face me. "She is an accountant, my father wrote wallpaper for Imagineering. It was a huge building; it seemed as if we were always getting into the elevator with ten neighbors we never knew we had. I was coming home from school one day when an old woman stopped me in the lobby. 'Little girl,' she said, 'how would you like to earn ten dollars?' My parents had warned me not to talk to strangers, but she obviously was a resident. Besides, she had an ancient pair of exolegs strapped on, so I knew I could outrun her if I needed to. She asked me to go to the store for her, handed me a grocery list and a cash card, and said I should bring everything up to her apartment, 10W. I should have been more suspicious because all the downtown groceries deliver, but as I soon found out, all she really wanted was someone to talk to her. And she was willing to pay for it, usually five or ten dollars, depending on how long I stayed. Before long I was stopping by almost every day after school. I think my parents would have made me stop if they had known; they were very strict. They would not have liked me taking her money. But neither of them got home until after six, so it was my secret to keep."

"Who was she?" I said. "What did you talk about?"

"Her name was Margaret Ase. She was ninety-seven years old, and I think she had been some kind of counselor. Her husband and her daughter had both died and she was alone. I didn't find out much about her; she made me do most of the talking. She asked me about my friends and what I was learning in school and my family. Things like that ..."

Her voice trailed off as my fingernail started to flash. I answered it.

=Michael, I am pleased to call you to here.= Silloin buzzed in my ear.

She was almost twenty minutes ahead of schedule.

"See, I told you we'd make the time fly." I stood; Kamala's eyes got very wide. "I'm ready if you are."

I offered her my hand. She took it and let me help her up. She wavered for a moment, and I sensed just how fragile her resolve was. I put my hand around her waist and steered her into the corridor. In the micrograv of Tuulen Station, she already felt as insubstantial as a memory. "So tell me, what happened that was so sad?"

At first I thought she hadn't heard. She shuffled along, said nothing.

"Hey, don't keep me in suspense here, Kamala," I said. "You have to finish the story."

"No," she said. "I don't think I do."

I didn't take this personally. My only real interest in the conversation had been to distract her. If she refused to be distracted, that was her choice. Some migrators kept talking right up to the moment they slid into the big blue marble, but lots of them went quiet just before. They turned inward. Maybe in her mind she was already on Gend, blinking in the hard white light.

We arrived at the scan center, the largest space on Tuulen Station. Immediately in front of us was the marble, containment for the quantum nondemolition sensor array — QNSA for the acronymically inclined. It was the milky blue of glacial ice and big as two elephants. The upper hemisphere was raised, and the scanning table protruded like a shiny gray tongue. Kamala approached the marble and touched her reflection, which writhed across its polished surface. To the right was a padded bench, the fogger, and a toilet. I looked left, through the control room window. Silloin stood watching us, her impossible head cocked to one side.

=She is docile?= She buzzed in my ear stone.

I held up crossed fingers.

=Welcome, Kamala Shastri.= Silloin's voice came over the speakers with a soothing hush. = You are ready to open your translation?=

Kamala bowed to the window. "This is where I take my clothes off?"

=If you would be so convenient.=

She brushed past me to the bench. Apparently I had ceased to exist; this was between her and the dino now. She undressed quickly, folding her clingy into a neat bundle, tucking her slippers beneath the bench. Out of the corner of my eye, I could see tiny feet, heavy thighs, and the beautiful dark smooth skin of her back. She stepped into the fogger and closed the door.

"Ready," she called.

From the control room, Silloin closed circuits, which filled the fogger with a dense cloud of nanolenses. The nano stuck to Kamala and deployed, coating the surface of her body. As she breathed them, they passed from her lungs into her bloodstream. She only coughed twice; she had been well trained. When the eight minutes were up, Silloin cleared the air in the fogger and she emerged. Still ignoring me, she again faced the control room.

=Now you must arrange yourself on the scanning table,= said Silloin, =and enable Michael to fix you.=

She crossed to the marble without hesitation, climbed the gantry beside it, eased onto the table, and lay back.

I followed her up. "Sure you won't tell me the rest of the secret?"

She stared at the ceiling, unblinking.

"Okay, then." I took the canister and a sparker out of my hip pouch. "This is going to happen just like you've practiced it." I used the canister to respray the bottoms of her feet with nano. I watched her belly rise and fall, rise and fall. She was deep into her breathing exercise. "Remember, no skipping rope or whistling while you're in the scanner."

She did not answer. "Deep breath now," I said, and touched a sparker to her big toe. There was a brief crackle as the nano on her skin wove into a net and stiffened, locking her in place. "Bark at the ferrets for me." I picked up my equipment, climbed down the gantry, and wheeled it back to the wall.

With a low whine, the big blue marble retracted its tongue. I watched the upper hemisphere close, swallowing Kamala Shastri, then joined Silloin in the control room.

I'm not of the school who thinks the dinos stink, another reason I got assigned to study them up close. Parikkal, for example, has no smell at all that I can tell. Normally Silloin had the faint but not unpleasant smell of stale wine. When she was under stress, however, her scent became vinegary and biting. It must have been a wild morning for her. Breathing through my mouth, I settled onto the stool at my station.

She was working quickly, now that the marble was sealed. Even with all their training, migrators tend to get claustrophobic fast. After all, they're lying in the dark, in nanobondage, waiting to be translated. Waiting. The simulator at the Singapore training center makes a noise while it's emulating a scan. Most compare it to a light rain pattering against the marble; for some, it's low-volume radio static. As long as they hear the patter, the migrators think they're safe. We reproduce it for them while they're in our marble, even though scanning takes about three seconds and is utterly silent. From my vantage I could see that the sagittal, axial, and coronal windows had stopped blinking, indicating full data capture. Silloin was skirring busily to herself; her comm didn't bother to interpret. Wasn't saying anything baby Michael needed to know, obviously. Her head bobbed as she monitored the enormous spread of readouts; her claws clicked against touch screens that glowed orange and yellow.

At my station, there was only a migration status screen — and a white button.

I wasn't lying when I said I was just the doorman. My field is sapientology, not quantum physics. Whatever went wrong with Kamala's migration that morning, there was nothing *I* could have done. The dinos tell me that the quantum nondemolition sensor array is able to circumvent Heisenberg's Uncertainty Principle by measuring spacetime's most crogglingly small quantities without collapsing the wave/particle duality. How small? They say that no one can ever "see" anything that's only 1.62×10^{-33} centimeters long, because at that size, space and time come apart. Time ceases to exist and space becomes a random probabilistic foam, sort of like quantum spit. We humans call this the Planck-Wheeler length. There's a Planck-Wheeler time, too: 10^{-45} of a second. If something happens and something else happens and the two events are separated by an interval of a mere 10^{-45} of a second, it is impossible to say which came first. It was all dino to me — and that's just the scanning. The Hanen use different tech to create artificial wormholes, hold them open with electromagnetic vacuum fluctuations, pass the superluminal signal through, and then assemble the migrator from elementary particles at the destination.

On my status screen I could see that the signal that mapped Kamala Shastri had already been compressed and burst through the wormhole. All that we had to wait for was for Gend to confirm acquisition. Once they officially told us that they had her, it would be my job to balance the equation.

Pitter-patter, pitter-pat.

Some Hanen technologies are so powerful that they can alter reality itself. Wormholes could be used by some time-traveling fanatic to corrupt history; the scanner/assembler could be used to create a billion Silloins — or Michael Burrs. Pristine reality, unpolluted by such anomalies, has what the dinos call harmony. Before any sapients get to join the galactic club, they must prove total commitment to preserving harmony.

Since I had come to Tuulen to study the dinos, I had pressed the white button maybe three hundred times. It was what I had to do in order to keep my assignment. Pressing it sent a killing pulse of ionizing radiation through the cerebral cortex of the migrator's duplicated, and therefore unnecessary, body. No brain, no pain; death followed within seconds. Yes, the first few times I'd balanced the equation had been traumatic. It was still ... unpleasant. But this was the price of a ticket to the stars. If certain unusual people like Kamala Shastri had decided that price was reasonable, it was their choice, not mine.

=This is not a happy result, Michael.= Silloin spoke to me for the first time since I'd entered the control room. =Discrepancies are unfolding.= On my status screen I watched as the error-checking routines started turning up hits.

"Is the problem here?" I felt a knot twist suddenly inside me. "Or there?" If our original scan checked out, then all Silloin would have to do is send it to Gend again.

There was a long infuriating silence. Silloin concentrated on part of her board as if it showed her firstborn hatchling chipping out of its egg. The respirator between her shoulders had ballooned to twice its normal size. My screen showed that Kamala had been in the marble for four minutes plus.

=It may be fortunate to recalibrate the scanner and begin over.=

"*Shit.*" I slammed my hand against the wall, felt the pain tingle to my elbow. "I thought you had it fixed." When error-checking turned up problems, the solution was almost always to retransmit. "You're sure, Silloin? Because this one was right on the edge when I tucked her in."

Silloin gave me a dismissive sneeze and slapped at the error readouts with her bony little hand, as if to knock them back to normal. Like Linna and the other dinos, she had little patience with what she regarded as our weepy fears of migration. Unlike Linna, however, she was convinced that someday, after we had used Hanen technologies long enough, we would learn to think like dinos. Maybe she's right. Maybe when we've been squirting through wormholes for hundreds of years, we'll cheerfully discard our redundant bodies. When the dinos and other sapients migrate, the redundants zap themselves — very harmonious. They tried it with humans, but it didn't always work. That's why I'm here. =The need is most clear. It will prolong about 30 minutes,= she said.

Kamala had been alone in the dark for almost six minutes, longer than any migrator I'd ever guided. "Let me hear what's going on in the marble."

The control room filled with the sound of Kamala screaming. It didn't sound human to me — more like the shriek of tires skidding toward a crash.

"We've got to get her out of there," I said.

=That is baby-thinking, Michael.=

"So she's a baby, damn it." I knew that bringing migrators out of the marble was big trouble. I could have asked Silloin to turn the speakers off and sat there while Kamala suffered. It was my decision.

"Don't open the marble until I get the gantry in place." I ran for the door. "And keep the sound effects going."

At the first crack of light, she howled. The upper hemisphere seemed to lift in slow motion; inside the marble she bucked against the nano. Just when I was sure it was impossible that she couldn't scream any louder, she did. We had accomplished something extraordinary, Silloin and I; we had stripped the brave biomaterials engineer away completely, leaving in her place a terrified animal.

"Kamala, it's me. Michael."

Her frantic screams cohered into words. "Stop ... *don't* ... oh, my god, someone *help*!" If I could have, I would've jumped into the marble to release her, but the sensor array is fragile and I wasn't going to risk causing any more problems with it. We both had to wait until the upper hemisphere swung fully open and the scanning table offered poor Kamala to me.

"It's okay. Nothing's going to happen, all right? We're bringing you out, that's all. Everything's all right."

When I released her with the sparker, she flew at me. We pitched back and almost toppled down the steps. Her grip was so tight I couldn't breathe.

"Don't *kill* me, don't, *please*, don't."

I rolled on top of her. "Kamala!" I wriggled one arm free and use it to pry myself from her. I scrabbled sideways to the top step. She lurched clumsily in the microgravity and swung at me; her fingernails raked across the back of my hand, leaving bloody welts. "Kamala, stop!" It was all I could do not to strike back at her. I retreated down the steps.

"You bastard. What are you assholes trying to do to me?" She drew several deep shuttering breaths and began to sob.

"The scan got corrupted somehow. Silloin is working on it."

=The difficulty is obscure,= said Silloin from the control room.

"But that's not your problem." I backed toward the bench.

"They lied," she mumbled and seemed to fold in upon herself as if she were just skin, no flesh or bones. "They said I wouldn't feel anything and here ... do you know what it's like ... it's ... "

I reached for her clingy. "Look, here are your clothes. Why don't you get dressed? We'll get you out of here."

"You bastard," she repeated, but her voice was empty.

She let me coax her down off the gantry. I counted nubs on the wall while she fumbled back into her clingy. They were the size of the old dimes my grandfather used to hoard, and they glowed with a soft golden bioluminescence. I was up to forty-seven before she was dressed and ready to return to Reception D.

Where before she had perched expectantly at the edge of the couch, now she slumped back against it. "So what do I do?" she said.

"I don't know." I went to the kitchen station and took the carafe from the distiller. "What now, Silloin?" I poured water over the back of my hand to wash the blood off. It stung. My earstone was silent. "I guess we wait," I said finally.

"For what?"

"For her to fix ... "

"I'm not going back in there."

I decided to let that pass. It was probably too soon to argue with her about it, although once Silloin recalibrated the scanner, she'd have very little time to change her mind. "You want something from the kitchen? Another cup of tea, maybe?"

"How about a gin and tonic — hold the tonic?" She rubbed beneath her eyes. "Or a couple of hundred milliliters of Serentol?"

I tried to pretend she'd made a joke. "You know the dinos won't let us open the bar for migrators. The scanner might misread your brain chemistry, and your visit to Gend would be nothing but a three-year drunk."

"Don't you under*stand*?" She was right back at the edge of hysteria. "I am not *going*!" I didn't really blame her for the way she was acting, but at that moment, all I wanted was to get rid of Kamala Shastri. I didn't care if she went on to Gend or back to Lunex or over the rainbow to Oz, just as long as I didn't have to be in the same room with this miserable creature who was trying to make me feel guilty about an accident I had nothing to do with.

"I thought I could do it." She clamped her hands to her ears as if to keep from hearing her own despair. "I wasted the last two years convincing myself that I could just lie there and not think and then suddenly I'd be far away. I was going someplace wonderful and strange." She made a strangled sound and let her hands drop into her lap. "I was going to help people see."

"You did it, Kamala. You did everything we asked."

She shook her head. "I couldn't *not* think. That was the problem. And then there she was, trying to touch me. In the dark. I had not thought of her since ... " She shivered. "It's your fault for reminding me."

"Your secret friend," I said.

"Friend?" Kamala seemed puzzled by the word. "No, I wouldn't say she was a friend. I was always a little bit scared of her, because I was never quite sure what she wanted from me." She paused. "One day I went up to 10W after school. She was in her chair, staring down at Bloor Street. Her back was to me. I said, 'Hi, Ms. Ase.' I was going to show her a genie I had written, only she didn't say anything. I came around. Her skin was the color of ashes. I took her hand. It was like picking up something plastic. She was stiff, hard — not a person anymore. She had become a thing, like a feather or a bone. I ran; I had to get out of there. I went up to our apartment and I hid from her."

She squinted, as if observing — judging — her younger self through the lens of time. "I think I understand now what she wanted. I think she knew she was dying; she probably wanted me there with her at the end, or at least to find her body afterward and report it. Only I could *not*. If I told anyone she was dead, my parents would find out about us. Maybe people would suspect me of doing something to her — I don't know. I could have called security, but I was only ten; I was afraid somehow they might trace me. A couple of weeks went by and still nobody had found her. By then it was too late to say anything. Everyone would have blamed me for keeping quiet for so long. At night I imagined her turning black and rotting into her chair like a banana. It made me sick; I couldn't sleep or eat. They had to put me in the hospital, because I had touched her. Touched *death*."

=Michael,= Silloin whispered, without any warning flash. =An impossibility has formed.=

"As soon as I was out of that building, I started to get better. Then they found her. After I came home, I worked hard to forget Ms. Ase. And I did, almost." Kamala wrapped her arms around herself. "But just now she was with me again, inside the marble ... I couldn't see her, but somehow I knew she was reaching for me."

=Michael, Parikkal is here with Linna.=

"Don't you see?" She gave a bitter laugh. "How can I go to Gend? I'm *hallucinating*."

=It has broken the harmony. Join us alone.=

I was tempted to swat at the annoying buzz in my ear.

"You know, I've never told anyone about her before."

"Well, maybe some good has come of this after all." I patted her on the knee. "Excuse me for a minute?" She seemed surprised that I would leave. I slipped into the hall and hardened the door bubble, sealing her in.

"What impossibility?" I said, heading for the control room.

=She is pleased to reopen the scanner?=

"Not pleased at all. More like scared shitless."

=This is Parikkal.= My earstone translated his skirring with a sizzling edge, like bacon frying. =The confusion was made elsewhere. No mishap can be connected to our station.=

I pushed through the bubble into the scan center. I could see the three dinos through the control window. Their heads were bobbing furiously. "Tell me," I said.

=Our communications with Gend were marred by a transient false-hood,= said Silloin. =Kamala Shastri has been received there and reconstructed.=

"She migrated?" I felt the deck shifting beneath my feet. "What about the one we've got here?"

=The simplicity is to load the redundant into the scanner and finalize ... =

"I've got news for you. She's not going anywhere near that marble."

=Her equation is not in balance.= This was Linna, speaking for the first time. Linna was not exactly in charge of Tuulen Station; she was more like a senior partner. Parikkal and Silloin had overruled her before — at least I thought they had.

"What do you expect me to do? Wring her neck?"

There was a moment's silence — which was not as unnerving as watching them eye me through the window, their heads now perfectly still.

"No," I said.

The dinos were skirring at each other; their heads wove and dipped. At first they cut me cold and the comm was silent, but suddenly their debate crackled through my earstone.

=This is just as I have been telling,= said Linna. =These beings have no realization of harmony. It is wrongful to further unleash them on the many worlds.=

=You may have reason,= said Parikkal. =But that is a later discussion. The need is for the equation to be balanced.=

=There is no time. We will have to discard the redundant ourselves.= Silloin bared her long brown teeth. It would take her maybe five seconds to rip Kamala's throat out. And even though Silloin was the dino most sympathetic to us, I had no doubt she would enjoy the kill.

=I will argue that we adjourn human migration until this world has been rethought,= said Linna.

This was typical dino condescension. Even though they appeared to be arguing with each other, they were actually speaking to me, laying the situation out so that even the baby sapient would understand. They were informing me that I was jeopardizing the future of humanity in space. That the Kamala in Reception D was dead whether I quit or not. That the equation had to be balanced and it had to be now.

"Wait," I said. "Maybe I can coax her back into the scanner." I had to get away from them. I pulled my earstone out and slid it into my pocket. I was in such a hurry to escape that I stumbled as I left the scan center and had to catch myself in the hallway. I stood there for a second, staring at the hand pressed against the bulkhead. I seemed to see the splayed fingers through the wrong end of a telescope. I was far away from myself.

She had curled into herself on the couch, arms clutching knees to her chest, as if trying to shrink so that nobody would notice her.

"We're all set," I said briskly. "You'll be in the marble for less than a minute, guaranteed."

"*No*, Michael."

I could actually feel myself receding from Tuulen Station. "Kamala, you're throwing away a huge part of your life."

"It is my right." Her eyes were shiny.

No, it wasn't. She was redundant; she had no rights. What had she said about the dead old lady? She had become a thing, like a bone.

"Okay, then." I jabbed at her shoulder with a stiff forefinger. "Let's go." She recalled. "Go where?"

"Back to Lunex. I'm holding the shuttle for you. It just dropped off my afternoon list; I should be helping them settle in, instead of having to deal with you."

She unfolded herself slowly.

"Come on." I jerked her roughly to her feet. "The dinos want you off Tuulen as soon as possible, and so do I." I was so distant, I couldn't see Kamala Shastri anymore.

She nodded and let me march her to the bubble door.

"And if we meet anyone in the hall, keep your mouth shut."

"You're being so mean." Her whisper was thick.

"You're being such a baby."

When the inner door glided open, she realized immediately that there was no umbilical to the shuttle. She tried to twist out of my grip but I put my shoulder into her, hard. She flew across the airlock, slammed against the outer door, and caromed onto her back. As I punched at the switch to close the inner door, I came back to myself. *I* was doing this terrible thing — me, Michael Burr. I couldn't help myself: I giggled. When I last saw her, Kamala was scrabbling across the deck toward me but she was too late. I was surprised that she wasn't screaming again; all I heard was her ferocious breathing.

As soon as the inner door sealed, I opened the outer door. After all, how many ways are there to kill someone on a space station? There were no guns. Maybe someone else could have stabbed or strangled her, but not me. Poison how? Besides, I wasn't thinking, I had been trying desperately not to think of what I was doing. I was a sapientologist, not a doctor. I always thought that exposure to space meant instantaneous death. Explosive decompression or something like. I didn't want her to suffer. I was trying to make it quick. Painless.

I heard the *whoosh* of escaping air and thought that was it; the body had been ejected into space. I had actually turned away when thumping started, frantic, like the beat of a racing heart. She must have found something to hold onto. *Thump, thump, thump!* It was too much. I sagged against the inner door — *thump, thump* — slid down it, laughing. Turns out that if you empty the lungs, it is possible to survive exposure to space for at least a minute, maybe two. I thought it was funny. *Thump!* Hilarious, actually. I had tried my best for her — risked my career — and this was how she repaid me? As I laid my cheek against the door, the *thumps* started to weaken. There were just a few centimeters between us, the difference between life and death. Now she knew all about balancing the equation. I was laughing so hard I could scarcely breathe. Just like the meat behind the door. Die already, you weepy bitch!

I don't know how long it took. The *thumping* slowed. Stopped. And then I was a hero. I had preserved harmony, kept our link to the stars open. I chuckled with pride; I could think like a dinosaur.

— • —

I popped through the bubble door into reception D. "It's time to board the shuttle."

Kamala had changed into a clingy and velcro slippers. There were at least ten windows open on the wall; the room filled with the murmur of talking heads. Friends and relatives had to be notified; their hero had returned, safe and sound. "I have to go," she said to the wall. "I will call you all when I land."

She gave me a smile that seemed stiff from disuse. "I want to thank you again, Michael." I wondered how long it took migrators to get used to being human. "You were such a help and I was such a ... I was not myself." She glanced around the room one last time and then shivered. "I was really scared."

"You were."

She shook her head. "Was it that bad?"

I shrugged and led her out into the hall.

"I feel so silly now. I mean, I was in the marble for less than a minute and then" — she snapped her fingers — "there I was on Gend, just like you said." She brushed up against me as we walked; her body was hard under the clingy. "Anyway, I am glad we got this chance to talk. I really *was* going to look you up when I got back. I certainly did not expect to see you here."

"I decided to stay on." The inner door to the airlock glided open. "It's a job that grows on you." The umbilical shivered as the pressure between Tuulen Station and the shuttle equalized.

"You have got migrators waiting," she said.

"Two."

"I envy them." She turned to me. "Have *you* ever thought about going to the stars?"

"No," I said.

Kamala put her hand to my face. "It changes everything." I could feel the prick of her long nails — claws, really. For a moment I thought she meant to scar my cheek the way she had been scarred.

"I know," I said. ■

WALKING THE MOONS

BY JONATHAN LETHEM

Jonathan Lethem (born 1964 in Brooklyn, New York) studied art at the High School for Music and Art in New York City, and in the late 1970s started a magazine called *The Literary Exchange*, a mixture of artwork and writing. He began selling short stories in the science fiction field in 1989, though his novels from the beginning have blended fantastical elements with other genres, such as the hard-boiled detective tale (*Gun, With Occasional Music*, 1994, winner of the International Association of the Fantastic in the Arts's William L. Crawford Award for Best First Novel and finalist for the Nebula Award), the road story (*Amnesia Moon*, 1995), the campus comedy (*As She Climbed Across the Table*, 1997), the Western (*Girl in Landscape*, 1998), and the *roman à clef*

(*Motherless Brooklyn*, 1999, winner of the National Book Critics Circle Award, the Macallan Gold Dagger for crime fiction, and the *Salon* Book Award, and named Book of the Year by *Esquire*; and the *New York Times* Best Seller *The Fortress of Solitude*, 2003). His 1996 collection *The Wall of the Sky, the Wall of the Eye* won the World Fantasy Award. His several dozens of short stories include further Nebula nominees, such as "Ninety Percent of Everything" (1999), which was written with James Patrick Kelly and John Kessel. His website is at jonathanlethem.com.

Lethem admits that he has a tendency to problematize the science fictional, futuristic, and fantastic tropes in his works. In a 1998 interview with me ("Private Hells and Radical Doubts," *Science Fiction Studies* online, July 1998), he described "Walking the Moons" as one of a sequence of stories that are "specifically skeptical about claims being made for virtual reality technologies ... claims that were being made that seemed to me naive, founded in a lack of awareness of the corruption inherent in most technological opportunities, and a search for zipless transcendence which seems to me usually a mistake. Virtual reality's reception was a combination of some of the utopian, consciousness-revolutionizing claims that had been made for radio and film when they appeared, and the utopian nuttiness that surrounded the first experiments with LSD. 'We finally have a mechanism by which we can take human consciousness to another level and abandon tired, earthly concerns.' And so I found these resistance stories coming out of me."

WALKING THE MOONS

"LOOK," SAYS THE MOTHER OF THE MAN WHO IS WALKING
Around The Moons Of Jupiter, "he's going so fast."

She snickers to herself and scuttles around the journalist to a table littered with wiring tools and fragmented mechanisms. She loops a long,
tangled cord over her son's intravenous tube and plugs one end into his
headset, jostling him momentarily as she works it into the socket. His stride
on the treadmill never falters. She runs the cord back to a modified four-
track recorder sitting in the dust of the garage floor, then picks up the
recorder's microphone and switches it on.

"Good morning, Mission Commander," she says.

"Yes," grunts The Man Who, his slack jaw moving beneath the massive
headset. It startles the journalist to hear the voice of The Man Who boom out
into the tiny garage.

"Interview time, Eddie."

"Who?"

"Mr. Kaffey. *Systems* Magazine, remember?"

"O.K.," says Eddie, The Man Who. His weakened, pallid body trudges
forward. He is clothed only in jockey undershorts and orthopedic sandals,

and the journalist can see his heart beat beneath the skin of his chest.

The Mother Of smiles artificially and hands the journalist the microphone. "I'll leave you boys alone," she says. "If you need anything, just yodel."

She steps past the journalist, over the cord, and out into the sunlight, pulling the door shut behind her.

The journalist turns to the man on the treadmill.

"Uh, Eddie?"

"Yeah."

"Uh, I'm Ron Kaffey. Is this O.K.? Can you talk?"

"Mr. Kaffey, I've got nothing but time." The Man Who smacks his lips and tightens his grip on the railing before him. The tread rolls away steadily beneath his feet, taking him nowhere.

The journalist covers the mike with the palm of his hand and clears his throat, then begins again. "So you're out there now. On Io. Walking."

"Mr. Kaffey, I'm currently broadcasting my replies to your questions from a valley on the northwestern quadrant of Io, yes. You're coming in loud and clear. No need to raise your voice. We're fortunate in having a pretty good connection, a good Earth-to-hookup, so to speak." The journalist watches as The Man Who moistens his lips, then dangles his tongue in the open air. "Please feel free to shoot with the questions, Mr. Kaffey. This is pretty uneventful landscape even by Io standards and I'm just hanging on your every word."

"Explain to me," says the journalist, "what you're doing."

"Ah. Well, I designed the rig myself. Took pixel satellite photographs and fed them into my simulator, which gives me a steadily unfolding virtual-space landscape." He reaches up and taps at his headset. "I log the equivalent mileage at the appropriate gravity on my treadmill and pretty soon I've had the same experience an astronaut would have. If we could afford to send them up anymore. Heh." He scratches violently at his ribs, until they flush pink. "Ask me questions," he says. "I'm ready at this end. You want me to describe what I'm seeing?"

"Describe what you're seeing."

"The desert, Mr. Kaffey. God, I'm so goddamned bored of the desert. That's all there is, you know. There isn't any atmosphere. We'd hope for some atmosphere, we had some hopes, but it didn't turn out that way. Nope. The dust all lays flat here, because of that. I try kicking it up, but there isn't any wind." The Man Who scuffs in his Dr. Scholl's sandals at the surface of the treadmill, booting imaginary pebbles, stirring up nonexistent dust. "You probably know I can't see Jupiter right now. I'm on the other side, so I'm pretty much out here alone under the stars. There isn't any point in my describing *that* to you."

The Man Who scratches again, this time at the patch where the intravenous tube intersects his arm, and the journalist is afraid he'll tear it off. "Bored?" asks the journalist.

"Yeah. Next time I think I'll walk across a grassy planet. What do you think of that? Or across the Pacific Ocean. On the bottom, I mean. 'Cause they're mapping it with ultrasound. Feed it into the simulator. Take me a couple of weeks. Nothing like this shit.

"I'm thinking more in terms of smaller scale walks from here on in, actually. Get back down to Earth, find ways to make it count for more. You know what I mean? Maybe even the ocean isn't such a good idea, actually. Maybe my fans can't really identify with my off-world walks, maybe they're feeling, who knows, a little, uh, alienated by this Io thing. I know I am. I feel out of touch, Mr. Kaffey. Maybe I ought to walk across the cornbelt or the sunbelt or something. A few people in cars whizzing past, waving at me, and farmers' wives making me picnic lunches, because they've heard I'm passing through. I could program that. I could have every goddamn Mayor from Pinole to Akron give me the key to their goddamn city."

"Sounds O.K., Eddie."

"Sounds O.K.," echoes The Man Who. "But maybe even that's a little much. Maybe I ought to walk across the street to the drugstore for a pack of gum. You don't happen to have a stick of gum in your pocket, Mr. Journalist?

I'll just open my mouth and you stick it in. I trust you. We don't have to tell my mother. If you hear her coming you just let me know, and I'll swallow it. You won't get in any trouble."

"I don't have any," says the journalist.

"Ah well."

The Man Who walks on, undaunted. Only now something is wrong. There's a hiss of escaping liquid, and the journalist is certain that The Man Who's nutrient serum is leaking from his arm. Then he smells the urine and sees the undershorts of The Man Who staining dark and adhering to the cave-white flesh of his thigh.

"What's the matter, Kaffey? No more questions?"

"You've wet yourself," says the journalist.

"Oh, damn. Uh, you better call my mom."

But The Mother Of has already sensed that something is amiss. She steps now back into the garage, smoking a cigarette and squinting into the darkness at her son. She frowns as she discerns the stain, and takes a long drag on her cigarette, closing her eyes.

"I guess you're thinking that there might not be a story here," says The Man Who. "Least not the story you had in mind."

"Oh no, I wouldn't say that," says the journalist quickly. He's not sure if he hasn't detected a note of sarcasm in the voice of The Man Who by now. "I'm sure we can work something up."

"Work something up," parrots The Man Who. The Mother Of has his shorts down now, and she's swabbing at his damp flank with a paper towel. The Man Who sets his mouth in a grim smile and trudges forward. He's not here, really. He's out on Io, making tracks. He's going to be in the Guinness Book of World Records.

The journalist sets the microphone back down in the dust and packs his bag. As he walks the scrubby driveway back to the street he hears The Man Who Is Walking Around The Moons Of Jupiter, inside the garage, coughing on cigarette fumes. ■

FLASHES

BY ROBERT J. SAWYER

Robert J. Sawyer (born 1960 in Ottawa, Ontario) is often referred to as "the dean of Canadian science fiction," and Canada, of course, is a more humanist, more secular, country than the United States. It's significant that in 2007 he received China's Galaxy Award for most-popular foreign science-fiction author — an officially atheist nation embracing his work, work that often questions organized religion and blind faith.

Still, although Sawyer may represent his country well on the international stage, he's an uneasy ambassador for atheism, taking on what he calls, with sarcastic capital letters, "the Modern Skeptical Movement" not just in novels such as 2000's *Calculating God*, but also in a pointed op-ed piece for *The Ottawa Citizen* ("A Bright Idea

for Atheists," online at sfwriter.com/atheists.htm).
His is a kinder, gentler humanism, still savage but
in a polite, quintessentially Canadian way (*The
New York Review of Science Fiction* once referred to
him as "a gentle giant of a writer").

The most-honored of Sawyer's 17 novels are
those that directly engage the science-vs.-religion
dialogue: the Hugo Award-winning *Hominids*
(2002), which postulates an alternate Earth that
was never tainted by religion, belief in God, or the
poisonous notion of an afterlife; the Nebula
Award-winning *The Terminal Experiment* (1995),
in which a biomedical engineer discovers scientific proof for the existence of a human soul only
to learn that no individuality — no essential
humanity — can survive death; and the John W.
Campbell Memorial Award-winning *Mindscan*
(2005), in which a courtroom battle strips bare
our archaic dualism and desperate desire to cling
to the notion of souls.

Sawyer received an honorary doctorate
from Ontario's Laurentian University in 2007,
and in 2008 the Canadian publishing trade
journal *Quill & Quire* named him one of the "30
most influential, innovative, and just plain powerful people in Canadian publishing." That
innovation goes way back: he was the first science-fiction writer to have a website; see
sfwriter.com.

Sawyer frequently writes about first contact
between humans and aliens, portraying that con-

tact in humorous or tragic ways, and with comedic or lethal consequences. In the unique first-contact scenario that follows, he evokes Sir Isaac Newton's celebrated phrase, "If I have seen further, it is by standing upon the shoulders of giants" — but readers should consider how sometimes the giants kick you when you're down.

FLASHES

MY HEART POUNDED AS I SURVEYED THE SCENE. IT WAS A horrific, but oddly appropriate, image: a bright light pulsing on and off. The light was the setting sun, visible through the window, and the pulsing was caused by the rhythmic swaying of the corpse, dangling from a makeshift noose, as it passed in front of the blood-red disk.

"Another one, eh, Detective?" said Chiu, the campus security guard, from behind me. His tone was soft.

I looked around the office. The computer monitor was showing a virtual desktop with a panoramic view of a spiral galaxy as the wallpaper; no files were open. Nor was there any sheet of e-paper prominently displayed on the real desktop. The poor bastards didn't even bother to leave suicide notes anymore. There was no point; it had all already been said.

"Yeah," I said quietly, responding to Chiu. "Another one."

The dead man was maybe sixty, scrawny, mostly bald. He was wearing black denim jeans and a black turtleneck sweater, the standard professorial look these days. His noose was fashioned out of fiber-optic cabling, giving it a pearlescent sheen in the sunlight. His eyes had bugged out, and his mouth was hanging open.

"I knew him a bit," said Chiu. "Ethan McCharles. Nice guy — he always remembered my name. So many of the profs, they think they're too important to say hi to a security guard. But not him."

I nodded. It was as good a eulogy as one could hope for — honest, spontaneous, heartfelt.

Chiu went on. "He was married," he said, pointing to the gold band on the corpse's left hand. "I think his wife works here, too."

I felt my stomach tightening, and I let out a sigh. My favorite thing: informing the spouse.

Cytosine Methylation: *All lifeforms are based on self-replicating nucleic acids, commonly triphosphoparacarbolicnucleic acid or, less often, deoxyribonucleic acid; in either case, a secondary stream of hereditary information is encoded based on the methylation state of cytosine, allowing acquired characteristics to be passed on to the next generation ...*

The departmental secretary confirmed what Chiu had said: Professor Ethan McCharles's wife did indeed also work at the University of Toronto; she was a tenured prof, too, but in a different faculty.

Walking down a corridor, I remembered my own days as a student here. Class of 1998 — "9T8," as they styled it on the school jackets. It'd been — what? — seventeen years since I'd graduated, but I still woke up from time to time in a cold sweat, after having one of those recurring student nightmares: the exam I hadn't studied for, the class I'd forgotten I'd enrolled in. Crazy dreams, left over from an age when little bits of human knowledge mattered; when facts and figures we'd discovered made a difference.

I continued along the corridor. One thing *had* changed since my day. Back then, the hallways had been packed between classes. Now, you could actually negotiate your way easily; enrollment was way down. This corridor was long, with fluorescent lights overhead, and was lined with wooden doors that had frosted floor-to-ceiling glass panels next to them.

I shook my head. The halls of academe.

The halls of death.

I finally found Marilyn Maslankowski's classroom; the arcane room-numbering system had come back to me. She'd just finished a lecture, apparently, and was standing next to the lectern, speaking with a redheaded male student; no one else was in the room. I entered.

Marilyn was perhaps ten years younger than her husband had been, and had light brown hair and a round, moonlike face. The student wanted more time to finish an essay on the novels of Robert Charles Wilson; Marilyn capitulated after a few wheedling arguments.

The kid left, and Marilyn turned to me, her smile thanking me for waiting. "The humanities," she said. "Aptly named, no? At least English literature is something that we're the foremost authorities on. It's nice that there are a couple of areas left like that."

"I suppose," I said. I was always after my own son to do his homework on time; didn't teachers know that if they weren't firm in their deadlines they were just making a parent's job more difficult? Ah, well. At least this kid had gone to university; I doubted my boy ever would.

"Are you Professor Marilyn Maslankowski?" I asked.

She nodded. "What can I do for you?"

I didn't extend my hand; we weren't allowed to make any sort of overture to physical contact anymore. "Professor Maslankowski, my name is Andrew Walker. I'm a detective with the Toronto Police." I showed her my badge.

Her brown eyes narrowed. "Yes? What is it?"

I looked behind me to make sure we were still alone. "It's about your husband."

Her voice quavered slightly. "Ethan? My God, has something happened?"

There was never any easy way to do this. I took a deep breath, then:

"Professor Maslankowski, your husband is dead."

Her eyes went wide and she staggered back a half-step, bumping up against the smartboard that covered the wall behind her.

"I'm terribly sorry," I said.

"What — what happened?" Marilyn asked at last, her voice reduced to a whisper.

I lifted my shoulders slightly. "He killed himself."

"Killed himself?" repeated Marilyn, as if the words were ones she'd never heard before.

I nodded. "We'll need you to positively identify the body, as next of kin, but the security guard says it's him."

"My God," said Marilyn again. Her eyes were still wide. "My God ... "

"I understand your husband was a physicist," I said.

Marilyn didn't seem to hear. "My poor Ethan ... " she said softly. She looked like she might collapse. If I thought she was actually in danger of hurting herself with a fall, I could surge in and grab her; otherwise, regulations said I had to keep my distance. "My poor, poor Ethan ... "

"Had your husband been showing signs of depression?" I asked.

Suddenly Marilyn's tone was sharp. "Of course he had! Damn it, wouldn't you?"

I didn't say anything. I was used to this by now.

"Those aliens," Marilyn said, closing her eyes. "Those God-damned aliens."

Demand-Rebound Equilibrium: *Although countless economic systems have been tried by various cultures, all but one prove inadequate in the face of the essentially limitless material resources made possible through low-cost reconfiguration of subatomic particles. The only successful system, commonly known as Demand-Rebound Equilibrium, although also occasionally called [Untranslatable proper name]'s Forge, after its principal chronicler, works because it* *responds to market forces that operate independently from individual psychology, thus ...*

By the time we returned to Ethan's office, he'd been cut down and laid out on the floor, a sheet the coroner had brought covering his face and body. Marilyn had cried continuously as we'd made our way across the campus. It was early January, but global warming meant that the snowfalls I'd known as a boy didn't occur much in Toronto anymore. Most of the ozone was gone, too, letting ultraviolet pound down. We weren't even shielded against our own sun; how could we expect to be protected from stuff coming from the stars?

I knelt down and pulled back the sheet. Now that the noose was gone, we could see the severe bruising where Ethan's neck had snapped. Marilyn made a sharp intake of breath, brought her hand to her mouth, closed her eyes tightly, and looked away.

"Is that your husband?" I asked, feeling like an ass for even having to pose the question.

She managed a small, almost imperceptible nod.

It was now well into the evening. I could come back tomorrow to ask Ethan McCharles's colleagues the questions I needed answered for my report, but, well, Marilyn was right here, and, even though her field was literature rather than physics, she must have some sense of what her husband had been working on. I repositioned the sheet over his dead face and stood up. "Can you tell me what Ethan's specialty was?"

Marilyn was clearly struggling to keep her composure. Her lower lip was trembling, and I could see by the rising and falling of her blouse — so sharply contrasting with the absolutely still sheet — that she was breathing rapidly. "His — he ... Oh, my poor, poor Ethan ... "

"Professor Maslankowski," I said gently. "Your husband's specialty ... ?"

She nodded, acknowledging that she'd heard me, but still unable to focus on answering the question. I let her take her time, and, at last, as if they were curse words, she spat out, "Loop quantum gravity."

"Which is?"

"Which is a model of how subatomic particles are composed." She shook her head. "Ethan spent his whole career trying to prove LQG was correct, and … "

"And?" I said gently.

"And yesterday they revealed the true nature of the fundamental structure of matter."

"And this — what was it? — this 'loop quantum gravity' wasn't right?"

Marilyn let out a heavy sigh. "Not even close. Not even in the ballpark." She looked down at the covered form of her dead husband, then turned her gaze back to me. "Do you know what it's like, being an academic?"

I actually did have some notion, but that's not what she wanted to hear. I shook my head and let her talk.

Marilyn spread her arms. "You stake out your turf early on, and you spend your whole life defending it, trying to prove that your theory, or someone else's theory you're championing, is right. You take on all comers — in journals, at symposia, in the classroom — and if you're lucky, in the end you're vindicated. But if you're unlucky … "

Her voice choked off, and tears welled in her eyes again as she looked down at the cold corpse lying on the floor.

[**Untranslatable proper name**] **Award:** *Award given every [roughly 18 Earth years] for the finest musical compositions produced within the Allied Worlds. Although most species begin making music even prior to developing written language, [The same untranslatable proper name] argued that no truly sophisticated composition had ever been produced by a being with a lifespan of less than [roughly 1,100 Earth years], and since such lifespans only become possible with technological maturity, nothing predating a race's overcoming of natural death is of any artistic consequence.*

*Certainly, the winning compositions bear out her position: the work
of composers who lived for [roughly 140 Earth years] or less seem
little more than atonal noise when compared to ...*

It had begun just two years ago. Michael — that's my son; he was thir-
teen then — and I got a call from a neighbor telling us we just *had* to put
on the TV. We did so, and we sat side by side on the couch, watching the
news conference taking place in Pasadena, and then the speeches by the
U.S. President and the Canadian Prime Minister.

When it was over, I looked at Michael, and he looked at me. He was a
good kid, and I loved him very much — and I wanted him to understand
how special this all was. "Take note of where you are, Michael," I said. "Take
note of what you're wearing, what I'm wearing, what the weather's like outside. For the rest of your life, people will ask you what you were doing when
you heard."

He nodded, and I went on. "This is the kind of event that comes along
only once in a great while. Each year, the anniversary of it will be marked;
it'll be in all the history books. It might even become a holiday. This is a
date like ... "

I looked round the living room, helplessly, trying to think of a date
that this one was similar to. But I couldn't, at least not from my lifetime,
although my dad had talked about July 20, 1969, in much the same way.

"Well," I said at last, "remember when you came home that day when
you were little, saying Johnny Stevens had mentioned something called
9/11 to you, and you wanted to know what it was, and I told you, and you
cried. This is like that, in that it's significant ... but ... but 9/11 was such a
bad memory, such an awful thing. And what's happened today — it's ... it's
joyous, that's what it is. Today, humanity has crossed a threshold. Everybody
will be talking about nothing but this in the days and weeks ahead, because,
as of right now" — my voice had actually cracked as I said the words — "we
are not alone."

Cosmic Microwave Background Radiation: *a highly isotropic radiation with an almost perfect blackbody spectrum permeating the entire universe, at a temperature of approximately [2.7 degrees Kelvin]. Although some primitive cultures mistakenly cite this radiation as proof of a commonly found creation myth — specifically, a notion that the universe began as a singularity that burst forth violently — sophisticated races understand that the cosmic microwave background is actually the result of ...*

It didn't help that the same thing was happening elsewhere. It didn't help one damned bit. I'd been called in to U of T seven times over the past two years, and each time someone had killed himself. It wasn't always a prof; time before McCharles, it had been a Ph.D. candidate who'd been just about to defend his thesis on some abstruse aspect of evolutionary theory. Oh, evolution happens, all right — but it turns out the mechanisms are way more complex than the ones the Darwinians have been defending for a century and a half. I tried not to get cynical about all this, but I wondered if, as he slit his wrists before reproducing, that student had thought about the irony of what he was doing.

The source of all his troubles — of so many people's troubles — was a planet orbiting a star called 54 Piscium, some thirty-six light-years away. For two years now, it had been constantly signaling Earth with flashes of intense laser light.

Well, not quite constantly: it signaled for eighteen hours, then paused for twenty, and it fell silent once every hundred and twelve days for a period just shy of two weeks. From this, astronomers had worked out what they thought were the lengths of the day and the year of the planet that was signaling us, and the diameter of that planet's sun. But they weren't sure; nobody was sure of anything anymore.

At first, all we knew was that the signals were artificial. The early patterns of flashes were various mathematical chains: successively larger primes, then Fibonacci sequences in base eight, then a series that no one has quite worked out the significance of but that was sent repeatedly.

But then real information started flowing in, in amazing detail. Our telecommunications engineers were astonished that they'd missed a technique as simple as fractal nesting for packing huge amounts of information into a very narrow bandwidth. But that realization was just the first of countless blows to our egos.

There was a clip they kept showing on TV for ages after we'd figured out what we were receiving: an astronomer from the last century with a supercilious manner going on about how contact with aliens might plug us into the *Encyclopedia Galactica*, a repository of the knowledge of beings millions of years ahead of us in science and technology, in philosophy and mathematics. What wonders it would hold! What secrets it would reveal! What mysteries it would solve!

No one was arrogant like that astronomer anymore. No one could be.

Of course, various governments had tried to put the genie back into the bottle, but no nation has a monopoly on signals from the stars. Indeed, anyone with a few hundred dollars worth of equipment could detect the laser flashes. And deciphering the information wasn't hard; the damned encyclopedia was designed to be read by anyone, after all.

And so the entries were made public — placed on the web by individuals, corporations, and those governments that still thought doing so was a public service. Of course, people tried to verify what the entries said; for some, we simply didn't have the technology. For others, though, we could run tests, or make observations — and the entries always turned out to be correct, no matter how outlandish their claims seemed on the surface.

I thought about Ethan McCharles, swinging from his fiber-optic noose. The poor bastard.

It was rumored that one group had sent a reply to the senders, begging them to stop the transmission of the encyclopedia. Maybe that was even true — but it was no quick fix. After all, any signal sent from Earth would take thirty-six years to reach them, and even if they replied — or stopped — immediately upon receipt of our message, it would take another thirty-six years for that to have an impact here.

Until then at least, data would rain down on us, poison from the sky.

Life After Death: *A belief, frequently encountered in unenlightened races, that some self-aware aspect of a given individual survives the death of the body. Although such a belief doubtless gives superstitious primitives a measure of comfort, it is easily proven that no such thing exists. The standard proofs are drawn from (1) moral philosophy, (2) quantum information theory, (3) non-[Untranslatable proper name] hyper-parallactic phase-shift phenomenology, and (4) comprehensive symbolic philosologic. We shall explore each of these proofs in turn ...*

"Ethan was a good man," said Marilyn Maslankowski. We had left her husband's office — and his corpse — behind. It was getting late, and the campus was mostly empty. Of course, as I'd seen, it was mostly empty earlier, too — who the hell wanted to waste years getting taught things that would soon be proven wrong, or would be rendered hopelessly obsolete?

We'd found a lounge to sit in, filled with vinyl-covered chairs. I bought Marilyn a coffee from a machine; at least I could do that much for her.

"I'm sure he was," I said. They were always good men — or good women. They'd just backed the wrong horse, and —

No. No, that wasn't right. They'd backed a horse when there were other, much faster, totally invisible things racing as well. We knew nothing.

"His work was his life," Marilyn continued. "He was so dedicated. Not just about his research, either, but as a teacher. His students loved him."

"I'm sure they did," I said. However few of them there were. "Um, how did you get to work today?"

"TTC," she replied. Public transit.

"Where abouts do you live?"

"We have a condo near the lake, in Etobicoke."

We. She'd probably say "we" for months to come.

She'd finished her coffee, and I drained mine in a final gulp. "Come on," I said. "I'll give you a lift home."

We headed down some stairs and out to the street. It was dark, and the sky seemed a uniform black: the glare of street lamps banished the stars. If only it were so easy ...

We got into my car, and I started driving. Earlier, she'd called her two adult children. One, her daughter, was rushing back to the city from a skiing trip — artificial snow, of course. The other, her son, was in Los Angeles, but was taking the red-eye, and would be here by morning.

"Why are they doing this?" she asked, as we drove along. "Why are the aliens doing this?"

I moved into the left lane and flicked on my turn signal. *Blink, blink, blink.*

Off in the distance we could see the tapered needle of the CN Tower, Toronto's — and, when I was younger — the world's tallest building, stretching over half a kilometer into the air. Lots of radio and television stations broadcast from it, and so I pointed at it. "Presumably they became aware of us through our radio and TV programs — stuff we leaked out into space." I tried to make my tone light. "Right now, they'd be getting our shows from the 1970s — have you ever seen any of that stuff? I suppose they think they're uplifting us. Bringing us out of the dark ages."

Marilyn looked out the passenger window. "There's nothing wrong with darkness," she said. "It's comforting." She didn't say anything further as we continued along. The city was gray and unpleasant. Christmas had come and gone, and —

Funny thing; I hadn't thought about it until just now. Used to be at Christmas, you'd see stars everywhere: on the top of trees, on lampposts, all over the place. After all, a star had supposedly heralded Jesus' birth. But I couldn't recall seeing a single one this past Christmas. Signals from the heavens just didn't have the same appeal anymore ...

Marilyn's condo tower was about twenty stories tall, and some of the windows had tinfoil covering them instead of curtains. It looked like it used to be an upscale building, but so many people had lost their jobs in the past two years. I pulled into the circular driveway. She looked at me, and her eyes were moist. I knew it was going to be very difficult for her to go into her apartment. Doubtless, there'd be countless things of her husband's left in a state that suggested he was going to return. My heart went out to her, but there was nothing I could do, damn it all. They should let us touch them. They should let us hold them. Human contact: it's the only kind that doesn't hurt.

After letting her off, I drove to my house, exhausted emotionally and physically; for most of the trip, the CN Tower was visible in my rearview mirror, as though the city was giving me the finger.

My son Michael was fifteen now, but he wasn't home, apparently. His mother and I had split up more than five years ago, so the house was empty. I sat on the living-room couch and turned on the wall monitor. As always, I wondered how I was going to manage to hold onto this place in my old age. The police pension fund was bankrupt; half the stocks it had invested in were now worthless. Who wanted to own shares in oil companies when an entry might be received showing how to make cold fusion work? Who wanted to own biotechnology stocks when an entry explaining some do-it-yourself gene resequencing technique might be the very next one to arrive?

The news was on, and, of course, there was the usual report about the encyclopedia entries whose translations had been released today. The entries came in a bizarre order, perhaps reflecting the alphabetical sequence of their names in some alien tongue; we never knew what would be next. There'd be an entry on some aspect of biology, then one on astronomy, then some arcane bit of history of some alien world, then something from a new science that we don't even have a name for. I listened halfheartedly; like most people, I did everything halfheartedly these days.

"One of the latest *Encyclopedia Galactica* entries," said the female reporter, "reveals that our universe is finite in size, measuring some forty-four billion light-years across. Another new entry contains information about a form of combustion based on neon, which our scientist had considered an inert gas. Also, a lengthy article provides a comprehensive explanation of dark matter, the long suspected but never identified source of most of the mass in the universe. It turns out that no such dark matter exists, but rather there's an interrelationship between gravity and tachyons that ... "

Doubtless some people somewhere were happy or intrigued by these revelations. But others were surely devastated, lifetimes of work invalidated. Ah, well. As long as none of them were here in Toronto. Let somebody else, somewhere else, deal with the grieving widows, the orphaned children, the inconsolable boyfriends. I'd had enough. I'd had plenty.

I got up and went to make some coffee. I shouldn't be having caffeine at this hour, but I didn't sleep well these days even when I avoided it. As I stirred whitener into my cup, I could hear the front door opening. "Michael?" I shouted out, as I headed back to the couch.

"Yeah," he called back. A moment later he entered the living room. My son had one side of his head shaved bald, the current street-smart style. Leather jackets, which had been *de rigueur* for tough kids when I'd been Michael's age — not that any tough kid ever said *de rigueur* — were frowned upon now; a synthetic fabric that shone like quicksilver and was as supple as silk was all young people wore these days; of course, the formula to make it had come from an encyclopedia entry.

"It's a school night," I said. "You shouldn't be out so late."

"School." He spat the word. "As if anyone cares. As if any of it matters."

We'd had this argument before; we were just going through the motions. I said what I said because that's what a parent is supposed to say.

He said what he said because ...

Because it was the truth.

I nodded, and shut off the TV. Michael headed on down to the basement, and I sat in the dark, staring up at the ceiling.

Chronics: *Branch of science that deals with the temporal properties of physical entities. Although most entities in the universe progress through time in an orthrochronic, or forward, fashion, certain objects instead regress in a retrochronic, or backward, fashion. The most common example ...*

Yesterday, it turned out, was easy. Yesterday, I only had to deal with *one* dead body.

The explosion happened at 9:42 a.m. I'd been driving down to division headquarters, listening to loud music on the radio with my windows up, and I still heard it. Hell, they probably heard it clear across Lake Ontario, in upstate New York.

I'd been speeding along the Don Valley Parkway when it happened, and had a good view through my windshield toward downtown. Of course, the skyline was dominated by the CN Tower, which —

My God!

— which was now leaning over, maybe twenty degrees off vertical. The radio station I'd been listening to went dead; it had been transmitting from the CN Tower, I supposed. Maybe it was a terrorist attack. Or maybe it was just some bored school kid who'd read the entry on how to produce antimatter that had been released last week.

There was a seven-story complex of observation decks and restaurants two-thirds of the way up the tower, providing extra weight. It was hard to —

Damn!

My car's brakes had slammed on, under automatic control; I pitched forward, the shoulder belt giving a bit. The car in front of mine had come to a complete stop — as, I could now see, had the car in front of it, and the one in front of that car, too. Nobody wanted to continue driving toward the tower. I undid my seat belt and got out of my car; other motorists were doing the same thing.

The tower was leaning over further now: maybe thirty-five degrees. I assumed the explosion had been somewhere near its base; if it had been antimatter, from what I understood, only a minuscule amount would have been needed.

"There it goes!" shouted someone behind me. I watched, my stomach knotting, as the tower leaned over farther and farther. It would hit other, lesser skyscrapers; there was no way that could be avoided. I was brutally conscious of the fact that hundreds, maybe thousands, of people were about to die.

The tower continued to lean, and then it broke in two, the top half plummeting sideways to the ground. A plume of dust went up into the air, and —

It was like watching a distant electrical storm: the visuals hit you first, well before the sound. And the sound was indeed like thunder, a reverberating, cracking roar.

Screams were going up around me. "*Oh, my God! Oh, my God!*" I felt like I was going to vomit, and I had to hold onto my car's fender for support.

Somebody behind me was shouting, "Damn you, damn you, damn you!" I turned, and saw a man shaking his fist at the sky. I wanted to join him, but there was no point.

This was just the beginning, I knew. People all over the world had read that entry, along with all the others. Antimatter explosions; designer diseases based on new insights into how biology worked; God only knew what else. We needed a firewall for the whole damn planet, and there was no way to erect one.

I abandoned my car and wandered along the highway until I found an off-ramp. I walked for hours, passing people who were crying, people who were screaming, people who, like me, were too shocked, too dazed, to do either of those things.

I wondered if there was an entry in the *Encyclopedia Galactica* about Earth, and, if so, what it said. I thought of Ethan McCharles, swinging back and forth, a flesh pendulum, and I remembered that spontaneous little eulogy Chiu, the security guard, had uttered. Would there be a eulogy for Earth? A few kind words, closing out the entry on us in the next edition of the encyclopedia? I knew what I wanted it to say.

I wanted it to say that we *mattered*, that what we did had worth, that we treated each other well most of the time. But that was wishful thinking, I suppose. All that would probably be in the entry was the date on which our first broadcasts were detected, and the date, only a heartbeat later in cosmic terms, on which they had ceased.

It would take me most of the day to walk home. My son Michael would make his way back there, too, I'm sure, when he heard the news.

And at least we'd be together, as we waited for whatever would come next. ■

VERITAS

BY JAMES MORROW

James Morrow (born 1947 in Philadelphia, Pennsylvania) has been writing fiction ever since shortly after his seventh birthday, when he dictated "The Story of the Dog Family" to his mother, who dutifully typed it up and bound the pages with yarn. This four-page, six-chapter fantasy, dated February 1, 1954, is still in the author's private archives. As he likes to say, "My current publisher is William Morrow, but my first publisher was Emily Morrow." Upon reaching adulthood, Morrow proceeded to write nine speculative-fiction novels and enough short stories to fill two collections. He has edited four anthologies, three of them in the *Nebula Awards* annual series. Among his literary honors are two World Fantasy Awards, for his novels *Only*

Begotten Daughter (1990) and *Towing Jehovah* (1994), and two Nebula Awards, for "Bible Stories for Adults, No. 17: The Deluge" (1988) and *City of Truth* (1991), an expansion of "Veritas." A collection of essays on his oeuvre was published in the 1999, Volume 5 issue of the journal *Para*Doxa: Studies in World Literary Genres*, republished as *The Divinely Human Comedy of James Morrow* and edited by James Winchell (Delta Publications, 2000). Recent novels included a critically acclaimed epic about the birth of the scientific worldview, *The Last Witchfinder* (2006), and its "thematic sequel," *The Philosopher's Apprentice* (2008), an homage to Mary Shelley's ground-breaking science fiction novel, *Frankenstein*. He also maintains a weblog, fittingly called The Passionate Rationalist, which you can find by tuning in to jamesmorrow.net.

Morrow has said that this story is about "how all dualisms and dichotomies almost seem to be *ipso facto* defeating" and the possibility that "any truth that gets out of hand becomes an evil." He regards all his fiction as "thought experiments" analogous to the Gedanken calculations — unstageable demonstrations conducted entirely within the confines of one's skull — routinely performed by physicists and philosophers. "Veritas" is no exception, being centered around a grand "What if?" question (What if a society outlawed falsehoods?) whose implications you are about to enjoy.

VERITAS

PIGS HAVE WINGS ...

Rats chase cats ...

Snow is hot ...

Even now the old lies ring through the charred interior of my skull. I cannot speak them. I shall never be able to speak them — not without being dropped from here to hell in a bucket of pain. But they still inhabit me, just as they did on that momentous day when the city began to fall.

Grass is purple ...

Two and two make five ...

I awoke aggressively that morning, tearing the blankets away as if they were all that stood between myself and total alertness. Yawning vigorously, I charged into the shower, where warm water poured forth the instant the sensors detected me. I'd been with Overt Intelligence for over five years, and this was the first time I'd drawn an assignment that might be termed a plum. Spread your nostrils, Orville. Sniff her out. Sherry Urquist: some name! It sounded more like a mixed drink than like what she allegedly was, a purveyor of falsehoods, an enemy of the city, a member of the Dissemblage. The day could not begin soon enough.

The Dissemblage was like a deity. Not much tangible evidence, but people still had faith in it. Veritas, they reasoned, must harbor its normal share of those who believe the status quo is ipso facto wrong. Paradise will have its dissidents. The real question was not, Do subversives live in our city? The real question was, How do they tell lies without going mad?

My in-shower cablevision receiver winked on. Grimacing under the studio lights, our Assistant Secretary of Imperialism discussed Veritas's growing involvement in the Lethean civil war. "So far, over four thousand of our soldiers have died," the interviewer noted. "A senseless loss," the secretary conceded. "Our policy is impossible to justify on logical grounds, which is why we've started invoking national security and other shibboleths."

Have no illusions. The Sherry Urquist assignment did not fall into my lap because somebody at Overt Intelligence liked me. It was simply this: I am a roué. If any agent had a prayer of planting this particular Dissembler, that agent was me. It's the eyebrows that do it, great bushy extrusions suggesting a predatory mammal of unusual prowess, though I must admit they draw copious support from my straight nose and full, pillowlike lips. Am I handsome as a god? Metaphorically speaking, yes.

The picture tube had fogged over, so I activated the wiper. On the screen, a seedy-looking terrier scratched its fleas. "We seriously hope you'll consider By-product Brand Dog Food," said the voice-over. "Yes, we do tie up an enormous amount of protein that might conceivably be used in relieving worldwide starvation. However, if you'll consider the supposed benefits of dogs, we believe you may wish to patronize us."

On the surface, Ms. Urquist looked innocent enough. The dossier pegged her a writer, a former newspaper reporter with several popular self-help books under her belt. She had some other commodities under her belt, too, mainly fat, unless the accompanying OIA photos exaggerated. The case against her consisted primarily of rumor. Last week a neighbor, or possibly a sanitation engineer — the dossier contradicted itself on this point — had gone through her garbage. The yield was largely what you'd expect from someone in Ms. Urquist's profession: vodka bottles, outdated caffeine tablets, computer disk boxes, an early draft of her last bestseller, *How to Find a Certain Amount of Inner Peace Some of the Time If You Are Lucky*. Then came the kicker. The figurative smoking gun. The nonliteral forbidden fruit. At the bottom of the heap, the report asserted, lay "a torn and crumpled page" from what was "almost certainly a work of fiction."

Two hundred and thirty-nine words of it, to be precise. A story, a yarn, a legend. Something made up.

ART IS A LIE, the electric posters in Washington Park reminded us. Truth was beauty, but it simply didn't work the other way around.

I left the shower, which instantly shut itself down, and padded naked into my bedroom. Clothes per se were deceitful, of course, but this was the middle of winter, so I threw on some underwear and a gray suit with the lapels cut off — no integrity in freezing to death. My apartment was peeled to a core of rectitude. Most of my friends had curtains, wall hangings, and rugs, but not I. Why take chances with one's own sanity?

The odor of stale urine hit me as I rushed down the hall toward the lobby. How unfortunate that some people translated the ban on sexually segregated restrooms — PRIVACY IS A LIE, the posters reminded us — into a general fear of toilets. Hadn't they heard of public health? Public health was guileless.

Wrapped in dew, my Plymouth Adequate glistened on the far side of Probity Street. In the old days, I'd heard, you never knew for sure that your car would be unmolested, or even there, when you left it overnight. Twenty-eight degrees Fahrenheit, yet the thing started smoothly. I took off, zooming past the wonderfully functional cinderblocks that constituted city hall and heading toward the shopping district. My interview with Sherry Urquist was scheduled for ten, so I still had time to buy a gift for my nephew's brainburn party, which would happen around two-thirty that afternoon, right after he recovered. "Yes, I did take quite a few bribes during the Wheatstone Tariff affair," a thin-voiced senatorial candidate squeaked from out of my radio, "but you have to understand ... " His voice faded, pushed aside by the pressure of my thoughts. Today my nephew would learn to hate a lie. Today we would rescue him from deceit's boundless sea, tossing out our lifelines and hauling him aboard the ark called Veritas. So to speak.

Money grows on trees ...

Horses have six legs ...

And suddenly you're a citizen.

What could life have been like before the cure? How did the mind tolerate a world where politicians misled, advertisers overstated, women wore makeup, and people professed love for each other at the nonliteral drop of a hat? I shivered. Did the Dissemblers know what they were playing with? How I relished the thought of advancing their doom, how badly I wanted Sherry Urquist's bulky ass hanging figuratively over the mantel of my fireplace.

I was armed for the fight. Two days earlier, the clever doctors down at the agency's Medical Division had done a bit of minor surgery, and now one of my seminal vesicles contained not only its usual cargo but also a microscopic radio transmitter. My imagination showed it to me, poised in the duct like the Greek infantry waiting for the wooden horse to arrive inside Troy.

What will they think of next?

The problem was the itch. Not a literal itch — the transmitter was one thousandth the size of a pinhead. My discomfort was philosophical. Did the beeper lie or didn't it, that was the question. It purported to be only itself, a thing, a microtransmitter, and yet some variation of duplicity seemed afoot here.

I didn't like it.

— • —

Molly's Rather Expensive Toy Store, the sign said. Expensive: that was okay. Christmas came every year, but a kid got cured only once.

"My, aren't *you* a pretty fellow?" a female citizen sang out as I strode through the door. Marionettes dangled from the ceiling like victims of a mass lynching. Stuffed animals stampeded gently toward me from all directions.

"Your body is desirable enough," I said, casting a candid eye up and down the sales clerk. A tattered wool sweater molded itself around her emphatic breasts. Grimy white slacks encased her tight thighs. "But that nose," I added forlornly. A demanding business, citizenship.

"What brings you here?" She had one of those rare brands in which every digit is the same. 9999W, her forehead said. "You playboys are never responsible enough for parenthood."

"A fair assessment. You have kids?"

"I'm not married."

"It figures. My nephew's getting burned today."

"And you're waiting till the last minute to buy him a gift?"

"Right."

"Electric trains are popular. We sold eleven sets last week. Two were returned as defective."

She led me to a raised platform overrun by a kind of Veritas in miniature and kicked up the juice on the power-pack. A streamlined locomotive whisked a string of gleaming coaches past a factory belching an impressive facsimile of smoke.

"I wonder — is this thing a lie?" I opened the throttle, and the locomotive nearly jumped the track.

"What do you mean?"

"It claims to be a train. But it's not."

"It claims to be a *model* of a train, which it is."

I eased the locomotive into the station. "Is your price as good as anybody else's?"

"You can get the same thing for six dollars less at Marquand's."

"Don't have the time. Can you gift-wrap it?"

"Not skillfully."

"Anything will do. I'm in a hurry."

The downtown traffic was light, the lull before lunch hour, so I arrived early at Sherry Urquist's Washington Park apartment, a crumbling glass-and-steel ziggurat surmounted by a billboard that said, ASSUMING THAT GOD EXISTS, JESUS MAY HAVE BEEN HIS SON. I rode the elevator to the twentieth floor, exiting into a foyer where a handsome display of old military recruitment posters covered the fissured plaster. It was nice when somebody took the trouble to decorate a place. One could never use paint, of course. Paint was a lie. But with a little imagination ...

I rang the bell. Nothing. Had I gotten the time wrong? CHANNEL YOUR VIOLENT IMPULSES IN A SALUTARY DIRECTION, the nearest poster said. BECOME A MARINE.

The door swung open, and there stood our presumed subversive, a figurative cloud of confusion hovering about her heavy face, darkening her soft-boiled eyes and pulpy lips, features somewhat more attractive than the agency's photos suggested. "Did I wake you?" I asked. Her thermal pajamas barely managed to hold their contents in check, and I gave her an honest ogle. "I'm two minutes early."

"You woke me," she said. Frankness. A truth-teller, then? No, if there was one thing a Dissembler could do, it was deceive.

"Sorry," I said. I remembered the old documentary films of the oil paintings being burned. Rubens, that was the kind of sensual plumpness Sherry had going for her. Good old Peter Paul Rubens. Sneaking the Greek army inside Troy might be more entertaining than I'd thought.

She frowned, stretching her forehead brand into El Greco numerals. No one down at headquarters doubted its authenticity. Ditto her cerebroscan, voicegram, fingerprints ...

A citizen, and yet she had written fiction.

Maybe.

"Who are you?" Her voice was wet and deep.

"Orville Prawn," I said. A permanent truth. "I work for *Tolerable Distortions*." A more transient one; the agency had arranged for the magazine to hire me — payroll, medical plan, pension fund, the works — for the next forty-eight hours. "Our interview ... " I took out a pad and pencil.

Her pained expression seemed like the real thing. "Oh, damn, I'm *sorry*." She snapped her fingers. "It's on my calendar, but I've been up against a dozen deadlines, and I —"

"Forgot?"

"Yeah." She patted my forearm and guided me into her sparsely appointed living room. "Excuse me. These pajamas are probably driving you crazy."

"Not the pajamas per se."

She disappeared, returning shortly in a dingy yellow blouse and a red skirt circumscribed by a cracked and blistered leather belt.

The interview went well, which is to say she never asked whether I worked for Overt Intelligence, whereupon the whole show would have abruptly ended. She did not wish to discuss her old books, only her current project, a popular explanation of psychoanalytic theory to be called *From Misery to Unhappiness*. My shame was like a fever, threading my body with sharp, chilled wires. A toy train was not a lie, that clerk believed. Then maybe my little transmitter wasn't one either...

And maybe wishes were horses.

And maybe pigs had wings.

There was also this: Sherry Urquist was charming me. No doubt about it. A manufacturer of bestsellers is naturally stuffed with vapid thoughts and ready-made opinions, right? But instead I found myself sitting next to a first-rate mind (oh, the premier eroticism of intellect intersecting Rubens), one that could be severe with Freud for his lapses of integrity while still grasping his essential genius.

"You seem to love your work, Ms. Urquist."

"Writing is my life."

"Tell me, honestly — do you ever get any ideas for ... fiction?"

"Fiction?"

"Short stories. Novels."

"That would be suicidal, wouldn't it?"

A blind alley, but I expected as much.

The diciest moment occurred when Sherry asked in which issue the interview would be published, and I replied that I didn't know. True enough, I told myself. Since the thing would never see print at all, it was accurate to profess ignorance of the corresponding date. Still, there came a sudden, mercifully brief surge of unease, the tides of an ancient nausea ...

"All this sexual tension," I said, returning the pad and pencil to my suit jacket. "Alone with a sensually plump woman in her apartment, and your face is appealing too, now that I see the logic of it. You probably even have a bedroom. I can hardly stand it."

"Sensually plump, Mr. Prawn? I'm fat."

"Eye of the beholder."

"You'd have to go through a lot of beholders in my case."

"I find you very attractive." I did.

She raised her eyebrows, corrugating her brand. "It's only fair to give warning — you try anything funny, I'll knock you flat."

I cupped her left breast, full employment for any hand, and asked, "Is this funny?"

"On one level, your action offends me deeply." She brushed my knee. "I find it presumptuous, adolescent, and symptomatic of the worst kind of male arrogance." If faking her candor, she was certainly doing a god job. "On another level ... well, you *are* quite handsome."

"An Adonis analogue."

We kissed. She went for my belt buckle. Reaching under her blouse, I sent her bra on a well-deserved sabbatical.

"Any sexually-transmittable diseases?" she asked.

"None." I stroked her dry, stringy hair. The Trojan horse was poised to change history. "You?"

"No," she said.

The truth? I couldn't know.

To bed, then. Time to plant her and, concomitantly, the transmitter. Nice work if you can get it. I slowed myself down with irrelevant thoughts — dogs can talk, rain is red — and left her a satisfied woman.

Full of Greeks.

— • —

I had promised Gloria that I wouldn't just come to the party, I would attend the burn as well. Normally both parents were present, but Dixon's tropological scum-bucket of a father couldn't be bothered. It will take only an hour, Gloria had told me. I'd rather not, I replied. He's your nephew, for Christ's sake, she pointed out. All right, I said.

Burn hospitals were in practically every neighborhood, but Gloria insisted on the best, Veteran's Shock Institute. Taking Dixon's badly wrapped gift from the back seat, I started toward the building, a smoke-stained pile of bricks overlooking the Thomas More Bridge. I paused. Business first. In theory the transmitter was part of Sherry now, forever fixed to her uterine wall. Snug as a bug in a ... I went back to my Adequate and slid the sensorchart out of the dash. Yes, there she was, my fine Dissembler, a flashing red dot floating near Washington Park. I wished for greater detail, so I could know exactly when she was in her kitchen, her bathroom, her bedroom. Peeping Tom goes high tech. No matter. The thing worked. We could stalk her from here to Satan's backyard. As it were.

Inside the hospital, the day's collection of burn patients was every-where, hugging dads, clinging tearfully to moms' skirts. I'd never understood this child-worship nonsense our culture wallows in, but, even so, the whole thing started getting to me. Every eight-year-old had to do it, of course, and the disease was certainly worse than the cure. Still ...

I punished myself by biting my inner cheeks. Sympathy was fine, but sentimentality was wasteful. If I wanted to pity somebody, I should go up to Ward Six. Cystic fibrosis. Cancer. Am I going to die, Mommy?

Yes, dear.

Soon?

Yes, dear.

Will I see you in heaven?

Nobody knows.

I went to the front desk, where I learned that Dixon had been admitted half an hour earlier. "Room one-forty-five," said the nurse, a rotund man with a warty face. "The party will be in one-seventeen."

My nephew was already in the glass cubicle, dressed in a green smock and bound to the chair via leather thongs, one electrode strapped to his his left arm, another to his right leg. Black wires trailed from the copper terminals like threads spun by a carnivorous spider. He welcomed me with a brave smile, and I held up his gift, hefting it to show that it had substance, it wasn't clothes. A nice enough kid — what I knew of him. Cute freckles, a wide, apple face. I remembered that for somebody his age, Dixon understood a great deal of symbolic logic.

A young, willowy, female nurse entered the cubicle and began snugging the helmet over his cranium. I gave Dixon a thumbs-up signal. (Soon it will be over, kid. Pigs have wings, rats chase cats, all of it.)

"Thanks for coming." Drifting out of her chair, Gloria took my arm. She was an attractive woman — same genes as me — but today she looked lousy: the anticipation, the fear. Sweat collected in her forehead brand. I had stopped proposing incest years ago. Not her game. "You're his favorite uncle, you know."

Uncle Orville. God help me, I was actually present when Gloria's marriage collapsed. The three of us were sitting in a Reconstituted Burgers when suddenly she said, I sometimes worry that you're having an affair — are you? And Tom said, yes, he was. And Gloria said, you fucker. And Tom said, right. And Gloria asked how many. And Tom said lots. And Gloria asked why. Did he do it to strengthen the marriage? And Tom said no, he just liked to screw other women.

Clipboard in hand, a small, homely doctor with MERRICK affixed to his tunic waddled into the room. "Good afternoon, folks," he said, his cheer a precarious mix of the genuine and the forced. "Bitter cold day out, huh? How are we doing here?"

"Do you care?" my sister asked.

"Hard to say." Dr. Merrick fanned me with his clipboard. "Friend of the family?"

"My brother," Gloria explained.

"He has halitosis. Glad there are two of you." Merrick smiled at the boy in the cubicle. "With just one, the kid'll sometimes go into clinical depression on us." He pressed the clipboard toward Gloria. "Informed consent, right?"

"They told me all the possibilities." She studied the clipboard. "Cardiac —"

"Cardiac arrest, cerebral hemorrhage, respiratory failure, kidney damage," Merrick recited.

"When was the last time anything like that happened?"

"They killed a little girl down at Mount Sinai on Tuesday. A freak thing, but now and then we really screw up."

After patting Dixon on his straw-colored bangs, the nurse left the cubicle and told Dr. Merrick that she was going to get some coffee.

"Be back in ten minutes," he ordered.

"Oh, but of course." Such sarcasm from one so young. "We mustn't have a *doctor* cleaning up, not when we can get some underpaid nurse to do it."

Gloria scrawled her signature.

The nurse edged out of the room.

Dr. Merrick went to the control panel.

And then it began. This bar mitzvah of the human conscience, this electro-convulsive rite of passage. A hallowed tradition. An unvarying text. Today I am a man ... We believe in one Lord, Jesus Christ ... I pledge allegiance to the flag ... Why is this night different from all other nights ... Dogs can talk ... Pigs have wings. To tell you the truth, I was not really thinking about Dixon's cure just then. My mind was abloom with Sherry Urquist.

Merrick pushed a button, and PIGS HAVE WINGS appeared before my nephew on a lucite tachistoscope screen. "Can you hear me, lad?" the doctor called into the microphone.

Dixon opened his mouth, and a feeble "Yes" dribbled out of the loudspeaker.

"You see those words?" Merrick asked. The lurid red characters hovered in the air like lethargic butterflies.

"Y-yes."

"When I give the order, read them aloud. Okay?"

"Is it going to hurt?" my nephew quavered.

"It's going to hurt a lot. Will you read the words when I say so?"

"I'm scared. Do I have to?"

"You have to." Merrick rested a pudgy finger on the switch. "Now!"

"P-pigs have wings." The volts ripped through Dixon. He yelped and burst into tears. "But they don't," he moaned. "Pigs don't ... "

My own burn flooded back. The pain. The anger.

"You're right, lad — they don't." Merrick gave the voltage regulator a subtle twist, and Gloria flinched. "You did reasonably well, boy," the doctor continued. "We're not yet disappointed in you." He handed the mike to Gloria.

"Oh, yes, Dixon," she said. "Keep up the awfully good work."

"It's not fair." Sweat speckled Dixon's forehead. "I want to go home."

As Gloria surrendered the mike, TWO AND TWO MAKE FIVE materialized.

"Now, lad! Read it!"

"T-t-two and two make ... f-five." Lightning struck. The boy shuddered, howled. Blood rolled over his lower lip. During my own burn, I had practically bitten my tongue off. "I don't want this any more," he wailed.

"It's not a choice, lad."

"Two and two make *four*." Tears threaded Dixon's freckles together. "Please stop hurting me."

"Four. Right. Smart lad." Merrick cranked up the voltage. "Ready, Dixon? Here it comes."

HORSES HAVE SIX LEGS.

"Why do I have to do this? *Why*?"

"Everybody does it. All your friends."

"H-h-horses have ... have ... They have *four* legs, Dr. Merrick."

"Read the words, Dixon!"

"I hate you! I hate all of you!"

"Dixon!"

He raced through it. Zap. Two hundred volts. The boy began to cough and retch, and a string of white mucus shot from his mouth like a lizard's tongue. Nothing followed: burn patients fasted for sixteen hours prior to therapy.

"Too much!" cried Gloria. "Isn't that too much?"

"The goal is five hundred," said Merrick. "It's all been worked out. You want the treatment to take, don't you?"

"Mommy! Where's my Mommy?"

Gloria tore the mike away. "Right here, dear!"

"Mommy, make them stop!"

"I can't, dear. You must try to be brave."

The fourth lie appeared. Merrick upped the voltage. "Read it, lad!"

"No!"

"Read it!"

"Uncle Orville! I want Uncle Orville!"

My throat constricted, my stomach went sour. Uncle: such a strange sound. I really was one, wasn't I? "You're doing pretty swell, Dixon," I said, taking the mike. "I think you'll like your present."

"Uncle Orville, I want to go home!"

"I got you a fine toy."

"What is it?"

"Here's a hint. It has —"

"Dixon!" Merrick grabbed the mike. "Dixon, if you don't do this, you'll never get well. They'll take you away from your mother." A threat, but wholly accurate. "Understand? They'll take you away."

Dixon balled his face into a mass of wrinkles. "Grass!" he screamed, spitting blood. "Is!" he persisted. "Purple!" He jerked like a gaffed flounder, spasm after spasm. A broad urine stain blossomed on his crotch, and despite the obligatory enema a brown fluid dripped from the hem of his smock.

"Excellent!" Merrick increased the punishment to four hundred volts. "Your cure's in sight, lad!"

"No! Please! Please! Enough!" Sweat encased Dixon's face. Foam leaked from his mouth.

"You're almost halfway there!"

"Please!"

The war continued, five more pain-tipped rockets shooting through Dixon's nerves and veins, detonating inside his mind. He asserted that rats chase cats. He lied about money, saying that it grew on trees. Worms taste like honey, he said. Snow is hot. Rain is red.

He fainted just as the final lie arrived. Even before Gloria could scream, Merrick was inside the cubicle, checking the boy's heartbeat. A begrudging admiration seeped through me. The doctor had a job, and he did it.

A single dose of smelling salts brought Dixon around.

Guiding the boy's face toward the screen, Merrick turned to me. "Ready with the switch?"

"Huh? You want me —" Ridiculous.

"Let's just get it over with. Hit the switch when I tell you."

"I'd rather not." But already my finger rested on the damn thing. Doctor's orders.

"Read, Dixon," muttered Merrick.

"I c-can't."

"One more, Dixon. Just one more and you'll be a citizen."

Blood and spittle mingled on Dixon's chin. "You all hate me! Mommy hates me!"

"I love you as much as myself," said Gloria, leaning over my shoulder. "You're going to have a wonderful party. Almost certainly."

"Really?"

"Highly likely."

"Presumably wonderful," I said. The switch burned my finger. "I love you too."

"Dogs can talk," said Dixon.

And it truly was a wonderful party. All four of Dixon's grandparents showed up, along with his teacher and twelve of his friends, half of whom had been cured in recent months, one on the previous day. Dixon marched around Room 117 displaying the evidence of his burn like war medals. The brand, of course — performed under local anesthesia immediately after his cure — plus copies of his initial cerebroscan, voicegram, and fingerprint set.

Brand, scan, gram, prints: Sherry Urquist's had all been in perfect order. She had definitely been burned. And yet there was fiction in her garbage.

The gift-opening ceremony contained one bleak moment. Pulling the train from its wrapping, Dixon blanched, garroted by panic, and Gloria had to rush him into the bathroom, where he spent several minutes throwing up. I felt like a fool. To a boy who's just been through a brainburn, an electric train has gruesome connotations.

"Thanks for coming," said Gloria. She meant it.

"I *do* like my present," Dixon averred. "A freight train would have been nicer," he added. A citizen now.

I apologized for leaving early. A big case, I explained. Very hot, very political.

"Good-bye, Uncle Orville."

Uncle. Great stuff.

— • —

I spent the rest of the day tracking my adorable Dissembler, never letting her get more than a mile from me or closer than two blocks. What agonizing hopes that dot on the map inspired, what rampant expectations. With each flash my longing intensified. Oh, Sherry, Sherry, you pulsing red angel, you stroboscope of my desire. No mere adolescent infatuation this. I dared to speak its name. "Neurotic obsession," I gushed, kissing the dot as it crossed Aquinas Avenue. "Mixed with bald romantic fantasy and lust," I added. The radio shouted at me: a hot-blooded evangelist no less enraptured than I. "Does faith tempt you, my friends? Fear not! Look into your metaphoric hearts, and you will discover how subconscious human needs project themselves onto putative revelations!"

For someone facing a wide variety of deadlines, my quarry didn't push herself particularly hard. Sherry spent the hour from four to five at the Museum of Secondary Fossil Finds. From five to six she did the Imprisoned Animals Garden. From six to seven she treated herself to dinner at Danny's Digestibles, after which she went down to the waterfront.

I cruised along Third Street, twenty yards from the Pathogen River. This was the city's frankest district, a gray mass of warehouses and abandoned stores jammed together like dead cells waiting to be sloughed off. Sherry walked slowly, aimlessly, as if ... could it be? Yes, damn, as if arm-in-arm with another person, as if meshing her movements with those of a second, intertwined body. Probably she had met the guy at Danny's, a conceited pile of muscles named Guido or something, and now they were having a cozy stroll along the Pathogen. I pressed the dot, as if to draw

Sherry away. What if she spent the night in another apartment? That would pretty much cinch it. I wondered how their passion would register. I pictured the dot going wild, love's red fibrillation.

After pausing for several seconds on the bank, the dot suddenly began prancing across the river. Odd. I fixed on the map. The Saint Joan Tunnel was half a mile away, the Thomas More Bridge even farther. I doubted that she was swimming — not in this weather, and not in the Pathogen, where the diseases of the future were born. Flying, then? The dot moved too slowly to signify an airplane. A hot-air balloon? Probably she was in a boat. Sherry and Guido, off on a romantic cruise.

I hung a left on Beach Street and sped down to the docks. Moonlight coated the Pathogen, settling into the waves, figuratively bronzing a lone, swiftly moving tugboat. I checked the map. The dot placed Sherry at least ten yards from the tug, in the exact middle of the river and heading for the opposite shore. I studied her presumed location. Nothing. Submerged, then? I knew she hadn't committed suicide; the dot's progress was too resolute. Was she in scuba gear?

I abandoned the car and attempted to find where she had entered the water, a quest that took me down concrete steps to a pier hemmed by pylons smeared with gull dung. Jagged odors shot from the dead and rotting river; water lapped over the landing with a harsh sucking sound, as if a pride of invisible lions was drinking here. My gaze settled on a metal grate, barred like the ribcage of some promethean robot. It seemed slightly askew ... Oh, great, Orville, let's go traipsing through the sewers, with rats nipping at our heels and slugs the size of bagels falling on our shoulders. Terrific idea.

The grate yielded readily to my reluctant hands. Had she truly gone down there? Should I follow? A demented notion, but duty called, using its shrillest voice, and, beside, this was Sherry Urquist, this was irrational need. I secured a flashlight from the car and proceeded down the ladder. It was like entering a lung. Steamy, warm. The flashlight blazed through the blackness. A weapon, I decided. Look out, all you rats and slugs. Make way. Here comes Orville Prawn, the fastest flashlight in Veritas.

I moved through a multilayered maze of soggy holes and dripping cat-acombs. So many ways to descend: ladders, sloping tunnels, crooked little stairways — I used them all, soon moving beyond the riverbed into other territories, places not on the OIA map.

All around me Veritas's guts were spread: its concrete intestines, gushing lead veins, buzzing nerves of steel and gutta-percha. Much to my surprise, the city even had its parasites — shacks of corrugated tin leaned against the wet brick walls, sucking secretly on the power cables and water mains. This would not do. No, to live below Veritas like this, appropriating its juices, was little more than piracy. Overt Intelligence would hear of it.

My astonishment deepened as I advanced. I could understand a few hobos setting up a shantytown down here, but how might I explain these odd chunks of civilization? These blazing streetlamps, these freshly painted picket fences, these tidy grids of rose bushes, these fountains with their stone dolphins spewing water? Paint, flowers, sculpture: so many lies in one place! Peel back the streets of any city and do you find its warped reflection, its doppelgänger mirrored in distorting glass? Or did Veritas alone harbor such anarchy, this tumor spreading beneath her unsuspecting flesh?

A sleek white cat shot out of the rose bushes and disappeared down an open manhole. At first I thought that its pursuer was a dog, but no. Wrong shape. And that tail.

The shudder began in my lower spine and expanded.

A rat.

A rat the size of an armadillo.

Chasing a cat.

I moved on. Vegetable gardens now. Two bright yellow privies. Cottages defaced with gardenia plots and strings of clematis scurrying up trellises. A building that looked suspiciously like a chapel. A park of some kind, with flagstone paths and a duck pond. Ruddy puffs of vapor bumped against the treetops.

Rain is red ...

I entered the park.

A pig glided over my head like a miniature dirigible, wheeling across the sky on cherub wings. At first I assumed it was a machine, but its squeal was disconcertingly organic.

"You!"

A low, liquid voice. I dropped my gaze.

Sherry shared the bench with an enormous dog, some grotesque variation on the malamute, his chin snugged into her lap. "You!" she said again, erecting the word like a barrier, a spiked vocable stopping my approach. The dog lifted his heard and growled.

"Correct," I said, stock still.

"You followed me?"

"I cannot tell a lie." I examined the nearest tree. No fruit, of course, only worms and paper money.

"Dirty spy."

"Half true. I am not dirty."

She wore a buttercup dress, decorated with lace. Her thick braid lay on her shoulder like a loaf of challah. Her eyes had become cartoons of themselves, starkly outlined and richly shaded. "If you try to return" — she patted the malamute — "Max will eat you alive."

"You bet your sweet ass," said the dog.

She massaged Max's head, as if searching for the trigger that would release his attack. "I expected better of you, Mr. Prawn."

We were in a contest. Who could act the more betrayed, the more disgusted? "I'd always assumed the Dissemblage was just a group." Spit dripped off my words. "I didn't know it was ... all this."

"Two cities," muttered Sherry, launching her index finger upward. "Truth above, dignity below." The finger descended. Her nails, I noticed, were a fluorescent green.

"Her father built it," explained the dog.

"His life's work," added Sherry.

"Are there many of you?" I asked.

"I'm the first to reach adulthood," said Sherry.

"The prototype liar?"

Her sneer evolved into a grin. "Others are hatching."

"How can you betray your city like this?" I drilled her with my stare. "Veritas, who nurtured you, suckled you?"

"Shall I kill him now?" asked the dog.

Sherry chucked Max under the chin, told him to be patient. "Veritas did not suckle me." Her gesture encompassed the entire park and, by extension, the whole of Veritas's twisted double. "*This* was my cradle — my nursery." She took a lipstick from her purse. "It's not hard to make a lie. The money trees are props. The rats and pigs trace to avant-garde microbiology."

"All I needed were vocal cords," said the dog.

She began touching up her lips. "Thanks to my father, I reached my eighth birthday knowing that pigs had wings, that snow was hot, that two and two equaled five, that worms tasted like honey ... all of it. So when my burn came —"

"You were incurable," I said. "You walked away from the hospital ready to swindle and cheat and —"

"Write fiction. Four novels so far. Maybe you'd like to read them. You might be a bureaucratic drudge, but I'm fond of you, Orville."

"How do I know you're telling the truth?"

"You don't. And when my cadre takes over and the burn ends — it won't be hard, we'll lie our way to the top — when that happens, you won't know when *anybody's* telling the truth."

"Right," said the dog, leaping off the bench.

"Truth is beauty," I said.

Sherry winced. "My father did not mind telling the truth." Here she became an actress, that consummate species of liar, dragging out her lines.

"But he hated his inability to do otherwise. Honesty without choice, he said, is slavery with a smile."

A glorious adolescent girl rode through the park astride a six-legged horse, her skin dark despite her troglodytic upbringing, her eyes alive with deceit. The *gift* of deceit, as Sherry would have it. I wondered whether Dixon was playing with his electric chain just then. Probably not. Past his bedtime. I kept envisioning his cerebrum, brocaded with necessary scars.

Sherry patted the spot where the dog had been, and I sat down cautiously. "Care for one?" she asked, plucking a worm off a money tree.

"No."

"Go ahead. Try it."

"Well ... "

"Open your mouth and close your eyes."

The creature wriggled on my tongue, and I bit down. Pure honey. Sweet, smooth, but I did not enjoy it.

Truth above, dignity below. My index finger throbbed, prickly with that irrevocable little tug of the switch in Room 145. Five hundred volts was a lot, but what was the alternative? To restore the age of thievery and fraud?

History has it I joined Sherry's city that very night. A lie, but what do you expect — all the books are written by Dissemblers. True, sometime before dawn I did push my car into the river, the better to elude Overt Intelligence. But fully a week went by before I told Sherry about her internal transmitter. She was furious. She vowed to have the thing cut out. Go ahead, I told her, do it — but don't expect my blessing. That's another thing the historians got wrong. They say I paid for the surgery.

Call me a traitor. Call me a coward. Call me love's captive. I have called myself all these things. But — really — I did not join Sherry's city that night. That night I merely sat on a park bench staring into her exotically adorned eyes, fixing on her bright lips, holding her fluorescent fingertips.

"I want to believe whatever you tell me," I said.

"Then you'll need to have faith in me," she said.

"It's raining," noted the dog, and then he launched into a talking-dog joke.

"My cottage is over there." Sherry replaced her lipstick in her purse. She tossed her wondrous braid over her shoulder.

We rose and started across the park, hand in hand, lost in the sweet uncertainty of the moment, oblivious to the chattering dark and the lashing wind and bright red rain dancing on the purple grass. ■

"A HISTORY OF THE TWENTIETH CENTURY, WITH ILLUSTRATIONS"

BY KIM STANLEY ROBINSON

Kim Stanley Robinson (born 1952 in Waukegan, Illinois) grew up in Southern California, a region in which much of his fiction is set, notably in what is often called "The Orange County trilogy": the acclaimed and multiple-award-nominated novels *The Wild Shore* (1984), *The Gold Coast* (1988), and *Pacific Edge* (1990, a John W. Campbell Memorial Award Best Novel winner). These books envisioned humanity struggling to reinvent civilization after its collapse in a future California, and they heralded the arrival of a new master of disaster. Among his finest eco-thriller novels in which his characters face disaster and strive against bureaucracy, willful ignorance, and well-intentioned sabotage we must include his multiple-award-winning "Mars trilogy," consisting of *Red*

Mars (1992), *Green Mars* (1993), and *Blue Mars* (1996); and, blending the catastrophe of global warming with breathtaking adventure and romance in a way that nobody except Robinson could, the series including *Antarctica* (1997), *Forty Signs of Rain* (2004), *Fifty Degrees Below* (2005), and *Sixty Days and Counting* (2007). His highly praised shorter works include "Black Air" (1984), a World Fantasy Best Novella winner, and "The Blind Geometer" (1988), a Nebula Best Novella winner.

Often a very funny writer, here his humor is wry and black (for example, in a comparison of "small" wars following the World Wars, his character, Frank, comments: "Improvement of a sort"). As in much of Robinson's fiction, the portrayal of disasters, like barrages of information, are beyond Frank's control and yet compel him to respond to and interpret them. Note, also, the many ways in which Robinson uses light and darkness to punch up his protagonist's evolution from a dark mood to a state of enlightenment.

"A HISTORY OF THE TWENTIETH CENTURY, WITH ILLUSTRATIONS"

"If truth is not to be found on the shelves of the British Museum,
where, I asked myself, picking up a notebook and a pencil, is truth?"
— Virginia Woolf

DAILY DOSES OF BRIGHT LIGHT MARKEDLY IMPROVE THE MOOD of people suffering from depression, so every day at eight in the evening Frank Churchill went to the clinic on Park Avenue, and sat for three hours in a room illuminated with sixteen hundred watts of white light. This was not exactly like having the sun in the room, but it was bright, about the same as if sixteen bare lightbulbs hung from the ceiling. In this case the bulbs were probably long tubes, and they were hidden behind a sheet of white plastic, so it was the whole ceiling that glowed.

He sat at a table and doodled with a purple pen on a pad of pink paper. And then it was eleven and he was out on the windy streets, blinking as traffic lights swam in the gloom. He walked home to a hotel room in the west Eighties. He would return to the clinic at five the next morning for a predawn treatment, but now it was time to sleep. He looked forward to that. He'd been on the treatment for three weeks, and he was tired. Though the treatment did seem to be working — as far as he could tell; improvement was supposed to average twenty percent a week, and he wasn't sure what that would feel like.

In his room the answering machine was blinking. There was a message from his agent, asking him to call immediately. It was now nearly midnight, but he push buttoned the number and his agent answered on the first ring.

"You have DSPS," Frank said to him.

"What? What?"

"Delayed sleep phase syndrome. I know how to get rid of it."

"Frank! Look, Frank, I've got a good offer for you."

"Do you have a lot of lights on?"

"What? Oh, yeah, say, how's that going?"

"I'm probably sixty percent better."

"Good, good. Keep at it. Listen, I've got something should help you a hundred percent. A publisher in London wants you to go over there and write a book on the twentieth century."

"What kind of book?"

"Not your usual thing, Frank, but this time putting together the big picture. Reflecting on all the rest of your books, so to speak. They want to bring it out in time for the turn of the century, and go oversize, use lots of illustrations, big print run —"

"A coffee table book?"

"People'll want it on their coffee tables, sure, but it's not —"

"I don't want to write a coffee table book."

"Frank —"

"What do they want, ten thousand words?"

"They want thirty thousand words, Frank. And they'll pay a hundred thousand pound advance."

That gave him pause.

"Why so much?"

"They're new to publishing, they come from computers and this is the kind of numbers they're used to. It's a different scale."

"That's for sure. I still don't want to do it."

"Frank, come on, you're the one for this! The only successor to Barbara Tuchman!" That was a blurb found on paperback editions of his work. "They want you in particular — I mean, Churchill on the twentieth century, ha ha. It's a natural."

"I don't want to do it."

"Come on, Frank. You could use the money, I thought you were having trouble with the payments —"

"Yeah yeah." Time for a different tack. "I'll think it over."

"They're in a hurry, Frank."

"I thought you said turn of the century!"

"I did, but there's going to be a lot of this kind of book then, and they want to beat the rush. Set the standard and then keep it in print for a few years. It'll be great."

"It'll be remaindered within a year. Remaindered before it even comes out, if I know coffee table books."

His agent sighed. "Come on, Frank. You can use the money. As for the book, it'll be as good as you make it, right? You've been working on this stuff your whole career, and here's your chance to sum up. And you've got a lot of readers, people will listen to you." Concern made him shrill: "Don't let what's happened get you so down that you miss an opportunity like this! Work is the best cure for depression anyway. And this is your chance to influence how we think about what's happened!"

"With a coffee table book?"

"God damn it, don't think of it that way!"

"How should I think of it."

His agent took a deep breath, let it out, spoke very slowly. "Think of it as a hundred thousand pounds, Frank."

His agent did not understand.

— • —

Nevertheless, the next morning as he sat under the bright white ceiling, doodling with a green pen on yellow paper, he decided to go to England. He didn't want to sit in that room anymore; it scared him, because he suspected it might not be working. He was not sixty percent better. And he didn't want to shift to drug therapy. They had found nothing wrong with his brain, no physical problems at all, and though that meant little, it did make him resistant to the idea of drugs. He had his reasons and he wanted his feelings!

The light room technician thought that this attitude was a good sign in itself. "Your serotonin level is normal, right? So it's not that bad. Besides London's a lot farther north than New York, so you pick up the light you lose here. And if you need more you can always head north again, right?"

— • —

He called Charles and Rya Dowland to ask if he could stay with them. It turned out they were leaving for Florida the next day, but they invited him to stay anyway; they liked having their flat occupied while they were gone. Frank had done that before, he still had the key on his key-ring. "Thanks," he said. It would be better this way, actually. He didn't feel like talking.

So he packed his backpack, including camping gear with the clothes, and the next morning flew to London. It was strange how one travelled these days: he got into a moving chamber outside his hotel, then shifted from one chamber to the next for several hours, only stepping outdoors again when he emerged from the Camden tube station, some hundred yards from Charles and Rya's flat.

The ghost of his old pleasure brushed him as he crossed Camden High Street and walked by the cinema, listening to London's voices. This had been his method for years: come to London, stay with Charles and Rya until he found digs, do his research and writing at the British Museum, visit the used bookstores at Charing Cross, spend the evenings at Charles and Rya's, watching TV and talking. It had been that way for four books, over the course of twenty years.

The flat was located above a butcher shop. Every wall in it was covered with stuffed bookshelves, and there were shelves nailed up over the toilet, the bath, and the head of the guest bed. In the unlikely event of an earthquake the guest would be buried in a hundred histories of London.

Frank threw his pack on the guest bed and went past the English poets downstairs. The living room was nearly filled by a table stacked with papers and books. The side street below was an open-air produce market, and he could hear the voices of the vendors as they packed up for the day. The sun hadn't set, though it was past nine; these late May days were already long. It was almost like still being in therapy.

He went downstairs and bought vegetables and rice, then went back up and cooked them. The kitchen windows were the color of sunset, and the little flat glowed, evoking its owners so strongly that it was almost as if they were there. Suddenly he wished they were.

After eating he turned on the CD player and put on some Handel. He opened the living room drapes and settled into Charles's armchair, a glass of Bulgarian wine in his hand, an open notebook on his knee. He watched salmon light leak out of the clouds to the north, and tried to think about the causes of the First World War.

— • —

In the morning he woke to the dull *thump thump thump* of frozen slabs of meat being rendered by an axe. He went downstairs and ate cereal while leafing through *The Guardian*, then took the tube to Tottenham Court Road and walked to the British Museum.

Because of *The Belle Époque* he had already done his research on the pre-war period, but writing in the British Library was a ritual he didn't want to break; it made him part of a tradition, back to Marx and beyond. He showed his still-valid reader's ticket to a librarian and then found an empty seat in his usual row; in fact he had written much of *Entre Deux Guerres* in that very carrel, under the frontal lobes of the great skull dome. He opened a notebook and stared at the page. Slowly he wrote, *1900 to 1914*. Then he stared at the page.

His earlier book had tended to focus on the sumptuous excesses of the pre-war European ruling class, as a young and clearly leftist reviewer in *The Guardian* had rather sharply pointed out. To the extent that he had delved into the causes of the Great War, he had subscribed to the usual theory; that it had been the result of rising nationalism, diplomatic brinksmanship, and several deceptive precedents in the previous two decades. The Spanish-American War, the Russo-Japanese War, and the two Balkan wars had all remained localized and non-catastrophic; and there had been several "incidents," the Moroccan affair and the like, that had brought the two great alliances to the brink, but not toppled them over. So when Austria-Hungary made impossible demands to Serbia after the assassination of Ferdinand, no one could have known that the situation would domino into the trenches and their slaughter.

History as accident. Well, no doubt there was a lot of truth in that. But now he found himself thinking of the crowds in the streets of all the major cities, cheering the news of the war's outbreak; of the disappearance of pacifism, which had seemed such a force; of, in short, the apparently unanimous support for war among the prosperous citizens of the European powers. Support for a war that had no real reason to be!

There was something irreducibly mysterious about that, and this time he decided he would admit it, and discuss it. That would require a consideration of the preceding century, the *Pax Europeana*; which in fact had been a century of bloody subjugation, the high point of imperialism, with most of the world falling to the great powers. These powers had prospered at the expense of their colonies, who had suffered in abject misery. Then the powers had spent their profits building weapons, and used the weapons on each other, and destroyed themselves. There was something weirdly just about that development, as when a mass murderer finally turns the gun on himself. Punishment, an end to guilt, an end to pain. Could that really explain it? While staying in Washington with his dying father, Frank had visited the Lincoln Memorial, and there on the right hand wall had been Lincoln's Second Inaugural Address, carved in capital letters with the commas omitted, an oddity which somehow added to the speech's Biblical massiveness, as when it spoke of the ongoing war. "YET IF GOD WILLS THAT IT CONTINUE UNTIL ALL THIS WEALTH PILED BY THE BONDSMAN'S TWO HUNDRED AND FIFTY YEARS OF UNRE-QUITED TOIL SHALL BE SUNK AND UNTIL EVERY DROP OF BLOOD DRAWN WITH THE LASH SHALL BE PAID BY ANOTHER DRAWN WITH THE SWORD AS WAS SAID THREE THOUSAND YEARS AGO SO STILL IT MUST BE SAID 'THE JUDGMENTS OF THE LORD ARE TRUE AND RIGHTEOUS ALTOGETHER.'"

A frightening thought, from that dark part of Lincoln that was never far from the surface. But as a theory of the Great War's origin it still struck him as inadequate. It was possible to believe it of the kings and presidents, the generals and diplomats, the imperial officers around the world; they had known what they were doing, and so might have been impelled by unconscious guilt to mass suicide. But the common citizen at home, ecstatic in the streets at the outbreak of general war? That seemed more likely to be just another manifestation of the hatred of the other. All my problems are your fault! He and Andrea had said that to each other a lot. Everyone did.

And yet ... it still seemed to him that the causes were eluding him, as they had everyone else. Perhaps it was a simple pleasure in destruction. What is the primal response to an edifice? Knock it down. What is the primal response to a stranger? Attack him.

But he was losing his drift, falling away into the metaphysics of "human nature." That would be a constant problem in an essay of this length. And whatever the causes, there stood the year 1914, irreducible, inexplicable, unchangeable. "AND THE WAR CAME."

— • —

In his previous books he had never written about the wars. He was among those who believed that real history occurred in peacetime, and that in war you might as well roll dice or skip ahead to the peace treaty. For anyone but a military historian, what was interesting would begin again only when the war ended.

Now he wasn't so sure. Current views of the Belle Époque were distorted because one only saw it through the lens of the war that ended it; which meant that the Great War was somehow more powerful than the Belle Époque, or at least more powerful than he had thought. It seemed he would have to write about it, this time, to make sense of the century. And so he would have to research it.

He walked up to the central catalogue tables. The room darkened as the sun went behind clouds, and he felt a chill.

— • —

For a long time the numbers alone staggered him. To overwhelm trench defenses, artillery bombardments of the most astonishing size were brought to bear. On the Somme the British put a gun every twenty yards along a fourteen-mile front, and hurled a million and a half shells. In April 1917 the French fired six million shells. The Germans' Big Bertha shot shells seventy-five miles high, essentially into space. Verdun was a "battle" that lasted ten months, and killed almost a million men.

The British section of the front was ninety miles long. Every day of the war, about seven thousand men along that front were killed or wounded — not in any battle in particular, but just as the result of incidental sniper fire or bombardment. It was called "wastage."

Frank stopped reading, his mind suddenly filled with the image of the Vietnam Memorial. He had visited it right after leaving the Lincoln Memorial, and the sight of all those names engraved on the black granite plates had powerfully affected him. For a moment it had seemed possible to imagine all those people, a little white line for each.

But at the end of every month or two of the Great War, the British had had a whole Vietnam Memorial's worth of dead. Every month or two, for fifty-one months.

— • —

He filled out book request slips and gave them to the librarians in the central ring of desks, then picked up the books he had requested the day before and took them back to his carrel. He skimmed the books and took notes, mostly writing down figures and statistics. British factories produced two hundred and fifty million shells. The major battles all killed a half million or more. About ten million men died on the field of battle, ten million more by revolution, disease, and starvation.

Occasionally he would stop reading and try to write; but he never got far. Once he wrote several pages on the economy of the war. The organization of agriculture and business, especially in Germany under Rathenau and England under Lloyd George, reminded him very strongly of the postmodern economy now running things. One could trace the roots of late capitalism to Great War innovations found in Rathenau's *Kriegsrohstoffabteilung* (the "War Raw Stuff Department"), or in his *Zentral Einkauf-Gesellsschaft*. All business had been organized to fight the enemy; but when the war was over and the enemy vanquished, the organization remained. People continued to sacrifice the fruits of their work, but now they did it for the corporations that had taken the wartime governments' positions in the system.

So much of the twentieth century, there already in the Great War. And then the Armistice was signed, at eleven A.M. on November 11th, 1918. That morning at the front the two sides exchanged bombardments as usual, so that by eleven A.M. many people had died.

That evening Frank hurried home, just beating a thundershower. The air was as dark as smoky glass.

— • —

And the war never ended.

This idea, that the two world wars were actually one, was not original to him. Winston Churchill said it at the time, as did the Nazi Alfred Rosenberg. They saw the twenties and thirties as an interregnum, a pause to regroup in the middle of a two-part conflict. The eye of a hurricane.

Nine o'clock one morning and Frank was still at the Dowlands', lingering over cereal and paging through *The Guardian*, and then through his notebooks. Every morning he seemed to get a later start, and although it was May, the days didn't seem to be getting any longer. Rather the reverse.

There were arguments against the view that it was a single war. The twenties did not seem very ominous, at least after the Treaty of Locarno in 1925: Germany had survived its financial collapse, and everywhere economic recovery seemed strong. But the thirties showed the real state of things: the Depression, the new democracies falling to fascism, the brutal Spanish Civil War; the starvation of the kulaks; the terrible sense of fatality in the air. The sense of slipping on a slope, falling helplessly back into war.

But this time it was different. *Total War.* German military strategists had coined the phrase in the 1890s, while analyzing Sherman's campaign in Georgia. And they felt they were waging total war when they torpedoed neutral ships in 1915. But they were wrong; the Great War was not total war. In 1914 the rumor that German soldiers had killed eight Belgian nuns was enough to shock all civilization, and later when the Lusitania was sunk, objections were so fierce that the Germans agreed to leave passenger ships alone. This could only happen in a world where people still held the notion that in war armies fought armies and soldiers killed soldiers, while civilians suffered privation and perhaps got killed accidentally, but were never deliberately targeted. This was how European wars had been fought for centuries: diplomacy by other means.

In 1939, this changed. Perhaps it changed only because the capability for total war had emerged from the technological base, in the form of mass long-range aerial bombardment. Perhaps on the other hand it was a matter of learning the lessons of the Great War, digesting its implications. Stalin's murder of the kulaks, for instance: five million Ukrainian peasants, killed because Stalin wanted to collectivize agriculture. Food was deliberately shipped out of that bread basket region, emergency supplies withheld, hidden stockpiles destroyed; and several thousand villages disappeared as all their occupants starved. This was total war.

— • —

Every morning Frank leafed around in the big catalogue volumes, as if he might find some other twentieth century. He filled out his slips, picked up the books requested the previous day, took them back to his carrel. He spent more time reading than writing. The days were cloudy, and it was dim under the great dome. His notes were getting scrambled. He had stopped working in chronological order, and kept returning compulsively to the Great War, even though the front wave of his reading was well into World War Two.

Twenty million had died in the first war, fifty million in the second. Civilian deaths made the bulk of the difference. Near the end of the war, thousands of bombs were dropped on cities in the hope of starting firestorms, in which the atmosphere itself was in effect ignited, as in Dresden, Berlin, Tokyo. Civilians were the target now, and strategic bombing made them easy to hit. Hiroshima and Nagasaki were in that sense a kind of exclamation point, at the end of a sentence which the war had been saying all along: we will kill your families at home. War is war, as Sherman said; if you want peace, surrender! And they did.

After two bombs. Nagasaki was bombed three days after Hiroshima, before the Japanese had time to understand the damage and respond. Dropping the bomb on Hiroshima was endlessly debated in the literature, but Frank found few who even attempted a defense of Nagasaki. Truman and his advisors did it, people said, to a) show Stalin they had more than one bomb, and b) show Stalin that they would use the bomb even as a threat or warning only, as Nagasaki demonstrated. A Vietnam Memorial's worth of civilians in an instantaneous flash, just so Stalin would take Truman seriously. Which he did.

When the crew of the *Enola Gay* landed, they celebrated with a barbeque.

— • —

In the evenings Frank sat in the Dowlands' flat in silence. He did not read, but watched the evening summer light leak out of the sky to the north. The days were getting shorter. He needed the therapy, he could feel it. More light! Someone had said that on their deathbed — Newton, Galileo, Spinoza, someone like that. No doubt they had been depressed at the time.

He missed Charles and Rya. He would feel better, he was sure, if he had them there to talk with. That was the thing about friends, after all: they lasted and you could talk. That was the definition of friendship.

But Charles and Rya were in Florida. And in the dusk he saw that the walls of books in the flat functioned like lead lining in a radioactive environment, all those recorded thoughts forming a kind of shield against poisonous reality. The best shield available, perhaps.

But now it was failing, at least for him; the books appeared to be nothing more than their spines.

And then one evening in a premature blue sunset it seemed that the whole flat had gone transparent, and that he was sitting in an armchair, suspended over a vast and shadowy city.

— • —

The Holocaust, like Hiroshima and Nagasaki, had precedents. Russians with Ukrainians, Turks with Armenians, white settlers with native Americans. But the mechanized efficiency of the Germans' murder of the Jews was something new and horrible. There was a book in his stack on the designers of the death camps, the architects, engineers, builders. Were these functionaries less or more obscene than the mad doctors, the sadistic guards? He couldn't decide.

And then there was the sheer number of them, the six million. It was hard to comprehend it. He read that there was a library in Jerusalem where they had taken on the task of recording all they could find about every one of the six million. Walking up Charing Cross Road that afternoon he thought of that and stopped short. All those names in one library, another transparent room, another memorial. For a second he caught a glimpse of how many people that was, a whole London's worth. Then it faded and he was left on a street corner, looking both ways to make sure he didn't get run over.

As he continued walking he tried to calculate how many Vietnam Memorials it would take to list the six million. Roughly two per hundred thousand; thus twenty per million. So, one hundred and twenty. Count them one by one, step by step.

— • —

He took to hanging out through the evenings in pubs. The Wellington was as good as any, and was frequented occasionally by some acquaintances he had met through Charles and Rya. He sat with them and listened to them talk, but often he found himself distracted by his day's reading. So the conversations tumbled along without him, and the Brits, slightly more tolerant than Americans of eccentricity, did not make him feel unwelcome.

The pubs were noisy and filled with light. Scores of people moved about in them, talking, smoking, drinking. A different kind of lead-lined room. He didn't drink beer, and so at first remained sober; but then he discovered the hard cider that pubs carried. He liked it and drank it like the others drank their beer, and got quite drunk. After that he sometimes became very talkative, telling the rest things about the twentieth century that they already knew, and they would nod and contribute some other bit of information, to be polite, then change the subject back to whatever they had been discussing before, gently and without snubbing him.

But most of the time when he drank he only got more remote from their talk, which jumped about faster than he could follow. And each morning after, he would wake late and slow, head pounding, the day already there and a lot of the morning light missed in sleep. Depressives were not supposed to drink at all. So finally he quit going to the Wellington, and instead ate at the pubs closest to the Dowlands'. One was called The Halfway House, the other World's End, a poor choice as far as names were concerned, but he ate at World's End anyway, and afterwards would sit at a corner table and nurse a whisky and stare at page after page of notes, chewing the end of a pen to plastic shrapnel.

— • —

The Fighting Never Stopped, as one book's title put it. But the atomic bomb meant that the second half of the century looked different than the first. Some, Americans for the most part, called it the *Pax Americana*. But most called it the Cold War, 1945-1989. And not that cold, either. Under the umbrella of the superpower stalemate local conflicts flared everywhere, wars which compared to the two big ones looked small; but there had been over a hundred of them all told, killing about 350,000 people a year, for a total of around fifteen million, some said twenty; it was hard to count. Most occurred in the big ten: the two Vietnam wars, the two Indo-Pakistan wars, the Korean war, the Algerian war, the civil war in Sudan, the massacres in Indonesia in 1965, the Biafran war, and the Iran-Iraq war. Then another ten million civilians had been starved by deliberate military action; so that the total for the period was about the equal of the Great War itself. Though it had taken ten times as long to compile. Improvement of a sort.

And thus perhaps the rise of atrocity war, as if the horror of individualized murders could compensate for the lack of sheer number. And maybe it could; because now his research consisted of a succession of accounts and color photos of rape, dismemberment, torture — bodies of individual people, in their own clothes, scattered on the ground in pools of blood. Vietnamese villages, erupting in napalm. Cambodia, Uganda, Tibet — Tibet was genocide again, paced to escape the world's notice, a few villages destroyed every year in a process called *thamzing*, or re-education: the villages seized by the Chinese and the villagers killed by a variety of methods, "burying alive, hanging, beheading, disemboweling, scalding, crucifixion, quartering, stoning, small children forced to shoot their parents; pregnant women given forced abortions, the fetuses piled in mounds on the village squares."

— • —

Meanwhile power on the planet continued to shift into fewer hands. The Second World War had been the only thing to successfully end the

Depression, a fact leaders remembered; so the economic consolidation begun in the First War continued through the Second War and the Cold War, yoking the whole world into a war economy.

At first 1989 had looked like a break away from that. But now, just seven years later, the Cold War losers all looked like Germany in 1922, their money worthless, their shelves empty, their democracies crumbling to juntas. Except this time the juntas had corporate sponsors; multinational banks ran the old Soviet bloc just as they did the Third World, with "austerity measures" enforced in the name of "the free market," meaning half the world went to sleep hungry every night to pay off debts to millionaires. While temperatures still rose, populations still soared, "local conflicts" still burned in twenty different places.

One morning Frank lingered over cereal, reluctant to leave the flat. He opened *The Guardian* and read that the year's defense budgets worldwide would total around a trillion dollars. "More light," he said, swallowing hard. It was a dark, rainy day. He could feel his pupils enlarging, making the effort. The days were surely getting shorter, even though it was May; and the air was getting darker, as if London's Victorian fogs had returned, coal smoke in the fabric of reality.

He flipped the page and started an article on the conflict in Sri Lanka. Singhalese and Tamils had been fighting for a generation now, and some time in the previous week, a husband and wife had emerged from their house in the morning to find the heads of their six sons arranged on their lawn. He threw the paper aside and walked through soot down the streets.

— • —

He got to the British Museum on automatic pilot. Waiting for him at the top of the stack was a book containing estimates of total war deaths for the century. About a hundred million people.

He found himself on the dark streets of London again, thinking of numbers. All day he walked, unable to gather his thoughts. And that night as he fell asleep the calculations returned, in a dream or a hypnogogic vision: it would take two thousand Vietnam Memorials to list the century's war dead. From above he saw himself walking the Mall in Washington, D.C., and the whole park from the Capitol to the Lincoln Memorial was dotted with the black Vs of Vietnam Memorials, as if a flock of giant stealth birds had landed on it. All night he walked past black wing walls, moving west toward the white tomb on the river.

— • —

The next day the first book on the stack concerned the wars between China and Japan, 1931-1945. Like most of Asian history this war was poorly remembered in the West, but it had been huge. The whole Korean nation became in effect a slave labor camp in the Japanese war effort, and the Japanese concentration camps in Manchuria had killed as many Chinese as the Germans had killed Jews. These deaths included thousands in the style of Mengele and the Nazi doctors, caused by "scientific" medical torture. Japanese experimenters had, for instance, performed transfusions in which they drained Chinese prisoners of their blood and replaced it with horses' blood, to see how long the prisoners would live. Survival rates varied from twenty minutes to six hours, with the subjects in agony throughout.

Frank closed that book and put it down. He picked the next one out of the gloom and peered at it. A heavy old thing, bound in dark green leather, with a dull gold pattern inlaid on the spine and boards. *A History of the Nineteenth Century, with Illustrations* — the latter tinted photos, their colors faded and dim. Published in 1902 by George Newnes Ltd; last century's equivalent of his own project, apparently. Curiosity about that had caused him to request the title. He opened it and thumbed through, and on the last page the text caught his eye: "I believe that Man is good. I believe that we stand at the dawn of a century that will be more peaceful and prosperous than any in history."

— • —

He put down the book and left the British Museum. In a red phone box he located the nearest car rental agency, an Avis outlet near Westminster. He took the Tube and walked to this agency, and there he rented a blue Ford Sierra station wagon. The steering wheel was on the right, of course. Frank had never driven in Great Britain before, and he sat behind the wheel trying to hide his uneasiness from the agent. The clutch, brake, and gas pedal were left to right as usual, thank God. And the gear shift was arranged the same, though one did have to operate it with the left hand.

Awkwardly he shoved the gearshift into first and drove out of the garage, turning left and driving down the left side of the street. It was weird. But the oddity of sitting on the right insured that he wouldn't forget the necessity of driving on the left. He pulled to the curb and perused the Avis street map of London, plotted a course, got back in traffic, and drove to Camden High Street. He parked below the Dowlands' and went upstairs and packed, then took his backpack down to the car. He returned to leave a note: *Gone to the land of the midnight sun.* Then he went down to the car and drove north, onto highways and out of London.

— • —

It was a wet day, and low full clouds brushed over the land, dropping here a black broom of rain, there a Blakean shaft of sunlight. The hills were green, and the fields yellow or brown or light green. At first there were a lot of hills, a lot of fields. Then the highway swung by Birmingham and Manchester, and he drove by fields of row houses, line after line after line of them, on narrow treeless streets — all orderly and neat, and yet still among the bleakest human landscapes he had ever seen. Streets like trenches. Certainly the world was being overrun. Population densities must be near the levels set in those experiments on rats which had caused the rats to go insane. It was as good an explanation as any. Mostly males affected, in both cases: territorial hunters, bred to kill for food, now trapped in little boxes. They had gone mad. "I believe that Man is this or that," the Edwardian author had written, and why not; it couldn't be denied that it was mostly men's doing. The planning, the diplomacy, the fighting, the raping, the killing.

The obvious thing to do was to give the running of the world over to women. There was Thatcher in the Falklands and Indira Gandhi in Bangladesh, it was true; but still it would be worth trying, it could hardly get worse! And given the maternal instinct, it would probably be better. Give every first lady her husband's job. Perhaps every woman her man's job. Let the men care for the children, for five thousand years or fifty thousand, one for every year of murderous patriarchy.

— • —

North of Manchester he passed giant radio towers, and something that looked like nuclear reactor stacks. Fighter jets zoomed overhead. The twentieth century. Why hadn't that Edwardian author been able to see it coming? Perhaps the future was simply unimaginable, then and always. Or perhaps things hadn't looked so bad in 1902. The Edwardian, looking forward in a time of prosperity, saw more of the same; instead there had followed a century of horrors. Now one looked forward from a time of horrors; so that, by analogy, what was implied for the next century was grim beyond measure. And with the new technologies of destruction, practically anything was possible: chemical warfare, nuclear terrorism, biological holocaust; victims killed by nano-assassins flying through them, or by viruses in their drinking supply, or by a particular ringing of their telephone; or reduced to zombies by drugs or brain implants, torture or nerve gas; or simply dispatched with bullets, or starved; hi-tech, low-tech, the methods were endless. And the motivations would be stronger than ever; with populations rising and resources depleted; people were going to be fighting not to rule, but to survive. Some little country threatened with defeat could unleash an epidemic against its rival and accidentally kill off a continent, or everyone, it was entirely possible. The twenty-first century might make the twentieth look like nothing at all.

— · —

He would come to after reveries like that and realize that twenty or thirty or even sixty miles had passed without him seeing a thing of the outside world. Automatic pilot, on roads that were reversed! He tried to concentrate.

He was somewhere above Carlisle. The map showed two possible routes to Edinburgh: one left the highway just below Glasgow, while a smaller road left sooner and was much more direct. He chose the direct route and took an exit into a roundabout and onto the A702, a two lane road heading northeast. Its black asphalt was wet with rain, and the clouds rushing overhead were dark. After several miles he passed a sign that said "Scenic Route," which suggested he had chosen the wrong road, but he was unwilling to backtrack. It was probably as fast to go this way by now, just more work: frequent roundabouts, villages with traffic lights, and narrow stretches where the road was hemmed by hedges or walls. Sunset was near, he had been driving for hours; he was tired, and when black trucks rushed at him out of the spray and shadows it looked like they were going to collide with him head-on. It became an effort to stay to the left rather than the right, where his instincts shrieked he should be. Right and left had to be reversed on that level, but kept the same at foot level — reversed concerning which hand went on the gearshift, but not reversed for what the gearshift did — and it all began to blur and mix, until finally a huge lorry rushed head-first at him and he veered left, but hit the gas rather than the brakes. At the unexpected lurch forward he swerved farther left to be safe, and that ran his left wheels off the asphalt and into a muddy gutter, causing the car to bounce back onto the road. He hit the brakes hard and the lorry roared by his ear. The car skidded over the wet asphalt to a halt.

He pulled over and turned on the emergency blinker. As he got out of the car he saw that the driver's side mirror was gone. There was nothing there but a rectangular depression in the metal, four rivet holes slightly flared to the rear, and one larger hole for the mirror adjustment mechanism, missing as well.

He went to the other side of the car to remind himself what the Sierra's side mirrors looked like. A solid metal and plastic mounting. He walked a hundred yards back down the road, looking through the dusk for the missing one, but he couldn't find it anywhere. The mirror was gone.

— • —

Outside Edinburgh he stopped and called Alec, a friend from years past.

"What? Frank Churchill? Hello! You're here? Come on by, then."

Frank followed his directions into the city center, past the train station to a neighborhood of narrow streets. Reversed parallel parking was almost too much for him; it took four tries to get the car next to the curb. The Sierra bumped over paving stones to a halt. He killed the engine and got out of the car, but his whole body continued to vibrate, a big tuning fork humming in the twilight. Shops threw their illumination over passing cars. Butcher, baker, Indian deli.

Alec lived on the third floor. "Come in, man, come in." He looked harried. "I thought you were in America! What brings you here?"

"I don't know."

Alec glanced sharply at him, then led him into the flat's kitchen and living area. The window had a view across rooftops to the castle. Alec stood in the kitchen, uncharacteristically silent. Frank put down his backpack and walked over to look out at the castle, feeling awkward. In the old days he and Andrea had trained up several times to visit Alec and Suzanne, a primatologist. At that time those two had lived in a huge three-storied flat in the New Town, and when Frank and Andrea had arrived the four of them would stay up late into the night, drinking brandy and talking in a high-ceilinged Georgian living room. During one stay they had all driven into the Highlands, and another time Frank and Andrea had stayed through a festival week, the four attending as many plays as they could. But now Suzanne and Alec had gone their ways, and Frank and Andrea were divorced, and Alec lived in a different flat; and that whole life had disappeared.

"Did I come at a bad time?"

"No, actually." A clatter of dishes as Alec worked at the sink. "I'm off to dinner with some friends, you'll join us — you haven't eaten?"

"No. I won't be —"

"No. You've met Peg and Rog before, I think. And we can use the distraction, I'm sure. We've all been to a funeral this morning. Friends of ours, their kid died. Crib death, you know."

"Jesus. You mean it just ... "

"Sudden infant death syndrome, yeah. Dropped him off at day care and he went off during his nap. Five months old."

"Jesus."

"Yeah." Alec went to the kitchen table and filled a glass from a bottle of Laphroaig. "Want a whisky?"

"Yes, please."

Alec poured another glass, drank his down. "I suppose the idea these days is that a proper funeral helps the parents deal with it. So Tom and

Elyse came in carrying the coffin, and it was about this big." He held his hands a foot apart.

"No."

"Yeah. Never seen anything like it."

They drank in silence.

— • —

The restaurant was a fashionably bohemian seafood place, set above a pub. There Frank and Alec joined Peg and Rog, another couple, and a woman named Karen. All animal behaviorists, and all headed out to Africa in the next couple of weeks — Rog and Peg to Tanzania, the rest to Rwanda. Despite their morning's event the talk was quick, spirited, wide-ranging; Frank drank wine and listened as they discussed African politics, the problems of filming primates, rock music. Only once did the subject of the funeral come up, and then they shook their heads; there wasn't much to say. Stiff upper lip.

Frank said, "I suppose it's better it happened now than when the kid was three or four."

They stared at him. "Oh no," Peg said. "I don't think so."

Acutely aware that he had said something stupid, Frank tried to recover: "I mean, you know, they've more time to ... " He shook his head, foundering.

"It's rather comparing absolutes, isn't it," Rog said gently.

"True," he said. "It is." And he drank his wine. He wanted to go on: True, he wanted to say, any death is an absolute disaster, even that of an infant too young to know what was happening; but what if you had spent your life raising six such children and then went out one morning and found their heads on your lawn? Isn't the one more absolute than the other? He was drunk, his head hurt, his body still vibrated with the day's drive and the shock of the brush with the lorry; and it seemed likely that the dyslexia of exhaustion had invaded all his thinking, including his moral sense, making everything backward. So he clamped his lips together and concentrated on the wine, his fork humming in his hand, his glass chattering against his teeth. The room was dark.

— • —

Afterwards Alec stopped at the door to his building and shook his head. "Not ready for that yet," he said. "Let's try Preservation Hall, it's your kind of thing on Wednesday nights. Traditional jazz."

Frank and Andrea had been fans of traditional jazz. "Any good?"

"Good enough for tonight, eh?"

The pub was within walking distance, down a wide cobblestone promenade called the Grassmarket, then up Victoria Street. At the door of the pub they were stopped; there was a cover charge, the usual band had been replaced by a buffet dinner and concert, featuring several different bands. Proceeds to go to the family of a Glasgow musician, recently killed in a car crash. "Jesus Christ," Frank exclaimed, feeling like a curse. He turned to go.

"Might as well try it," Alec said, and pulled out his wallet. "I'll pay."

"But we've already eaten."

Alec ignored him and gave the man twenty pounds. "Come on."

Inside a very large pub was jammed with people, and an enormous buffet table stacked with meats, breads, salads, seafood dishes. They got drinks from the bar and sat at the end of a crowded picnic table. It was noisy, the Scots accents so thick that Frank understood less than half of what he heard. A succession of local acts took the stage: the traditional jazz band that usually played, a stand-up comedian, a singer of Forties' music hall songs, a country-western group. Alec and Frank took turns going to the bar to get refills. Frank watched the bands and the crowd. All ages and types were represented. Each band said something about the late musician, who apparently had been well-known, a young rocker and quite a hellion from the sound of it. Crashed driving home drunk after a gig, and no one a bit surprised.

About midnight an obese young man seated at their table, who had been stealing food from all the plates around him, rose whalelike and surged to the stage. People cheered as he joined the band setting up. He picked up a guitar, leaned into the mike, and proceeded to rip into a selection of r&b and early rock and roll. He and his band was the best group yet, and the pub went wild. Most of the crowd got to their feet and danced in place. Next to Frank a young punk had to lean over the table to answer a gray-haired lady's questions about how he kept his hair spiked. A Celtic wake, Frank thought, and downed his cider and howled with the rest as the fat man started up Chuck Berry's "Rock And Roll Music."

So he was feeling no pain when the band finished its last encore and he and Alec staggered off into the night and made their way home. But it had gotten a lot colder while they were inside, and the streets were dark and empty. Preservation Hall was no more than a small wooden box of light, buried in a cold stone city. Frank looked back in its direction and saw that a streetlight reflected off the black cobblestones of the Grassmarket in such a way that there were thousands of brief white squiggles underfoot, looking like names engraved on black granite, as if the whole surface of the Earth were paved by a single memorial.

— • —

The next day he drove north again, across the Forth Bridge and then west along the shores of a loch to Fort William, and north from there through the Highlands. Above Ullapool, steep ridges burst like fins out of boggy treeless hillsides. There was water everywhere, puddles to lochs, with the Atlantic itself visible from most high points. Out to sea the tall islands of the Inner Hebrides were just visible.

He continued north. He had his sleeping bag and foam pad with him, and so he parked in a scenic overlook, and cooked soup on his Bluet stove, and slept in the back of the car. He woke with the dawn and drove north. He talked to nobody.

Eventually he reached the northwest tip of Scotland and was forced to turn east, on a road bordering the North Sea. Early that evening he arrived in Scrabster, at the northeast tip of Scotland. He drove to the docks, and found that a ferry was scheduled to leave for the Orkney Islands the next day at noon. He decided to take it. There was no secluded place to park, so he took a room in a hotel. He had dinner in the restaurant next door, fresh shrimp in mayonnaise with chips, and went to his room and slept. At six the next morning the ancient crone who ran the hotel knocked on his door and told him an unscheduled ferry was leaving in forty minutes: did he want to go? He said he did. He got up and dressed, then felt too exhausted to continue. He decided to take the regular ferry after all, took off his clothes and returned to bed. Then he realized that exhausted or not he wasn't going to be able to fall back to sleep. Cursing, almost crying, he got up and put his clothes back on. Downstairs the old woman had fried bacon and made him two thick bacon sandwiches, as he was going to miss her regular breakfast. He ate the sandwiches sitting in the Sierra, waiting to get the car into the ferry. Once in the hold, he locked the car and went up to the warm stuffy passenger cabin, and lay on padded vinyl seating and fell back asleep.

He woke when they docked in Stromness. For a moment he didn't remember getting on the ferry, and he couldn't understand why he wasn't in his hotel bed in Scrabster. He stared through salt stained windows at fishing boats, amazed, and then it came to him. He was in the Orkneys.

— • —

Driving along the southern coast of the main island, he found that his mental image of the Orkneys had been entirely wrong. He had expected an extension of the Highlands; instead it was like eastern Scotland, low, rounded, and green. Most of it was cultivated or used for pasture. Green fields, fences, farmhouses. He was a bit disappointed.

Then in the island's big town of Kirkwall he drove past a Gothic Cathedral — a very little Gothic cathedral, a kind of pocket cathedral. Frank had never seen anything like it. He stopped and got out to have look. Cathedral of St. Magnus, begun in 1137. So early, and this far North! No wonder it was so small. Building it would have required craftsmen from the continent, shipped up here to a rude fishing village of drywall and turf roofs; a strange influx it must have been, a kind of cultural revolution. The finished building must have stood out like something from another planet.

But as he walked around the bishop's palace next door, and the little museum, he learned that it might not have been such a shock to Kirkwall after all. In those days the Orkneys had been a crossroads of a sort, where Norse and Scots and English and Irish had met, infusing an indigenous culture that went right back to the Stone Age. The fields and pastures he had driven by had been worked, some of them, for five thousand years!

And such faces walking the streets, so intent and vivid. His image of the local culture had been as wrong as his image of the land. He had thought he would find decrepit fishing villages dwindling to nothing as people moved south to the cities. But it wasn't like that in Kirkwall, where teenagers roamed in self-absorbed talky gangs, and restaurants open to the street were packed for lunch. In the book-stores he found big sections on local topics: nature guides, archaeological guides, histories, sea tales, novels. Several writers, obviously popular, had as their entire subject the islands. To the locals, he realized, the Orkneys were the center of the world.

— • —

He bought a guidebook and drove north, up the east coast of Mainland to the Broch of Gurness, a ruined fort and village that had been occupied from the time of Christ to the Norse era. The broch itself was a round stone tower about twenty feet tall. Its wall was at least ten feet thick, and was made of flat slabs, stacked so carefully that you couldn't have stuck a dime in the cracks. The walls in the surrounding village were much thinner: if attacked, the villagers would have retired into the broch. Frank nodded at the explanatory sentence in the guidebook, reminded that the twentieth century had no monopoly on atrocities. Some had happened right here, no doubt. Unless the broch had functioned as a deterrent.

Gurness overlooked a narrow channel between Mainland and the smaller island of Rousay. Looking out at the channel, Frank noticed white ripples in its blue water; waves and foam were pouring past. It was a tidal race, apparently, and at the moment the entire contents of the channel were rushing north, as fast as any river he had ever seen.

— • —

Following suggestions in the guidebook, he drove across the island to the Neolithic site of Brodgar, Stenness, and Maes Howe. Brodgar and Stenness were two rings of standing stones; Maes Howe was a nearby chambered tomb.

The Ring of Brodgar was a big one, three hundred and forty feet across. Over half of the original sixty stones were still standing, each one a block of roughly dressed sandstone, weathered over the millennia into shapes of great individuality and charisma, like Rodin figures. Following the arc they made, he watched the sunlight break on them. It was beautiful.

Stenness was less impressive, as there were only four stones left, each tremendously tall. It roused more curiosity than awe: how had they stood those monsters on end? No one knew for sure.

From the road, Maes Howe was just a conical grass mound. To see the inside he had to wait for a guided tour, happily scheduled to start in fifteen minutes.

He was still the only person waiting when a short stout woman drove up in a pickup truck. She was about twenty-five, and wore Levi's and a red windbreaker. She greeted him and unlocked a gate in the fence surrounding the mound, then led him up a gravel path to the entrance on the southwest slope. There they had to get on their knees and crawl, down a tunnel three feet high and some thirty feet long. Midwinter sunsets shone directly down this entryway, the woman looked over her shoulder to tell him. Her Levi's were new.

The main chamber of the tomb was quite tall. "Wow," he said, standing up and looking around.

"It's big, isn't it," the guide said. She told him about it in a casual way. The walls were made of the ubiquitous sandstone slabs, with some monster monoliths bracketing the entryway. And something unexpected: a group of Norse sailors had broken into the tomb in the twelfth century (four thousand years after the tomb's construction!) and taken shelter in it through a three-day storm. This was known because they had passed the time carving runes on the walls, which told their story. The woman pointed to lines and translated: "'Happy is he who finds the great treasure.' And over here: 'Ingrid is the most beautiful woman in the world.'"

"You're kidding."

"That's what it says. And look here, you'll see they did some drawing as well."

She pointed out three graceful line figures, cut presumably with axe blades: a walrus, a narwhal, and a dragon. He had seen all three in the shops of Kirkwall, reproduced in silver for earrings and pendants. "They're beautiful," he said.

"A good eye, that Viking."

He looked at them for a long time, then walked around the chamber to look at the runes again. It was a suggestive alphabet, harsh and angular. The guide seemed in no hurry, she answered his questions at length. She was a guide in the summer, and sewed sweaters and quilts in the winter. Yes, the winters were dark. But not very cold. Average temperature around thirty.

"That warm?"

"Aye, it's the Gulf Stream, you see. It's why Britain is so warm, and Norway too for that matter."

Britain so warm. "I see," he said carefully.

Back outside he stood and blinked in the strong afternoon light. He had just emerged from a five-thousand-year-old tomb. Down by the loch the standing stones were visible, both rings. Ingrid is the most beautiful woman in the world. He looked at Brodgar, a circle of black dots next to a silver sheen of water. It was a memorial too, although what it was supposed to make its viewers remember was no longer clear. A great chief; the death of one year, birth of the next; the planets, moon and sun in their courses. Or something else, something simpler. *Here we are.*

— • —

It was still mid-afternoon judging by the sun, so he was surprised to look at his watch and see it was six o'clock. Amazing. It was going to be just like his therapy! Only better because outdoors, in the sunlight and the wind. Spend summer in the Orkneys, winter in the Falklands, which were said to be very similar ... He drove back to Kirkwall and had dinner in a hotel restaurant. The waitress was tall, attractive, about forty. She asked him where he was from, and he asked her when it would get busy (July), what the population of Kirkwall was (about ten thousand, she guessed) and what she did in the winter (accounting). He had broiled scallops and a glass of white wine. Afterward he sat in the Sierra and looked at his map. He wanted to sleep in the car, but hadn't yet seen a good place to park for the night.

The northwest tip of Mainland looked promising, so he drove across the middle of the island again, passing Stenness and Brodgar once more. The stones of Brodgar stood silhouetted against a western sky banded orange and pink and white and red.

At the very northwest tip of the island, the Point of Buckquoy, there was a small parking lot, empty this late in the evening. Perfect. Extending west from the point was a tidal causeway, now covered by the sea; a few hundred yards across the water was a small island called the Brough of Birsay, a flat loaf of sandstone tilted up to the west, so that one could see the whole grass top of it. There were ruins and a museum at the near end, a small lighthouse on the west point. Clearly something to check out the next day.

South of the point, the western shore of the island curved back in a broad, open bay. Behind its beach stood the well preserved ruins of a six-teenth century palace. The bay ended in a tall sea cliff called Marwick Head, which had a tower on its top that looked like another broch, but was, he discovered in his guidebook, the Kitchener Memorial. Offshore in 1916 the *HMS Hampshire* had hit a mine and sunk, and six hundred men, including Kitchener, had drowned.

Odd, to see that. A couple of weeks ago (it felt like years) he had read that when the German front lines had been informed of Kitchener's death, they had started ringing bells and banging pots and pans in celebration; the noisemaking had spread up and down the German trenches, from the Belgian coast to the Swiss frontier.

He spread out his sleeping bag and foam pad in the back of the station wagon and lay down. He had a candle for reading, but he did not want to read. The sound of the waves was loud. There was still a bit of light in the air, these northern summer twilights were really long. The sun had seemed to slide off to the right rather than descend, and suddenly he understood what it would be like to be above the Arctic Circle in midsummer: the sun would just keep sliding off to the right until it brushed the northern horizon, and then it would slide up again into the sky. He needed to live in Ultima Thule.

The car rocked slightly on a gust of wind. It had been windy all day; apparently it was windy all the time here, the main reason the islands were treeless. He lay back and looked at the roof of the car. A car made a good tent: flat floor, no leaks ... As he fell asleep he thought, it was a party a mile wide and a thousand miles long.

— · —

He woke at dawn, which came just before five A.M. His shadow and the car's shadow were flung out toward the brough, which was an island still, as the tidal bar was covered again. Exposed for only two hours each side of low tide, apparently.

He ate breakfast by the car, and then rather than wait for the causeway to clear he drove south, around the Bay of Birsay and behind Marwick Head, to the Bay of Skaill. It was a quiet morning, he had the one-lane track to himself. It cut through green pastures. Smoke rose from farmhouse chimneys and flattened out to the east. The farmhouses were white, with slate roofs and two white chimneys, one at each end of the house. Ruins of farmhouses built to the same design stood nearby, or in back pastures.

He came to another parking lot, containing five or six cars. A path had been cut through tall grass just behind the bay beach, and he followed it south. It ran nearly a mile around the curve of the bay, past a big nine-teenth-century manor house, apparently still occupied. Near the south point of the bay stretched a low concrete seawall and a small modern building, and some interruptions in the turf above the beach. Holes, it looked like. The pace of his walk picked up. A few people were bunched around a man in a tweed coat. Another guide?

Yes. It was Skara Brae.

The holes in the ground were the missing roofs of Stone Age houses buried in the sand; their floors were about twelve feet below the turf. The interior walls were made of the same slab as everything else on the island, stacked with the same precision. Stone hearths, stone bedframes, stone dressers: because of the islands' lack of wood, the guide was saying, and the ready availability of the slabs, most of the houses' furniture had been made of stone. And so it had endured.

Stacks of slabs held up longer ones, making shelves in standard college student bricks-and-boards style. Cupboards were inset in the walls. There was a kind of stone kitchen cabinet, with mortar and pestle beneath. It was instantly obvious what everything was for; everything looked deeply familiar.

Narrow passageways ran between houses. These too had been covered; apparently driftwood or whale rib beams had supported turf roofs over the entire village, so that during bad storms they need never go out. The first mall, Frank thought. The driftwood had included pieces of spruce, which had to have come from North America. The Gulf Stream again.

Frank stood at the back of a group of seven, listening to the guide as he looked down into the homes. The guide was bearded, stocky, fiftyish. Like the Maes Howe guide, he was good at his work, wandering about with no obvious plan, sharing what he knew without memorized speeches. The village had been occupied for about six hundred years, beginning around 3000 B.C. Brodgar and Maes Howe had been built during those years, so probably people from here had helped in their construction. The bay had likely been a fresh-water lagoon at that time, with a beach separating it from the sea. Population about fifty or sixty. A heavy dependence on cattle and sheep, with lots of seafood as well. Sand filled in the homes when the village was abandoned, and turf grew over it. In 1850 a big storm tore the turf off and exposed the homes, completely intact except for the roofs ...

Water seepage had rounded away every edge, so that each slab looked sculpted and caught at the light. Each house a luminous work of art. And five thousand years old, yet so familiar: the same needs, the same thinking, the same solutions ... A shudder ran through him, and he noticed that he was literally slack-jawed. He closed his mouth and almost laughed aloud. Open-mouthed astonishment could be so natural sometimes, so physical, unconscious, genuine.

When the other tourists left, he continued to wander around. The guide, sensing another enthusiast, joined him.

"It's like the Flintstones," Frank said, and laughed.

"The what?"

"You expect to see stone TVs and the like."

"Oh aye. It's very contemporary, isn't it."

"It's marvelous."

Frank walked from house to house, and the guide followed, and they talked. "Why is this one called the chief's house?"

"It's just a guess, actually. Everything in it is a bit bigger and better, that's all. In our world a chief would have it."

Frank nodded. "Do you live out here?"

"Aye." The guide pointed at the little building beyond the site. He had owned a hotel in Kirkwall, but sold it; Kirkwall had been too hectic for him. He had gotten the job here and moved out, and was very happy with it. He was getting a degree in archaeology by correspondence. The more he learned, the more amazed he was to be here; it was one of the most important archaeological sites in the world, after all. There wasn't a better one. No need to imagine furnishings and implements, "and to see so clearly how much they thought like we do."

Exactly. "Why did they leave, in the end?"

"No one knows."

"Ah."

They walked on.

"No sign of a fight anyway."

"Good."

The guide asked Frank where he was staying, and Frank told him about the Sierra.

"I see!" the man said. "Well, if you need the use of a bathroom, there's one here at the back of the building. For a shave, perhaps. You look like you haven't had the chance in a while."

Frank rubbed a hand over his stubble, blushing. In fact he hadn't thought of shaving since well before leaving London. "Thanks," he said. "Maybe I'll take you up on that."

They talked about the ruins a while longer, and then the guide walked out to the seawall, and let Frank wander in peace.

He looked down in the rooms, which still glowed as if lit from within. Six hundred years of long summer days, long winter nights. Perhaps they had set sail for the Falklands. Five thousand years ago.

He called good-bye to the guide, who waved. On the way back to the car park he stopped once to look back. Under a carpet of cloud the wind was thrashing the tall beach grass, every waving stalk distinct, the clouds' underside visibly scalloped; and all of it touched with a silvery edge of light.

— • —

He ate lunch in Stromness, down by the docks, watching the fishing boats ride at anchor. A very practical-looking fleet, of metal and rubber and bright plastic buoys. In the afternoon he drove the Sierra around Scapa Flow and over a bridge at the east channel, the one Winston had ordered blocked with sunken ships. The smaller island to the south was covered with green fields and white farm-houses.

Late in the afternoon he drove slowly back to the Point of Buckquoy, stopping for a look in the nearby ruins of the sixteenth-century earl's palace. Boys were playing soccer in the roofless main room.

The tide was out, revealing a concrete walkway set on a split bed of wet brown sandstone. He parked and walked over in the face of a stiff wind, onto the Brough of Birsay.

Viking ruins began immediately, as erosion had dropped part of the old settlement into the sea. He climbed steps into a tight network of knee high walls. Compared to Skara Brae, it was a big town. In the middle of all the low foundations rose the shoulder-high walls of a church. Twelfth-century, ambitious Romanesque design: and yet only fifty feet long, and twenty wide! Now this was a pocket cathedral. It had had a monastery connected to it, however; and some of the men who worshipped in it had travelled to Rome, Moscow, Newfoundland.

Picts had lived here before that; a few of their ruins lay below the Norse. Apparently they had left before the Norse arrived, though the record wasn't clear. What was clear was that people had been living here for a long, long time.

— • —

After a leisurely exploration of the site, Frank walked west, up the slope of the island. It was only a few hundred yards to the lighthouse on the cliff, a modern white building with a short fat tower.

Beyond it was the edge of the island. He walked toward it and emerged from the wind shelter the island provided; a torrent of gusts almost knocked him back. He reached the edge and looked down.

At last something that looked like he thought it would! It was a long way to the water, perhaps a hundred and fifty feet. The cliff was breaking off in great stacks, which stood free and tilted out precariously, as if they were going to fall at any moment. Great stone cliffs, with the sun glaring directly out from them, and the surf crashing to smithereens on the rocks below: it was so obviously, grandiloquently the End of Europe that he had to laugh. A place made to cast oneself from. End the pain and fear, do a Hart Crane off the stern of Europe ... except this looked like the bow, actually. The bow of a very big ship, crashing westward through the waves; yes, he could feel it in the soles of his feet. And foundering, he could feel that too, the shudders, the rolls, the last sluggish list. So jumping overboard would be redundant at best. The end would come, one way or another. Leaning out against the gale, feeling like a Pict or Viking, he knew he stood at the end — end of a continent, end of a century; end of a culture.

— • —

And yet there was a boat, coming around Marwick Head from the south, a little fishing tub from Stromness, rolling horribly in the swell. Heading northwest, out to — out to where? There were no more islands out there, not until Iceland anyway, or Greenland, Spitsbergen ... where was it going at this time of day, near sunset and the west wind tearing in?

He stared at the trawler for a long time, rapt at the sight, until it was nothing but a black dot near the horizon. Whitecaps covered the sea, and the wind was still rising, gusting really hard. Gulls skated around on the blasts, landing on the cliffs below. The sun was very near the water, sliding off to the north, the boat no more than flotsam: and then he remembered the causeway and the tide.

He ran down the island and his heart leaped when he saw the concrete walkway washed by white water, surging up from the right. Stuck here, forced to break into the museum or huddle in a corner of the church ... but no; the concrete stood clear again. If he ran —

He pounded down the steps and ran over the rough concrete. There were scores of parallel sandstone ridges still exposed to the left, but the right side was submerged already, and as he ran a broken wave rolled up onto the walkway and drenched him to the knees, filling his shoes with seawater and scaring him much more than was reasonable. He ran on cursing.

Onto the rocks and up five steps. At his car he stopped, gasping for breath. He got in the passenger side and took off his boots, socks, and pants. Put on dry pants, socks, and running shoes.

He got back out of the car.

The wind was now a constant gale, ripping over the car and the point and the ocean all around. It was going to be tough to cook dinner on his stove; the car made a poor windbreak, wind rushing under it right at stove level.

He got out the foam pad and propped it with his boots against the lee side of the car. The pad and the car's bulk gave him just enough wind shelter to keep the little Bluet's gas flame alive. He sat on the asphalt behind the stove, watching the flames and the sea. The wind was tremendous, the Bay of Birsay riven by whitecaps, more white than blue. The car rocked on its shock absorbers. The sun had finally slid sideways into the sea, but clearly it was going to be a long blue dusk.

When the water was boiling he poured in a dried Knorr's soup and stirred it, put it back on the flame for a few more minutes, then killed the flame and ate, spooning split pea soup straight from the steaming pot into his mouth. Soup, bit of cheese, bit of salami, red wine from a tin cup, more soup. It was absurdly satisfying to make a meal in these conditions: the wind was in a fury!

When he was done eating he opened the car door and put away his dinner gear, then got out his windbreaker and rain pants and put them on. He walked around the carpark, and then up and down the low cliffy edges of the point of Buckquoy, watching the North Atlantic get torn by a full force gale. People had done this for thousands of years. The rich twilight blue looked like it would last forever.

Eventually he went to the car and got his notebooks. He returned to the very tip of the point, feeling the wind like slaps on the ear. He sat with his legs hanging over the drop, the ocean on three sides of him, the wind pouring across him, left to right. The horizon was a line where purest blue met bluest black. He kicked his heels against the rock. He could see just well enough to tell which pages in the notebooks had writing on them; he tore these from the wire spirals, and bunched them into balls and threw them away. They flew off to the right and disappeared immediately in the murk and whitecaps. When he had disposed of all the pages he had written on, he cleared the long torn shreds of paper out of the wire rings, and tossed them after the rest.

— • —

It was getting cold, and the wind was a constant kinetic assault. He went back to the car and sat in the passenger seat. His notebooks lay on the driver's seat. The western horizon was a deep blue, now. Must be eleven at least.

After a time he lit the candle and set it on the dash. The car was still rocking in the wind, and the candle flame danced and trembled on its wick. All the black shadows in the car shivered too, synchronized perfectly with the flame.

He picked up a notebook and opened it. There were a few pages left between damp cardboard covers. He found a pen in his daypack. He rested his hand on the page, the pen in position to write, its tip in the quivering shadow of his hand. He wrote, "I believe that man is good. I believe we stand at the dawn of a century that will be more peaceful and prosperous than any in history." Outside it was dark, and the wind howled. ▪

ABOUT THE EDITOR

Fiona Kelleghan was born in West Palm Beach, Florida, in 1965. She has published scholarly work in *Extrapolation, The New York Review of Science Fiction, Science Fiction Studies, Journal of the Fantastic in the Arts,* and *SFRA Review.* Her books include *Mike Resnick: An Annotated Bibliography and Guide to His Work,* and, as editor, *100 Masters of Mystery and Detective Fiction* and *Magill's Choice: Science Fiction and Fantasy Literature.* She is a contributor to *Contemporary Novelists, Magill's Guide to Science Fiction and Fantasy Literature, St. James Guide to Science Fiction Writers,* and *The Greenwood Encyclopedia of Science Fiction and Fantasy.* She is a graduate of the Clarion West Science Fiction Workshop and is a cataloging and metadata librarian at the University of Miami.

PUBLICATION HISTORY

A few passages are slightly reworked from speeches given by Fiona Kelleghan at the International Conference for the Fantastic in the Arts or from previously published essays written by her.

ROBERT J. SAWYER BOOKS

Letters from the Flesh by Marcos Donnelly

Getting Near the End by Andrew Weiner

Rogue Harvest by Danita Maslan

The Engine of Recall by Karl Schroeder

A Small and Remarkable Life by Nick DiChario

Sailing Time's Ocean by Terence M. Green

Birthstones by Phyllis Gotlieb

The Commons by Matthew Hughes

Valley of Day-Glo by Nick DiChario

The Savage Humanists edited by Fiona Kelleghan

And from Red Deer Press:

Iterations and Other Stories by Robert J. Sawyer

Identity Theft and Other Stories by Robert J. Sawyer

www.robertjsawyerbooks.com